I0663161

ground
FICTION

Vol. 2, Issue 1
Spring/Summer 2021

Editor
Seth Harwood

Managing Editor
Rich Ferri

Assistant Editors
Jennifer Fickley-Baker
Alyce Werdel

Designer
Jaye Manus

Copyeditors
Chris Rhatigan
Babs Griswold

Visit groundfiction.com for more info. Yearly subscriptions and previous issues of *Ground* can be obtained at groundfiction.com.

Cover design by Aleksandra Dabic
On the cover: *Japanese Tea Garden Bridge,* 2012, Mark Coggins
See more at markcoggins.com

ground [1]

n.

1. an area used for a particular purpose
2. an area of knowledge or special interest
3. a basis for belief, action, or argument
4. a special soil, such as at the bottom of a body of water
5. an object that makes an electrical connection with the earth

v.

1. to provide a reason or justification for
2. to furnish with a foundation of knowledge
3. to bring to or place on the ground

ground [2]

adj.

reduced to small pieces or a powder by a grinding process

Table of Contents

Dear Reader,

Thanks for picking up our second issue of *Ground*. We couldn't be happier to have it out in the world.

Here again, we've got some great stories and novel excerpts from new authors you may not have heard of, though we hope that's starting to change. You'll recognize many returning authors from our first issue, some with new stories and others with more of their works-in-progress.

On top of these, we are overjoyed to have a story from Elizabeth Wetmore, the author of *Valentine*, one of 2020's absolute literary highlights and an instant *New York Times* bestseller. If you haven't read this novel yet, go get it! You're in for a treat.

One of *Valentine*'s striking features is the strong voices of its characters, all strong women from mid-1970s West Texas. Here we're lucky to have a rare outtake—a male voice of this novel—that of PFC Jesse Belden or, as I like to call him, "the guy in the pipe." I know you'll love this piece. Thanks so much, Beth, for adding your work to *Ground*.

In other news, we're now proud to offer subscriptions and individual issue sales at groundfiction.com—your one-stop shop for all things *Ground*, as well as info on our authors. Subscribe now and rest assured that each new issue will arrive at your door upon its release.

Interested writers can find out more about working with me or attending workshops with *Ground* authors at writewithseth.com.

Here's to a new year and new directions for us all.

> With great appreciation for all who read,
> Seth Harwood

Jesse Belden

Elizabeth Wetmore

WHEN YOU FINALLY get back home, keep your discharge papers in the front pocket of your shirt, like somebody might stop you and demand to see them, like maybe just coming back alive makes you a criminal. Nadine picks you up in Fort McClellan in the family Pinto wagon and drives you back to eastern Tennessee. For three hundred miles, you sit in the passenger seat with your eyes closed and your good ear next to the open window. When you think about home, try to remember the racket in those woods out behind your mama's house. Thrum of cicadas, frogs belching down by the creek, two crows trying to keep jays and cowbirds away from their nest, buzz of mosquitoes and yellow jackets. Animal noise, not people noise. Try to remember the splash of a rainbow trout when you pull it from the Clinch River, the scrape of aluminum dragging red mud when your fishing boat hits bottom, and that same red mud sucking and climbing up your legs when you step into the Clinch River to wash the smell of fish off your hands.

Nadine lays on the horn as soon as she turns off the highway and starts up the dirt road that snakes through your family's hollow. Your mom's trailer is filled with people smiling and shaking hands. Uncles talk about driving to eastern Kentucky for work in the mines, their mouths open and close like snapping turtles when they say you picked a bad time to come back to eastern Tennessee. They fixed your teeth when you joined the service, and now your mother covers her mouth when she laughs, her big hand marked with scratches, knuckles twisted and raw. Cousin Travis even drives from Texas to welcome you home. Pulling up in a new Ford F-150, shaking your hand and asking what's next. Ain't no jobs here, he says, that's sure as shit. He wears new boots and a new nickname, Boomer, because he nearly blew himself to kingdom come his first week on the job. You don't need to know diddly about petroleum, he says. Just do what they tell you and collect your pay on Friday. Three hundred a week, brother, and all the Texas pussy you can handle.

But everybody can't always be standing on your good side, and you miss a lot. After a while, it starts to sound like airplanes taking off. Nod and grin and let somebody fill your cup and when they ask where you've been, tell them: Hell if I know, I never learned to pronounce the goddamned name. And think of the two boys you had to shoot before you got your orders to come back home.

To hear that noise you remembered while you were overseas, walk a little ways into the woods behind the house and stand real still. Before the war, your hearing was so good your uncle used to brag about it. Us Beldens always were blessed with good hearing. Take Jesse there, he can hear a doe swat a housefly off her ass from a hundred yards off. He can hear a tick let go of a dog's ear, and a catfish farting from the bottom of a thirty-foot swimming hole. But on the day you come home to eastern Tennessee after three years serving your country for something you never figured out, you sit in the woods and listen, and when the sounds finally come—branch strikes dirt when a little breeze shakes it loose from the tree, whitetail deer tears up the woods, rifle reports from the other of side of your hollow, Belden Hollow—you can't decide if you are really hearing them, or just the memory of them.

In January, drive away from eastern Tennessee with your Army gear in the back of your truck and Boomer's phone number in your pocket. Drive with a particular kind of noise in your head, a Jesse Belden get your shit together kind of noise, and when the trees disappear on the other side of Dallas, wonder how anyplace on this earth can be so brown. In Tennessee, brown is the color of Nadine's eyes, or a white-tailed deer. Here, it is everything. Brown earth, brown fences, brown derricks and jacks. Even the shining blue sky will turn brown, if the wind blows hard enough. At the veteran's hospital in Big Spring, hand your discharge papers and medical card to the guard. Tell him, I don't know what's wrong with me. There's a ringing in my right ear, and a howling in my left. Some days, everything hurts and I don't know why. Stay for two weeks, sleeping in a ward with men whose arms and legs and eyes and minds are gone, and see how blessed you are.

Don't take it personally when one of the doctors hands you a stack of papers and curls his fingers around the bony knob of your shoulder. You are twenty-two years old, he reminds you, time to get your shit together. And you want to say, I'm trying! But I can't hold a thought in my head for more than a couple of minutes and I can't be busy but I can't be still, can't be in my skin and don't know how to leave it behind. Instead, feel the weight and shape of his class ring through your T-shirt and ask him, How far is it to Odessa? And when he walks you out to your truck and points west, follow his gaze and see nothing but flat, brown earth and telephone poles. When he tells you it's only sixty miles and be sure to lock up your truck at night, wish he could be your father.

At a work site in Stanton, the crew chief shakes your hand and introduces himself—Dale Strickland. He looks you over and smiles like he just won the coin toss for the last turkey leg at Thanksgiving. You mind small spaces, Shorty?

When you tell him you were a tunnel rat in the service, he says, You ain't gonna hit the deck screaming every time we blow a seal, are you?

No, sir.

He looks at your tennis shoes—you got boots?—and when you shake your head, he hands you a twenty and tells you where to go. He'll take it out of your first week's pay. Strickland talks some more, but the site is a hundred kinds of noise all happening at once. Men twist threading steel rods into bits as big around as your head, generators switch on and pipeline falls off the back of a flatbed. You nod and say yes sir, yes sir, and the next morning you climb into your first tank with a respirator, a broom, and a metal scraper taller than you. When you climb back out, you look like one of the onyx statues you saw in markets overseas, little girls holding them up to the light and telling you the names. *The Thinker. Laughing Buddha. Skinny little man,* they laughed. Like you!

Spend twenty minutes in the field shower and because mucking saltwater and waste can make a man sick if he does too much of it, spend the rest of the day digging drain trenches next to the drilling platform. Back home, there wasn't anything to do but fish the Clinch River and look for agates at Paint Rock and Greasy Cove, and drive over to the VA hospital where the doctor told you there wasn't one goddamned thing wrong with you, other than being deaf in one ear. But here in Odessa, you work. Like a man does.

Days are long. The driver picks you up at five, and it's a ninety-minute drive to the work site. On a good day, if the foreman is feeling kindly, y'all might wrap it up for the day at seven. Drink in the truck on the way home from the site, then drink some more at Boomer's house while his new bride scowls in the doorway from the kitchen. Start the night with a little blow, end it with a tranquilizer. Marvel that no matter how drunk and stoned everyone else gets the night before, they still get up and go to work the next morning. Half the time, the driver hasn't even been to bed when he hands you a thermos of coffee and a pill or two.

But even with all that money—three, four hundred a week, cash on the barrelhead—you can't get the hang of it. The sofa at Boomer's house is stone hard and Brittney makes you keep your bags in your pickup, just so you don't get too comfortable, and you aren't there a month before Brittney wants to know when you're leaving. By April, Boomer is standing at the end of the couch, knocking your feet off the arm, while you plead sick. When the driver honks a third time, your cousin shrugs and knocks you in the head with the flat of his hand. Suit yourself, fuck-up. By the time you drive over to meet Boomer and a couple of pipefitters from Abilene at the new gentlemen's club, you are already making plans to get yourself back home.

It's not dark yet, and the bar is mostly empty. After a long Skynyrd number, the dancers take a break and sit at a table in the corner with the bouncer while the bartender queues up some Joe Ely. You can hear every word when one man's girlfriend comes in and screams at him for being at the titty bar. And when another man's wife calls on the phone and yells at the bartender to send her man home right fucking now, you can hear that too. Then Boomer makes a cracking sound with his mouth, pussy-whipped, and you are laughing, feeling loose and being part of something, digging it all. So when Boomer starts talking about Brittney, the old ball and chain who has his balls in a vice, when he says your days of sleeping on the sofa are numbered, you laugh and join in the fun. Well, no shit, brother. Your woman's a stone-cold cunt.

And your cousin's eyes go flat as a copperhead's. Have another drink, cousin. This one's on me.

When one of the men hits you square in the back with something, a two-by-four maybe, or a steel pipe, you will drop like an egg blown from a nest. Never saw it coming. Do yourself a favor and stay down. Lie on your belly with your good ear up. When your cousin leans out the driver's side window and hollers that he's keeping your truck as collateral, you will hear him clearly. Ask him, What for?

Motherfucker, you think that sofa you been sleeping on all these weeks is free? You think beer grows on trees?

Watch your discharge papers from the VA hospital drift across the parking lot and catch on a chain-link fence. Watch them tremble when a small wind catches them. If she were here, Nadine would say that's lucky. Good thing that fence is there because you are going to need those papers.

It will be dark out by the time you're ready to move. The temperature has dropped thirty degrees, but the pavement is warm against your cheek. Gather up the papers that say you were well enough to leave the hospital. Find your copy of *Field Hygiene and Sanitation* lying next to the dumpster behind the gentlemen's club. Open it and make sure your photograph is still there—you kids standing on the bank of Coker Creek, you in your button-down shirt, Nadine in a dress that hit just above the knees, and both of you wearing shoes. Must have been a Sunday. Look through your open duffel bag. One of the best men helped himself to the box of rubbers Boomer gave you when you showed up at his door. These local girls can't wait to put a man's name on a birth certificate, he said. That didn't sound like a bad deal, a woman and some kids, but you took the box. Your copy of *Gallery* is still in the duffel bag. It is three years old and some pages are missing, but you like the cover, a round blonde lying on her back, an inch-thick sisal rope coiled around a pair of great big titties.

Stand behind the strip club and listen to the music on the other side of the sheet metal wall. Wonder what's on the other side of the fence. If you were a little more stunk up, this might not hurt so much. But hard liquor and you are like oil and water, you don't mix, and you will be steady when you throw your bags over the fence and hook the toe of your old canvas shoe into the bottom link, when you half walk, half slide down the steep concrete slope of the flood canal and see two steel drainpipes at one end of the channel. The first is full of trash and tumbleweeds, and snakes and scorpions probably, but the second is nearly empty, just a couple of bottles and a little dust, as if it has been waiting for someone to crawl into it, someone small and light, someone blown in on the wind.

By the time the music at the strip bar stops, you can see your own breath in the beam of your flashlight. Find your plaid shirt and the blue jean jacket that makes a good-enough winter coat. Lie with your bad ear pressed to the ground and think of the dancers, stepping down from the stage after their last dance of the night, the bartender playing a slow song, a little Nazareth to send people on their way. Listen as the parking lot fills with people, mostly men but a few women too, and think that some nights it seems like this whole town is nothing but people shouting at each another. By two o'clock, when things are as quiet as they're going to get, close your eyes and hope you don't roll over onto your good ear in the middle of the night. The floor of the pipe is hard and cold, and everything hurts, but it's quiet and dark, and you sleep.

THE FIRST GIFT is a brown grocery bag sitting at the mouth of the drainage pipe, and you reckon Boomer has found out where you landed and decided to fuck with you. Expect the bag to be filled with ta-rantulas, or at least a couple of cow patties. Open with care. The top is sticky and there is a smiley face drawn with black marker. Inside, find a can of creamed corn, three sticks of gum, and a brown crayon with a dull tip. There is a note, too, folded in half, the edges sticky and stained with candy. *Don't worry, I'll take care of you. Write down what you need and put it next to the fence. Don't tell anybody.*

And you just fall out laughing when you read that. Because who are you going to tell? Sharpen the brown crayon with your pocketknife.

blankit cookpot can opener + matches
Jesse Belden, PFC, U.S. Army

THE NIGHTS ARE cold and the drainage pipe is darker than some of the tunnels you crawled into when you were overseas. Most nights you are sorry to see closing time. When you overhear the bartender bitch-ing that his whole cleaning crew just got deported—every damn one of them and who the hell's going to hose down the floors now?—tell the bouncer you can dump ashtrays after the bar closes every night, sweep and mop the floors. Stand up straight and keep him on your right, close to your good ear. Try to look clean and dependable. Ask to be paid in cash. Tell him you can start tonight.

Because it is already light out when you finish work, start taking the long way back to your camp. Walk up the street and over to Larkspur Lane, then cut down the alley and across the empty lot. This way, you can avoid having someone see you climb over the chain-link fence behind the strip club. Think about breaking into the empty house that sits a little ways off by itself from the other houses on the street. Won-der if you could at least sleep in the backyard, where there's a fence and maybe a water spigot that's still turned on, but it is private property and you are no trespasser. Imagine Nadine pulling up next to the flood channel one morning and rolling down the window on her old beater. Imagine her yelling, Damn it, Jesse, what in the hell did you get into now? Wish you could hear her say, Well, shit. Sometimes you're the June bug and sometimes you're the windshield, I guess. You come get in this car right now. But it is a thousand miles from Belden Hollow to Odessa, and Nadine has worries of her own. On her very best day, your sister couldn't make that drive, and neither could her car.

When you get home, look for snakes and scorpions and maybe another brown grocery bag. Shrug and crawl into your little hiding place where you've got two blankets, one heavy and one light, one to make the ground a little softer, one to keep you warm until the sun shines down on the concrete pipe and you don't need it anymore. Dream about the two boys you killed overseas, when you were standing in an underground room so close to the water table you could smell it. See the shorter boy step out of a side tunnel and stand directly in front of you while the taller one jams the butt of his rifle into your left ear. Dream in color but also in noise and dark, and wake up as you always do, wondering whether they were brothers and if they were, did their mama sit up all night, waiting for them to come home and wondering what happened.

THE SECOND GIFT comes on Easter Sunday, a holiday you would have completely forgot if all the dancers hadn't dressed up like bunnies the night before. After the bar closed, the floor manager told the bartender to pass around as many shots of Tequila Rose as the staff could drink and when you puked next to one of the dumpsters on your way home, the liquid was pink as a dyed egg, or a newly hatched earthworm. The paper sack is from Piggly Wiggly, and a happy pig beams at you from the bag's side. Inside, there are three hardboiled eggs, a piece of cornbread wrapped in foil, and a half-thawed casserole. Somebody tried to pick the masking tape label off the lid, and COR- is all that's left. There are fresh tomatoes, which you love more than just about anything in this world, and there is candy. Candy! You haven't seen a piece of candy since the Hershey's bars your platoon leader used to hand out on afternoons when things were calm and everybody was just sitting around, leaning against their packs and talking about home. The note says, *Happy Easter, Jesse Belden PFC U.S. Army*

BY MAY, YOU have to take your shirt off and sleep on the bare concrete. Some mornings you fall asleep with a small rock in your mouth, but you still wake up so thirsty you can't swallow. The first piss of the day smells like the solvent you used for the tanks, back when you worked with Dale on the Stanton rig and dreamed of driving up the road to Belden Hollow in a brand new truck, handing a roll of money to Nadine and Mama, saying y'all don't have to worry no more. The dark spot you've made on the concrete has started to fade before you crawl back into your little home. Twenty feet deep in the drainpipe, you lie on the concrete in your underwear and wish you had the energy to jerk off. When you hear somebody moving around outside, pick up your small roll of money and your pocketknife, and listen. When someone shines a flashlight into the pipe, press yourself against the concrete and don't move a muscle. Try to become smaller.

Are you in here?

The voice is that of a little girl and you are so relieved to hear it, to know that it is not a man, you think you might cry if you had enough water in you to make tears. A little girl! What can she possibly do to someone like you?

I won't tell anybody you're here. Her voice drifts through the dark. Are you sick?

I'm all right, you say. It is the first time you have said anything more than yes sir or no sir for days.

You need anything? she says.

Your eyes are dry as the dust you sleep on every night, dry as the snakeskin some old tomcat drug up one morning and laid at the opening of the flood pipe, but they still manage to fill with water when you answer. I want to go home.

A Gift from the Crows

Elizabeth Coleman

THE GIRL PRETENDS that she is the queen of the crows. From her pockets she scoops handfuls of peanuts, tossing them onto the ground in exchange for the gifts they bring her: bits of tinsel, buttons and coins, old nails and sequins, shiny objects that they've picked up in their black beaks and dropped at her feet before they gobble up their reward. All around her in the cemetery, the air is crisp, the branches on the tall trees barren, reaching into the pale, milky sky like spectral fingers. The crows circle about her, cawing, their wings flapping, breaking through the sharp silence like gunshots. They bob their heads, jumping from the brown, dried grass up to weathered gravestones and back, dancing for her, stamping their little crow feet in excitement and frenzy.

The last of the crows hops forward, dropping the offering to its queen into the pile of shinies. Its feathers gleam with a slight translucence, a rainbow slick upon oil. She likes to think the crows are shiny, too, just like the gifts they bring her. The girl tosses out the remaining peanuts and the crows descend in a mass, a writhing black pit next to her. She wipes the peanut shell dust from her fingers on her jeans and squats down in the dirt to examine her haul for the day.

She pokes at the pile, sifting through the mound of gifts. A broken earring, a washer, and a fishhook are among the shinies. A fine haul, befit for a queen. Her fingers come across a weathered baby carrot, and she picks it up, spinning it around as she realizes it's encircled by a large diamond ring.

The girl turns the object over in her hand. No, not a carrot. A finger. A bloody, severed finger. The girl's heart races as she inspects it.

The finger is stained with dark dirt and mottled, purple blood. The severed end is blackened with age, bits of dried skin hanging off the mud-encrusted bone. The diamond is covered with dirt as well, and the girl spits on her fingers and wipes the facets of the stone. It gleams in the pale light of day, bright against the decaying flesh behind it.

She gathers up the gifts from the crows, drops them into the pockets of her jacket, and heads toward home. Her feet fly like the flock of black birds that accompany her, making sure their queen returns home safely. She skips through the graveyard, stumbling a bit down the molehill-ridden grass, until she passes through the tall, wrought-iron gates of the cemetery. Then she turns onto the old county road: a tree-lined, compacted dirt lane that runs along a narrow, shallow river. The pockets of her jacket are heavy. She touches the finger, flesh upon flesh.

Before she reaches home, the girl veers off the road onto a deer path. She pushes through a dense thicket, ducking under the branches and brambles that cross the narrow trail. In a clearing, slivers of the late afternoon sunlight pierce through the shadowed treetops. The girl reaches her special tree: a large redwood, burnt hollow from years of wildfires. She slips into a narrow opening in the tree trunk where she's hidden a large metal cookie tin. A beam of sunlight from outside the hollowed tree cuts into the shadows, spilling over the packed ground.

Sitting cross-legged on the cool, damp earth, the girl pushes her tangled hair back from her face, and removes the tin lid. Inside are washed out jelly and pickle jars, and she starts sorting her treasure into the glass containers. A button here, a nail there. But she hesitates when it comes to the finger, wavering between the small jar filled with bits of snake and mice bone, and the jar filled with sequins and silver beads. Neither will do.

The girl shoves the finger into her pocket and stashes the rest of her treasure into her secret spot. She slips out through the opening of the tree, and starts running for home, back through the woods and out to the main road. Her lungs burn as she runs up the front steps to her house. The wooden porch creaks and moans with her hurried shuffle.

Inside to the right in the sunken living room, her stepmother sits on the couch talking on the phone. The girl tiptoes through the foyer to the staircase, trying not to get mud on her stepmother's rugs covering the wooden floor. The woman glances over at a squeak from the floor, and the girl jumps quickly behind the wall at the foot of the stairs so the woman can't see her, heart beating fast.

Cigarette smoke wafts around the corner. She can hear the clink of ice on glass as her stepmother sips her drink. The girl presses her back against the wall, listening to the conversation. She slips a hand into her pocket, fingering her gift from the crows, turning it over and over, rubbing the diamond ring. Her ears perk up at the mention of Mr. Hawthorne, the rugged neighbor who lives down a small gravel road in the adjoining woods. The girl likes to hide in the trees and watch him work in his garden, pushing around his wheelbarrow and chopping firewood. Around drinks out on the back porch, her stepmother's friends have often commented on his looks, comparing him to some popular Australian actor and pondering why he is still single.

"I don't know," says her stepmother. "I'm just not ready." A pause. "Sure, I think he's attractive. But it's only been a year since Peter . . .

since everything happened. I'm not sure I'm ready to just put myself out there again."

Another pause. "I know he was always away for work. But that doesn't make it hurt any less."

The girl strains to hear.

"Maybe you're right. I still have time. I just never thought I'd have to start over, you know? And now this time with a kid that isn't even mine." A pause. "Oh, she's fine. Kids are resilient. Spends all her time outdoors playing make believe." Another pause. "Hey, I've got to go . . . Okay, okay, I'll consider it. I'll talk to you later, okay? Bye."

The girl flinches at the sound of her stepmother shrieking and a glass shattering against the wall. The woman lets out an anguished wail and starts sobbing. The girl scrabbles up the carpeted stairs before her stepmother can throw a glass at her next. She runs down the hall into her bedroom, slamming the door behind her, and turns on the radio on her nightstand to drown out the painful cries that echo through the house.

SAFE IN HER bedroom, Patsy Cline crooning on the radio, the girl takes the finger out of her pocket and places it on her nightstand. She rummages through drawers until she finds what she is searching for: an old leather pouch tied together with a long bit of looped twine. She dumps out the few rocks she had collected onto the carpet, and places the ringed finger into the pouch, pulling the drawstring cord tight. She puts it on like a necklace, the pouch coming to rest mid-chest level, next to her heart.

Later that night, while lying in bed under the pink and white quilt that her grandmother gave her as a baby, the girl wears the necklace, and stares up at the shadows playing across the ceiling. The wind rustles the tree outside her window, the branches going *clack clack clack* against her window frame. Lightning zings across the sky, briefly illuminating the dark clouds, and several seconds later, a thunderclap booms. The girl pulls the quilt over her head, hiding.

The girl thinks about the finger, and the dead person it belonged to. She often thinks about death, the black cloud that swallows people up and takes them away. How easy it is to forget people as memories fade. Her mother's face has always been a blank spot in her mind, her father's face starting to blur. She wishes she had a place on earth she could visit to remember them, like others do in the cemetery.

She wonders about the dead people under her feet there, wonders what it's like to rot back into the earth. She imagines being buried, the cool earth pressing up around her, encircling her like an airless tomb, and she pulls the quilt off so she can breathe once again.

She holds her hands up in front of her face, turning them front side and back. She can barely make out the faint lines of her fingers, illuminated by the cloud-covered moon shining through her curtains. Her fingers curl into claws, and the girl imagines what it would be like to be buried alive, forced to dig through the hard, cold earth to freedom. She paws at the air pretending she is the dead woman. She envisions a dirt-crusted hand, her hand, breaking through the surface of the ground, shooting toward the heavens, before the hand collapses, withered and spent. A big fat diamond sits on the finger, her finger, glistening in the pale light.

The girl imagines a crow, shiny and black against the sparse gray light, pecking through the earth for seeds and bits of shiny things. The crow spies the diamond beckoning to it. It hops over, grabs the stone in its beak, and yanks. The diamond is stuck fast.

The crow, crafty and smart, knows it must tear the diamond loose. The crow pecks at the finger, her finger, creating ribbons of skin. Bits of flesh and dried blood fly off as the bird hacks away until it reaches the white of the bone, peeking out against the dark, bloody flesh. It snaps the bone quickly in two.

The crow picks up the diamond ring in its beak. Heavy, with finger attached. It flaps its wings, beating itself aloft, and flies up and away with its prize toward its queen.

The girl falls asleep, clutching the finger, her finger, in her fist.

THE GIRL LIKES to watch people. She watches Mr. Hawthorne from high up in a tree, a tall pine with large, climbing branches that overlooks his cottage in the neighboring woods. From her vantage point, she can see into his backyard. She watches as he chops wood and repairs fences in his heavy work boots. He stops to catch his breath, wiping his brow with a rag. He looks up and smiles, his handsome face lighting up, and waves at her. The girl is so surprised, she almost tumbles right out of the tree. She had thought she was invisible, so high up in the sky like the crows that no one would even notice her watching.

Timidly, she raises a hand and waves. Mr. Hawthorne returns to his work. Sprinkled throughout the tree like dark Christmas ornaments, the crows caw, one after the other, sounding off an unknown alarm.

From the surrounding cottonwood trees, the last of the fall leaves shudder in the wind, and die, floating gently down to the cold earth to rot into the ground like the bodies in the cemetery.

BY WINTER, MOST of the crows are gone. Only a few brave souls remain to guard their queen. They watch over her from the power lines and treetops as the girl waits at the bus stop. Off to the side, the other children huddle in a cluster, stamping their booted feet and rubbing their mittened hands together, their breath crystallizing into little puffs. Hanging around her neck under her winter parka, the leather pouch with the finger is safe and warm against the frosty winter air.

The school bus is late. The children grow anxious, shifting and milling about. The girl steps lightly back and forth to keep warm, like a crow dancing.

"Hey, freak," calls out a boy.

The girl ignores him, staring down at her boots as she shifts from foot to foot. They're black and shiny like the feathers of the crows.

"Hey, freak. I'm talking to you," says the boy again, this time a hint of a threat in his voice.

The girl looks up. A seventh grader, Tommy Miller, is walking toward her with a few of his friends, an evil smirk curling up the edges of his mouth in his fat, ruddy face. The other children edge closer, watching. The girl feels surrounded. She wishes she could fly away.

"You're that girl that's always hanging out in the cemetery," says Tommy. "What are you, some kind of weirdo?" He laughs. "You like hanging out there so much, I bet you wish you were dead!"

The girl tries to ignore him, but the words cut deep. She clutches the finger in the leather pouch at her chest, her heart thumping a fast beat against it. Tommy takes a menacing step forward, brushing his lank hair from his oily forehead before clenching a fist, but he stops when he sees the old school bus turn the corner at the end of the long dirt road along the river, and ramble toward them.

The children line up to step onto the bus. The girl is last on. She bobs her head quickly at the bus driver lady with the long, beaked nose, hunched over the wheel in a big, puffy black coat. She falls quickly into the cracked leather seat at the front, slouching down so that Tommy and the others can't see her. The bus driver glances in the rearview mirror, her beady eyes catching the girl's, nods once, and drives on.

THE SCHOOL DAY passes like many others. The girl spends morning recess hiding from Tommy and his Neanderthal friends in a stall in the girl's bathroom, a paper "Out of Order" sign taped to the door. She crouches on top of a toilet, legs pulled up, watching the other girls through the small gap near the hinge as they laugh and gossip and put on makeup from little pink palettes. Tommy busts in, sending the girls into a screaming frenzy, but he is quickly dragged out by a hall monitor who threatens to send him to the principal's office.

In class, the girl slinks down at her desk, trying to be as small as possible so Ms. Williams will not call on her. She watches the crows through the large classroom window, perched on the ledge outside as they hop from one little crow foot and back, taking turns guarding their queen. At the end of the day, Ms. Williams passes out graded papers, giving the girl a sad, pitying smile when she hands her a test marked with a big red D+ on it. Some of the other students see the score and snicker, whispering about her behind their hands. When the bell rings, the girl shoves the test into her backpack and hurries out to line up at the bus stop. She tries to stay out of Tommy's line of sight, ducking behind other students as they wait.

At her stop, the girl watches Tommy get off the bus first. After mumbling thanks to the driver, she steps off, her feet sinking into the snow. The bus pulls away. She starts walking along the side of the road toward her home when *wham!* Something slams into her from behind and the snow-covered ground reaches up to meet her face. She lands hard, dazed from the sudden, unexpected impact. Her backpack is heavy on top of her.

Laughter rings out. Crows circle overhead, cawing. The girl blinks, and comes to. The world is sideways, rotating, the ground tilting slightly on its axis. Slowly, she picks herself up, her knees and palms scraped and bloody from falling on ice, drops of her red blood stark against the white snow. Tommy Miller elbows his friend and points, snickering. Tears well up in the girl's eyes, her lip trembles, but she won't let them see her cry. She keeps her gaze lowered, and tries to quickly dart away. Tommy steps in front of her path.

"Where do you think you're going?" he demands. The girl looks up at him, imagining what it would be like to fight back, imagining the look of surprise on his face. But she's outnumbered, and she backs away, looking for a chance to run. The boys circle around her until there is no escape. Tommy cocks a fist back to punch. The girl closes her eyes and cowers, raising her arms to cover her face and head, bracing for the blow.

A pickup truck rolls to a stop next to them, interrupting Tommy's attack. Mr. Hawthorne pokes his head out of the window.

"What's going on here?" Mr. Hawthorne asks. The bullies scatter, and suddenly, the girl is alone with him.

Mr. Hawthorne looks over at the girl's bloody hands and knees, and clears his throat, a slight cough that sounds like a growl. He looks angrily at the boys running away down the old country road, becoming tinier in the distance.

"Let's get you cleaned up, shall we?" says Mr. Hawthorne. The girl hesitates, and Mr. Hawthorne smiles. "I have ice cream as a special treat."

The girl nods slightly, and walks to the pickup truck. Mr. Hawthorne reaches over and opens the door for her. The girl hops up onto the bench seat, and slams the door shut. She's nervous, but Mr. Hawthorne isn't a stranger. He smiles at her and turns up the song on the radio, a bluesy song the girl hasn't heard before. He sings along as he puts the truck into drive and turns down his driveway toward his house in the woods. The girl looks out the window, watching her opaque reflection bob her head to the music, as a flock of crows circles overhead.

AS THE GIRL sits on his marble kitchen counter, her legs dangling over the side, Mr. Hawthorne rolls up the leg of her jeans past her knee and inspects it. Her knee is a red scrape, and she winces at the sting, but Mr. Hawthorne smiles, tickling her under her knee, and she giggles at the touch. He takes a first aid kit from a cabinet and cleans up the girl's injuries, wiping away the blood and dirt with a damp washcloth before gently placing ointment and a Sesame Street Band-Aid on her knee. The girl feels dizzy being close to him, breathing in his strong, woodsy scent.

"All better now," he says, standing up from his crouching position in front of her with a smile. "How about some ice cream?"

The girl shyly nods yes. Mr. Hawthorne scoops big spoonfuls of vanilla ice cream into two bowls, and sits down at the kitchen table. He takes a bite, and the girl does the same. The cold sweetness coats her mouth and she takes another spoonful quickly.

"Careful, or you'll give yourself a cold headache," Mr. Hawthorne warns. The girl nods.

"Angela," asks Mr. Hawthorne, "do those boys pick on you often?"

The girl looks down at her ice cream, the creamy vanilla gathering against the sides of the bowl like a melting snowball. A lump in her throat chokes her, and she clutches the leather pouch, holding the finger in her fist.

"Yes," she whispers, not meeting his eyes.

"Angela, look at me," says Mr. Hawthorne. The girl looks up.

"I want you to know, you can always come to me if you need anything," says Mr. Hawthorne. His brown eyes are kind, warm. "Anything at all, okay? Even if it's just ice cream."

The girl nods, smiling slightly, her cheeks hot. She feels something odd, like butterflies in her stomach. She finishes her ice cream, hops down from the counter, and quickly leaves, skipping down his front porch to the gravel-covered clearing, her backpack bumping against her back. When she reaches the edge of the clearing, she looks back toward Mr. Hawthorne's house, where he is watching her from the front porch. He raises a hand and waves at her. She waves back, and then darts into the woods.

HER STEPMOTHER'S BEDROOM is strictly off limits. The last time her stepmother had caught her in her room, she'd flown into a rage and slapped the girl. The girl had escaped around the woman, down the stairs, and out the front door before she could be stopped. She had spent the remainder of the day out in the meadow until way past dinnertime, when the house was dark and she could sneak back in without being seen.

But the lure of the forbidden is too great. The girl tiptoes over to the closed door of her stepmother's room, and stares at the shiny brass doorknob waiting to be turned. With the sting of a reddening hand fading from her memory, replaced with memories of little boxes filled with jewelry and soft, pretty things, she turns the doorknob slowly. The door creaks slightly as she pushes it open. The girl flinches at the sound, though the woman isn't even home. Inside, the décor is feminine, all evidence of her father gone so that it's almost like he didn't exist in the first place.

The girl starts with the closet, opening shoeboxes and searching in pockets for secrets. She isn't sure what she's looking for, but she knows there has to be some clue, something that will tell her why her stepmother hates her so much, why the woman had thrown away all pictures of her parents and erased them from the girl's life. But soon the search is forgotten as the girl's love of shiny, pretty things takes over. She starts trying on her stepmother's straw hats and high heels. The underwear drawer comes next. The girl picks through dainty, lacey things, holding her stepmother's brassieres up to her own flat chest in the mirror. She imagines she is a woman with large breasts and a tiny waist like the women in the fashion magazines her stepmother gets in the mail.

The girl reaches into the leather pouch around her neck, and pries the diamond ring off the dead finger. She slips the ring on. It's too big and the diamond is heavy and slips to the side. She imagines she is older. A woman. And Mr. Hawthorne just proposed to her with the ring, kneeling in front of her as he slips the ring on her finger and kisses her hand. She holds her hand up and shows off the ring to an imaginary crowd, gushing like she's seen women in movies do.

She sits down at her stepmother's vanity, admiring the way the diamond glitters in the light of the green Tiffany lamp off to the side. She picks up her stepmother's tube of red lipstick and starts to paint her lips. Her hand wavers a bit and she messes up the line, but no bother, she wipes it away with the back of her hand. But that just makes things worse, and soon bright red streaks of lipstick cover her mouth and cheeks and hands, like smeared blood.

"What do you think you're doing?" the girl's stepmother screeches. The girl's head whips to the door. Her stepmother is standing in the doorframe, her eyes blazing. The girl scrambles to put away the lipstick, to hide what she was doing, but her stepmother is already upon her, one strong hand bruising the girl's upper arm as she drags her away from the vanity.

"Ow, you're hurting me!" the girl cries out. The woman shakes the girl, her face twisted into a mask of rage. She raises an open palm like she is going to slap her. But then she notices the diamond ring on the girl's finger, and the woman grabs her hand and rips the ring away.

"What is this? Have you been stealing again?" Her stepmother shakes the ring in the girl's face.

"It's nothing!"

"Where did you get it?"

"Nowhere!" the girl sobs.

Her stepmother drags the girl kicking and screaming out of her bedroom, down the stairs, and across the backyard to the toolshed. She rips open the old wooden door and throws the girl inside, slamming down the latch and locking her in. The girl scrabbles in the dark, crying out. Something sharp slices her palm. She clutches her bloodied, injured hand to her chest, resting it on the leather pouch in which the dead finger still hangs around her neck. Blood trickles down her palm to her wrist and her forearm, falling in drops from the tip of her elbow to the dirt.

The girl curls into a tiny ball and cries in the dark, her sobs coming in icy gasps. Soon, there are no more tears. She shivers with no jacket until a numbness settles over her. Her eyes adjust and she makes out shapes in the dim light. The wound on her palm throbs, but the initial sting has faded, and the girl sits up and tries to decide what to do. She's been locked in the cellar before with the cobwebs and spiders, but never the toolshed. It's filled with sharp metal objects, and the girl imagines there are monsters in the dark, monsters with gnashing teeth trying to eat her.

She thinks about the finger in the leather pouch. She pretends that she's buried alive in this shed, the dark enveloping and encroaching around her. She feels like she might suffocate. She needs to be strong, strong like the woman with the finger. And dig her way out.

The girl spies a trowel and grabs it, frantically digging at the edge of the dirt floor where it meets the far wall. She puts the trowel down and paws at the earth with her hands, clay clumps crumbling under her bloody fingers. Rays of cool sunlight illuminate the growing hole, and it's finally large enough for the girl to fit through. She goes head first, ducking under the sharp tin siding. A painful scrape rips her dress down to the skin, and she cries out as she escapes.

She breaks out in a dead run like a startled rabbit, away from the shed, away from her stepmother, away from home, and ducks into the woods. The girl stumbles through the dense underbrush, crossing over streams and scrambling up hills in her haste to escape. The cool air fills her lungs, drying the tears in her eyes. She falls along a path she knows well, the driveway that leads to Mr. Hawthorne's cabin in the middle of the clearing. Her footsteps crunch over the gravel and ice and snow as she runs. She glances behind her. Drops of her red blood leave a trail on the white snow like breadcrumbs.

The cabin looks like a fairytale gingerbread cottage, sitting in the clearing, a light dusting of snow covering the pitched roof. A fire in the hearth sends wisps of smoke up from the chimney. Lights are on inside, and she sees Mr. Hawthorne sitting in a chair by the fire, reading, his feet kicked up on a stool. The girl crouches by the wood pile outside, and imagines that Mr. Hawthorne will wrap her in a blanket, give her warm soup, and read her stories by the fire. He won't make her tell him what happened, and he won't return her to her stepmother.

The girl stands up from her hiding spot, and starts walking toward the front door. The air is icy on her bare back from the tear in her dress, and she shivers. She feels weak, cold, and gray, like a ghost fading into the dark. She looks down at her pale, bare legs and imagines them disappearing. She reaches out toward the warmth of the cottage, toward Mr. Hawthorne, before she can vanish.

But then, she notices something. A slight tapping on her chest. *Tap, tap, tap.* A pulsing, like the pointed tip of a finger is rapping out a rhythm. She looks down at the leather pouch around her neck, confused. She takes another step forward, and the tapping becomes stronger, like the finger in the pouch is beating out a warning. *TAP,*

TAP, TAP. The girl stills. The tapping steadies into a strong thumping rhythm. The girl realizes she is feeling her heartbeat, quick and steady, mirroring the tapping from the finger.

A wolf howls in the distance. The girl backs away, lifting one foot and then the next. She stumbles on a rock and catches herself before she falls. She turns and starts running away, glancing back over her shoulder at the cabin. What looked warm and inviting before now looks like a dangerous den. The tapping of the finger fades until all she can feel is the pounding of her own heart. She feels alive, feels the blood coursing through her veins, strong and red.

As Angela runs back through the darkening woods away from the cabin, the crows caw overhead, circling her, making sure their queen returns to safety.

THE NEXT MORNING in the cemetery, Angela drops on her knees next to an elm tree, the gnarled roots poking up through the icy snow and dirt. She takes a small trowel from the pocket of her parka and starts to dig through the frozen earth. When she has a hole about the size of her hand, she takes the finger from the leather pouch around her neck and holds it up, turning it this way and that.

The finger is just a carrot now. A plain old baby carrot with a rooty point, curved slightly at the middle. Dried and shriveled, the tip is bleached white with dirt crusted in the cracks. In her mind's eye, she sees it as a finger one last time. As she gives it thanks, the images slip away like wisps of smoke, and all she's left with is the carrot.

Angela says a silent prayer and places the carrot in the hole, covering it with cold, crumbling earth until only a small, raised lump of ground remains. She takes off the leather pouch, ducking her head under the loop around her neck, and wraps the cord around the pouch. She places it on top of the small dirt mound, marking the grave like a cairn. She wants to remember, doesn't want the carrot finger to be forgotten the way other important things in her life have been.

All around her, the crows nod their approval, cawing and stamping their little crow feet. Overhead, the gray sky breaks and beams of light pierce the clouds, starting to melt the snow and wake up the spring.

"Hey freak."

Angela turns her head at the words and watches as Tommy Miller strides toward her with determination, his friends flanking him on either side. He hops over a gravestone, a menacing look in his eyes. His hands are balled into fists.

The girl considers running. Flying away like the crows before the boys can reach her. She could hide in the woods, hide in the safety of the shadows. She could fade away until she is forgotten as well.

She looks down at the finger she has just buried and marked to remember. A feeling sparks and unfurls in her stomach, licking up her sides and consuming her. She barely recognizes the fire burning inside: rage. She shakes, her breath coming in shallow gasps, and she steels herself, reaching for the garden trowel. Her hand wraps around the wooden handle, squeezing it. All around her, the crows, feeling their queen's wrath, caw and cry out, beating their wings against the air. Behind her, Tommy and his friends come to a stop in a half circle, trapping her against the tree.

Angela gets to her feet, clutching the garden trowel in her fist. She turns to face the boys, relishing the looks of surprise on their faces as she strikes.

Eighteen at Cedar Junction
Andrew C. Peterson

I OPENED THE dark brown door to Dermody's Saloon. A gust of warm autumn wind and a few leaves followed me inside. Dark plywood paneling dotted with cheap bronze sconces covered the walls. A wedge of light as if from a Hopper painting fell on a lone figure sitting in front of an old cash register at the left end of the bar.

"Close the door, please," a voice rasped. "The light bothers my eyes."

I closed the door. The wedge disappeared. My eyes adjusted to the gloom. Cornelius Dermody stood up at the end of the bar.

"Mr. Tannhauser."

"Mr. Dermody."

I limped down three short steps to the main floor. A few Formica tables jutted out from the wall to the right of the door. Metal stools with vinyl seats were tucked underneath them. The small windows above the entranceway behind me didn't let in much of the wan, late afternoon autumnal light. The yellow glow from the lit wall sconces cast a funereal pall. My boot steps echoed in the empty dimness. My cane tapped as I walked toward Dermody, who sized me up the whole time.

Meeting with a client means that I always arrive neat, clean, and casual. Today that meant a black V-neck sweater, 5.11 khaki tactical pants, and a black leather jacket that hid the Glock nestled in the small of my back. My brown cowboy boots from Cavender's probably threw him off, as did my cane. Few people wear cowboy boots in Boston. Most PIs don't have canes.

I sized him up, too. Cornelius Dermody had a head of gray hair, a heavily lined face with compact features, and a thick neck. He was tall. His solid arms filled out the jacket of the black double-breasted suit. He had clearly used the prison gym to good effect. For a man in his late fifties, he was an imposing figure.

According to the *Boston Globe*, Dermody was convicted of shaking down local strip clubs for protection money. He was also riddled with inoperable pancreatic cancer. His only son drowned in a boating accident while Dermody was inside. His wife had abandoned him a decade ago. He had returned home to nothing and no one. In six months—probably less—he was going to die painfully and alone. His debt to society had been paid, but to what end? If I didn't also know that he used to willingly inflict pain on people for a living, then I may have pitied him. But I did know.

He stood to greet me. I motioned for him to stop. "Arms up, if you please."

"If you must," he sighed, raising his hands in surrender.

I leaned my cane against the bar. As I frisked him, I realized that his suit actually hung a bit loosely. Up close, I could see the gray pallor of his skin. Like my father used to wear, his cologne—Old Spice—dominated the bar's stale air. I removed a .22 from his shoulder holster and a knife from his pocket.

"Old habits, Mr. Tannhauser . . ."

"Which is exactly why I frisked you, Mr. Dermody."

"Smart lad."

I placed the .22 and the blade on the bar nearer to me. A closer look at Dermody showed that he had the black eyes of a shark swimming in a yellow pool of disease. So much for fake news, the *Globe* nailed this one. He's dying.

"Satisfied?" he asked.

"I am. Would you care to . . . ?" I stepped back, raising my hands slightly.

Dermody waved his hand, dismissively. "Nah. I'll just ask. Are you carrying?"

I nodded. "I am."

"Fine," he said, extending his hand. I took it. We shook. His hand was cold, like a stone in winter.

"Thank you for coming," he said. "May I offer you a drink?"

He gestured behind him. On the bar was a new bottle of Redbreast twenty-one-year-old Irish whiskey. Two crystal glasses accompanied it. I nodded. He turned to open the bottle. While he did, I looked around the saloon. Neon signs from long-defunct beer companies lined the wall on my left. The wood bar was carved with initials and marred with graffiti. I read a few lines. A woman named Brigit got around.

I heard the familiar sloshing sound of whiskey flowing. He handed me a glass. He raised his; I raised mine. I'm not sure what we were saluting, but it didn't matter. My salary didn't allow for top-shelf whiskey. I lifted my glass to my nose, breathing deep the musky aroma. We drank.

"That's the good stuff," he declared.

"Chandler once said, 'There is no bad whiskey. There are only some whiskeys that aren't as good as others,' " I said. "Who am I to argue?"

"Nothing like it." He sipped again.

I savored the taste of my drink. Dermody drained his glass and reached for the bottle. I emptied mine. After pouring us both another two fingers, he sat on his barstool again, with one foot on the footrest and his left elbow on the bar. Dermody looked about the room, his eyes focusing on elsewhen.

I knew the look. I had no idea what Dermody saw. My own elsewhen was the sun-blasted sands of Iraq. I rubbed my bad knee absentmindedly, a gift I received on those selfsame sands. I gave Dermody his moment. I glanced around, too—confident that I was just a man in a saloon while Dermody was a man who had come home again.

The bar hadn't been open to the public in quite some time. The empty dust-covered shelves behind it surrounded a wall-size mirror framed in gold. An old Wurlitzer jukebox sat at the other end of the bar. A kitchen door was next to it. Scanning back past Dermody, a clock hung silently on the wall above the old beer company signs. I never drank here, but I remembered places like this. Dermody's saloon was an old Boston mob hangout back in the day. That day was decades ago. Gentrification was swallowing old neighborhood haunts like this place. Soon the saloon, like Dermody himself, would be gone, replaced and forgotten.

"Family business?" I asked, not knowing what else to say.

"It was." He smiled. It didn't work. His face wasn't used to the motions. "My grandfather opened this place during the war—not the first one, the second one. It went to my Da and then to me. I was on the inside when I took ownership. I missed Da's passing."

He looked away from me, tapping the bar with an index finger, his brow furrowed.

"It should have gone to my son. Paperwork was screwed up, so it stayed in my name." Dermody rubbed his hand across his chin. "We never got the chance to correct it before Liam had the accident."

He paused as if startled by the honesty of his own voice.

So far, I was doing exactly what I had been paid handsomely to do.

Dermody's man had hired me to spend one half hour with his boss, just to talk over a good bottle of Irish whiskey. If Mr. Dermody liked what he heard after our time together, then he would offer me a job. I thought twice about it. After all, Dermody was rumored to have killed three people. He also survived three attempts on his own life. Yet, ten thousand dollars upfront was too good to pass up. I took his money, I drank his whiskey, and I was armed. Now our conversation was an Irish wake, and I was his sin-eater.

"I was no businessman," Dermody said. "But I couldn't let the place go. I closed it instead of selling it."

No words came. I nodded instead.

"I used to conduct my business right here," he said while tapping the bar. I shook people down and roughed them up right here," he said. "I was good at it, too. Real good." He smiled at this, wrecking his face.

"Apparently," I replied. "Good enough to do eighteen at Cedar Junction."

Anger flashed in Dermody's eyes. "Don't be crass, Mr. Tannhauser," he said hard.

"No insult intended, Mr. Dermody," I said, smiling. "Just an observation."

"You're not known as a tactless man."

"Begging your pardon, Mr. Dermody, but you don't know me from Adam."

"True enough," he replied. "But I know of you. You're known on these streets as a man with a knight's morals and a killer's instinct."

"I'll have to give my publicist a raise."

"So you don't deny the reputation?"

"Would it matter if I did? I am who I am." I drained my glass.

"I've also heard that you've killed a man before, Mr. Tannhauser.

A few, in fact." He leaned in closer as if we were talking out of turn during a sermon.

"What did you say earlier about being crass, Mr. Dermody?"

"Being a PI must be a bloody business. Is there blood on your hands, Mr. Tannhauser?"

"None that I'll discuss with you."

Dermody leaned back on his stool, finishing his whiskey.

"Why am I here, Mr. Dermody?"

"To talk, Mr. Tannhauser. You work here. You know these streets," his voice trailed off. "I don't know anyone here anymore."

"You left this neighborhood a long time ago, Mr. Dermody."

"No one ever really leaves the neighborhood, and please, call me 'Neely.' "

"It's your dime, Neely." I picked up the bottle and gestured toward his glass.

He nodded, extending his glass. "May I call you 'Adrian'?"

"It's a free country." I shrugged, pouring him a swallow. I refilled my own glass.

"Do you have an office now?" he asked.

"I had one in Jamaica Plain but briefly. I gave it up. Technology allows my office to be wherever I am. Why pay overhead?"

"Smart."

"I thought so."

"Is business good?"

"Good enough to pay the rent. Not good enough to turn down this meeting."

"I wasn't sure you'd come."

"For a moment, I wasn't sure either. I knew this meeting would be trouble."

"Did you now?" he repositioned himself slightly as he spoke.

"I did. I came anyway."

"Why is that?" he asked after taking another sip.

"Curiosity, I guess. The world can be so dull." I held my glass to my lips. "Whatever today brings, it won't be dull." I drank.

"No, Adrian, it won't," Neely rasped. He adjusted his position on the stool. A slight grimace spread over his features. He swallowed his pain and chased it with whiskey.

"Are you married, Adrian?"

"No."

"Haven't found the right girl? Or guy? Or whatever?" He shrugged. "You never know these days anymore."

"No, I haven't met the right girl yet, Neely."

"I met my wife here," he said. "I saw her come through that kitchen door on her first day on the job. Waitress. God, she was beautiful. Fucking perfect."

He smiled. This time it didn't look painful.

"We were married in less than a year. Liam was born eight months after that."

I laughed. "How did you explain that to the parish priest?"

He chuckled. "We tithed generously. Father Reardon knew well enough not to do the math." He sipped his drink. "We baptized Liam in the Lord's house, and then we baptized him here. I poured whiskey on his head, anointing him."

"Here?" I asked.

"Right here," he said, tapping the bar. "Whiskey and holy water—a potent combination."

I smiled at the mental image. "Indeed."

"My own Da arranged it. Of course, things were different back then. In those days, people like us were royalty. My Da dined with bishops and politicians and badmouthed them both."

"It's all a little before my time," I replied.

"Mine too," he said with regret. "Mine too."

Neely stood up, stretched a bit, and grimaced as he did so. "In '97 the press spilled the beans on the whole thing. Whitey was gone by this time, and the place fell to shit. I got pinched for, well, it doesn't matter for what. I got pinched and sent in."

"This is all public knowledge, Neely. Why the history lesson?"

He turned on me quick, quicker than I would have thought. "Oh yeah? Anywhere in those history lessons that you had, did you learn that I loved my wife? Or my son? Or how missing my son is an open fucking wound every day?"

"No," I replied softly. "I didn't."

"Fuck right, you didn't," he spat. Placing his drink down, he rested his hands on the edge of the bar, leaning forward in silence. "Fuck right you didn't . . ." he whispered, through a labored breath. He coughed a wet cough. Standing again, he ran his hands across his face and through his hair. Grabbing his drink, he walked toward the end of the bar while looking around the room.

"So many memories . . ." he said, composing himself once more.

"Don't wander too far, Neely," I said, watching him.

He stopped moving and sat on a stool at the bar's right-side end near the kitchen door. His gaze wandered to an antique clock on the far wall from his seat, nearer to me. He gestured at it.

"See that clock? My grandfather put that there when he opened this place."

I looked at it. It was a regulator pendulum wall clock, dark oak. Dust covered the cracked glass over the clock face.

"It only chimed at closing time. Everyone packed up and left after that. No muss, no fuss." He sighed. "Hasn't worked in years."

A pause. Neely's gaze was unfocused again.

"Liam used to sit right here, sliding glasses to our friends. He always pretended to be a bartender. He couldn't wait to own this place."

"I'm sorry for your loss. Your losses." I was surprised to find that I meant it.

Neely nodded, then stared into his glass. "I'm dying, Adrian," he rasped. "Friggin' cancer, can you believe it?"

"I know."

"A vet wouldn't let a dog die the way I'm going to."

"Probably not."

He placed his glass on the bar. "Do you have any thoughts on death, Adrian?"

My gaze faltered. Screams of the dying buffeted me. The sound of gunfire and flies swarming over the dead echoed in my ears. The stench of loose bowels filled my nostrils. "None worth sharing."

His bushy eyebrows shot up. "No? Why not?"

"We're all dying, Neely," I said. "Some of us just know our expiration date."

He whistled. "That's damned cold, Adrian, but true enough."

Neely caught my eye and held the glass up with his left hand. "To life."

I raised mine in return. "To life."

Neely put his own glass to his lips. I did the same, tilting both my head and the shot glass.

I heard a ripping sound. My eyes darted to Neely, who now stood, aiming a pistol at me. I moved toward my left as he squeezed the trigger—a sharp crack. A bullet cut into my right shoulder.

I threw my glass at Neely backhanded. He ducked as I reached for the Glock tucked in my waistband, yanking it free. I could still use my arm. Hurt though. A lot. I aimed for his chest but pulled the trigger too quickly as I moved. The loud report filled the room as my round went into the jukebox behind Neely. The Wurlitzer shattered.

Neely stood firm behind the end of the bar. His arm was now level; his features compacted like he was holding his breath. He pulled the trigger. Another crack. His shot flew wide, glass shattered behind me.

I stole a quick glance at him. Shark eyes. He'd fire again. I had no cover with him diagonally across from me at the far corner of the bar. With nowhere to go left or right, I went down. My lousy leg buckled under me as I crouched down to the floor; pain ripped up to my hip. I grunted in agony as I rolled onto my side, getting into position. My weight pressed on my right shoulder blade; my gaze focused on the corner of the bar, my gun at the ready. Neely was now out of my line of sight, but I heard his footsteps as he moved quickly to the other end of the bar. He turned the corner. Our eyes locked. I fired first and placed two rounds into his torso. He dropped his gun, grabbing his abdomen. Blood oozed between his fingers. He stood awkwardly now like a large marionette barely held up by a small hand. Then he crumpled to the floor, strings cut.

Blood trickled down my right arm as I stood and limped toward Neely. A loud ringing was in my ears. His gun was at my feet. It was a second .22 with duct tape stuck to it. I kicked the gun across the floor away from us.

Neely was having difficulty breathing. I put my Glock back in my waistband and pulled my cell phone from my pocket. I called 911. I knelt down beside him as I put my phone away again, looking him over as his breath rattled in his chest. "Help is on the way, Neely."

"I hope not," he choked. Blood soaked his abdomen, probably from his liver or a tear in his abdominal aorta. From the wheezing and gasping sounds, I knew I hit a lung. The EMTs would never arrive in time.

"Why not?"

"This is . . . a better death . . ."

"How so?"

"On my feet," he rasped, "like a man."

My hands shook with anger.

"Thank you," he gurgled. His gaze locked with mine.

"For what? Making me your executioner? There's enough blood on my hands, you bastard."

His lips moved. No sound came with it.

I leaned in closer, "What?"

"You were defending yourself," he said slowly and softly. "Killer's instinct, remember?"

"Not like this, Neely. Not like this," I barked.

"Just like this." He looked at me and wheezed, "Today is my expiration day . . ."

His eyelids half-closed, his breathing stopped. I heard the siren's wail of an ambulance approaching the saloon. Charon's ferry arrived as it always does: in silence.

SOMETIME LATER, I sat on the edge of a hospital bed with my bandaged arm. The bullet to my shoulder was a through and through that thankfully missed my subclavian artery. Otherwise, I'd be lying in the morgue beside Neely.

A detective was interviewing me, taking notes.

"Suicide by PI? That's a new one," he said while scribbling.

"I guess."

"Hey, I could just put the cause of death down as 'lead poisoning.' "
He laughed.

I didn't.

And I didn't for a long time afterward.

Extinct Things

Jennifer Fickley-Baker

"STELLA, THIS WAY! Stay close!" Marina called over her shoulder, then turned to continue pushing her younger daughter, Sadie, in her stroller, down the hallway past the museum's Grecian Hall of Sculpture. Sadie's blonde head turned from side to side as the toddler chattered to herself, excited to be going to a new place, to be going anywhere really.

Stella, Marina's seven-year-old, dashed up from behind.

"There are statues of naked people in there!" Stella said, her brunette ponytail swinging. "They have leaves on their privates! And they're playing Frisbee! Why would someone play Frisbee with no clothes on?"

For a split second, Marina felt her mood lift. Stella had no such thing as inner dialogue. Every thought dribbled out in sentence form.

"The Greek statues? Yeah, they're funny. And it's not a Frisbee, it's a discus, but . . . sort of the same idea I think."

Stella fell into step next to her and folded her spindly arms over her chest, her explosive kid energy reined in for the moment. "You *can* see their butts, though," Stella whispered a minute later.

Marina steered them farther down the right wing of the first floor, taking in every detail as they walked—the shivery smell of too much air-conditioning, the squeak of their shoes on the slick floor, the echo of their voices inside the empty hallway. Being back in the History Museum of Pittsburgh—her *father's* museum, as she grew up thinking of it—felt as familiar as stepping back into her long-gone childhood bedroom.

She glimpsed vented silver tubes that lined the ceiling as they walked—newly added state-of-the-art air purifiers. They were mandatory nearly everywhere now. She shook her head. God, how the world had changed since the last time she'd last been here, which was when? She tried to remember. Twenty-two-years old and about to leave for her marine biology grad program, maybe? Now she was a forty-year-old widow with two daughters. Her father, the most renowned paleontologist in the northeast, had also passed.

In a way, it'd felt like she'd been gone forever; in a way it'd felt like she'd been gone five minutes.

Marina tapped her phone screen and opened the museum app. Another change. Cell phones held everything now. Maps, ID cards, driver's licenses, passports, passes, tickets—even money. Paper could cause viral transfer. No one would touch it.

"It says it's down to the right." She clicked the screen to sleep and slid the phone into the pocket of her yellow cardigan.

The wing they were heading to had formerly housed a fusty insect collection she'd always avoided as a child. Someone else at the museum must've had the same opinion of its dullness because the entire wing had been blown open for the expansion. According to the email she'd received two months ago announcing the exhibit, it was to be dedicated to her father's work. She'd hardly believed it, that a museum—a *public* place—would bother expanding in a time like this. Then again, it was always bizarre what rich people would spend their money on.

Around the corner a set of fresh glass doors sat propped open. New gold lettering above the door read, DINOSAURS IN THEIR ERA!

Above them, an air purifier hissed.

"Okay, here we go." Marina rolled Sadie underneath the signage, moving off of the sleek marble and onto a floor of poured concrete that had been pockmarked and cracked to look like volcanic terrain. Stella hung close to Marina's elbow.

"Wow," Marina and Stella said in tandem as they stepped inside. Even Sadie leaned forward and babbled, jabbing a tiny finger forward.

The museum's previous dinosaur exhibit had been limited to a dimly lit room up on the second floor, with a T-rex poised ominously in the center and smaller Jurassic-era creatures in each corner. But DINO-SAURS IN THEIR ERA! stretched out before them as a walk-through diorama that wound through what looked like three, maybe four, bas-ketball-court-sized rooms. The path they stood on twisted and turned through clusters of dinosaurs that Marina recognized from the Me-sozoic, Jurassic, and Cretaceous eras, each in little habitats separated by knee-high rock work or thick clusters of faux paleo-plants. She was happily surprised to see that all the dinos were fossilized skeletons, no animatronics. Her father had always argued that people came to mu-seums to see "the real thing," not robots covered in rubber.

She'd taken just a few steps when a gold plaque on the wall inside the door caught her attention.

Dedicated to the work of
DR. ALFRED ST. JAMES,
Paleontologist

"Look, Stella," Marina nodded. "Your grandfather's name. Gosh, he would've loved this. He would've loved that the two of you would've seen all of this."

It had been a risk, bringing the girls here. Taking them anywhere really, since the virus had mutated, become more dangerous, killed faster. For a moment, it felt worth it, as if she were safe in her father's house again. That she'd made the right decision for the three of them.

"Cool! Can I have your phone to take a pic?" Stella thrust her hand out. As if on cue, the phone buzzed in the pocket of her cardigan, a silent text alert.

Marina's stomach plummeted. *Five times*, she could hear her father say.

"Not now," Marina said, glancing back at the plaque. "We'll take pics on the way out. Let's just enjoy it first. No phones."

"Okay! Let's go!" Stella dashed ahead, calling back as she ran, "What are all of these, Mom? Do they have a raptor?"

But Marina kept her eyes on the plaque a few seconds longer, slipping her fingers into her pocket and clicked the button on the side of the phone, acknowledging the text without reading it.

Five times . . .

Her mouth went dry. A brick of anxiety began to form in her stomach. She turned and pushed Sadie, who was now babbling at the top of her tiny voice, deeper into the exhibit.

Marina rolled alongside a brontosaurus on her left. Its tail bones grew from the size of tiny piano keys and arched up into its massive spine and back legs. Its long neck stretched up toward a tree, where its skull poked its jaws toward a palm tree, as if readying to eat leaves.

"Look, Sadie, a big guy!" Stella said.

"Grrrawr!" Sadie attempted a snarl and curled her fingers into a dinosaur claw. "GRRAWAR!"

Stella gasped. "Mom! Look up there!" She was standing in the center of the aisle ahead of them, pointing at a massive winged and lethal-beaked skeleton hanging from the ceiling.

"Oh, wow." Marina looked up, then stepped around Sadie's stroller. She stooped down next to her and pointed up. "Look Sadie, a birdie!"

"Birdie?" Sadie repeated, and stabbed a chubby baby finger in the air. Her ice blue eyes—Will's eyes—curiously absorbing it all.

"That was a *bird*? What kind of bird?" Stella asked, making a face and walked back toward them.

"A pterosaur," Marina said, straightening herself, still taking it in. Its wingspan, she guessed, was at least forty feet wide and its beak alone was the size of a rowboat. Its entire skeleton tilted downward as if it was about to swoop down and snatch them up in one bite. It looked marvelous and intimidating as hell, even though it was just bones. "It's the largest bird that ever lived on earth," Marina added, then pursed her lips, ending her explanation there.

"Cool!" Stella pivoted and walked backwards toward a pile of prehistoric lizards up ahead.

Marina steered Sadie's stroller past the brontosaurus. Her cell phone pinged in her pocket again. Another text. Seriously? She felt the brick in her gut ache. She snatched the phone from her pocket, clicked the mute button.

"Damn it," she whispered, then tossed it into the stroller's basket.

Five times . . .

Distract yourself, she thought. She paused the stroller in front of a patch of duck-billed dinosaurs, their necks perked up and backs straightened as if listening for a predator. She unclipped Sadie and gathered her up onto her hip.

"Look at the duckies, Sadie. Big duckies." Marina smoothed down Sadie's blonde curls and kissed her perfect, smooth skin, inhaled the gentle scent of the baby shampoo she still used to bathe her. She could feel Sadie's little heart beating against her chest as the toddler carelessly looked around, soaking in everything.

Down in the stroller basket, her cell phone vibrated silently. A call this time? Jesus.

Marina squeezed Sadie closer to her for a second as she tilted her wrist to look at her own Apple Health wrist monitor. She clicked the button. Ninety-eight degrees. Normal.

Five times . . .

"LIFE ON EARTH has been nearly obliterated from the planet five times," her father had told her once. They were in his lab at the museum and he was peering into a microscope, piecing together the skeleton of a tiny oculudentavis, one of the smallest prehistoric lizards ever discovered, using two sets of tweezers. "They were called mass extinction events," he said, without looking up.

At the time they'd had this conversation, Marina hadn't paid attention to his words—she'd always thought dinosaurs *themselves* were always more exciting to her than *how* they died.

Until the viral infection took hold in Asia. And then swept around the world.

Then Marina began Googling terms she'd remembered from her father's conversation, his warning that yes, their world could in fact end. Just as it had five times before.

The first mass extinction, the Ordovician-Silurian event, had happened 440 million years ago when falling carbon dioxide levels plunged the planet into a cataclysmic cooling phase and life literally froze to death.

Next was the Devonian Extinction, 359 million years ago, when a series of comets, meteorites (or both) smashed into Earth. The heat of the impact polluted the atmosphere and seventy-to-eighty percent of life suffocated.

Third was the Permian-Triassic extinction event, 250 million years ago. Volcanic eruptions in Siberia released toxic levels of methane gas and carbon dioxide, poisoning the air. Ninety-five percent of life suffocated again.

Fourth. The Triassic-Jurassic extinction, 210 million years ago—the first of two extinction events that wiped out dinosaurs. Insane volcanic activity turned the air into poison and the oceans into acid. Seventy-five percent of marine animals and vertebrae perished, including the pterosaur, whose massive wings couldn't achieve enough lift in the filthy atmosphere to take flight to hunt. Instead, pterosaurs, like hundreds of other species, starved to death where they stood.

And fifth. The Cretaceous-Paleogene extinction, 66 million years ago. An asteroid six-miles wide smashed into the Yucatan Peninsula with the power of 10 billion atomic bombs, cracking the Earth's crust and tsunaming the oceans. Debris flew so high up out of the planet's atmosphere that it blotted out the sun, plunging Earth into an eternal night. When the mess reentered Earth's atmosphere, it did so so fast that it burst into flames. Fire rained down on any life left. Seventy-five percent of life was destroyed.

But now . . . sixth. The Anthropocene Extinction . . . confirmed by even . . .

"MOM, THERE'S A MAN."

Marina felt Stella pulling at her elbow. Marina turned, shaken back to reality, still anxiously bouncing Sadie back and forth on her hip in front of the herd of duckbills.

"What?" She narrowed her eyes in the direction Stella was pointing. They were supposed to have the exhibit exclusively. Viral infection rules. She'd gotten a confirmation email reminder again this morning confirming it. But Stella was right. There was the outline of a man, face and features in shadow compared to the bright window behind him, walking toward them from deeper within the exhibit.

It couldn't be.

It took a second to recognize the gait of his walk. The way he dipped his head every few steps. The curve of his hand when he held it up to give them a wave as he moved toward them.

No. He was away on a dig. That's what the museum website said.

She swept a hand quickly through her hair and readjusted Sadie on her hip. "Jake. Hi." She smiled awkwardly, bouncing Sophie back and forth as the toddler made a sour face and kicked her in the hip, squirming in the way she did when she wanted down.

Jake paused a good ten feet or so before them and nodded. His hair was a bit thinner and he'd gained a bit of weight, especially around the middle, where she could see one button straining just slightly against the fabric. His smile was the same, and although Marina knew it had been twenty years, she still felt surprised to see wrinkles form at the corners of his eyes.

She suddenly felt self-conscious in her cardigan, T-shirt dress, and white tennis shoes. She couldn't remember the last time she'd thought about fashion, or even cared. Did she look too simple? When Jake had known her, nothing about her was simple.

"Marina," Jake nodded. He spoke in the same quiet tone he always had and pushed his hands into the pockets of his jeans. He wore an untucked blue button-down, jeans, and navy Converse tennis shoes. A green badge on his chest read his last test date, Sept. 9, 2026. Two days ago. Green for negative. His eyes swept over the girls. "She's adorable," he said, the instant Sophie decided to smack Marina in the chin with her open palm. He cracked a smile.

"Thank you. This is Sadie, who needs a nap, obviously," she said, dropping her toddler back into her stroller as she kicked her legs in protest. "And my older one is Stella." She turned to see Stella hovering behind her, half-curious and half-shy over meeting someone new. "Stella, come say hello. This is Dr. Jake. He's an old friend of mine from college. He took over running the museum after Grandpa retired."

Actually, that was only partly true. Marina's father had handpicked Jake to be his heir when they were both still in college. When the two of them were together.

"Hi," Stella said, giving him the side eye.

"I thought you were away," Marina said, fooling with her hair again and wishing she had a hairband to pull her hair back. Or not. "A dig in Peru or someplace?"

"Oh, you saw that on the website?" he said. "I never made it there. The border closed. We also lost our web guy, so the site hasn't been updated in a long time." Jake's eyes darted from Marina to around the exhibit. He shrugged. "So . . . ?"

"What do I think?" Marina clipped Sadie back in her stroller and crossed her arms in front of her chest, as if they'd block the simpleness of her outfit. "I love it. You did a great job. Hands down. And he would've loved it, too. You should know that."

Jake smiled a crooked smile, the one he gave when someone gave him a compliment but was too humble to let it in. "Thanks for coming," he said, then raised his eyebrows. "I honestly can't believe you made the trip."

"Well, you named the exhibit after him, so . . ." She lowered the back of Sadie's stroller, the two-year-old blinking with heavy eyelids. "My girls never knew him, just heard stories about him, so I thought why not brave it up here."

Marina's cell phone, still in the basket below, lit up. Six text alerts, two missed calls. She ignored it.

"It's crazy you could get here, what with so many borders on lockdown. I'm happy you made it." He scratched the back of his head. "Listen, I have a Board of Directors meeting at two. It's a virtual thing. More donations coming in." He rolled his eyes, then glanced over at Stella, who was placing her glitter tennis-shoed-foot inside an enormous brachiosaurus footprint to compare sizes. "But if you want to run down to the cafeteria we could talk about your email—"

"You still have a cafeteria?" Marina said. "Restaurants aren't banned here?"

"I use the term 'cafeteria' loosely." Jake grimaced. "It's basically a cluster of vending machines that sell really bad prepackaged food. Subway just installed one, though, if you don't mind subs with wilted lettuce." He stepped around them, leading them back the way they'd entered. "Just this way."

"Oh, I think I remember the way," Marina said.

Out in the hallway, Jake called the elevator by waving his palm up in front of a glossy black panel. The doors immediately slid open. It was a weird juxtaposition, vintage Art Deco elevator doors hiding a sleek steel interior. Marina rolled Sadie's stroller inside and backed up into the right corner. Stella slipped in on the other side.

"Stella, don't touch anything, okay?"

"It's okay, the elevators have air purifiers, too, now," Jake pointed to the ceiling as he joined Marina on Sadie's right. "They were super expensive—another donation. The elevators clean themselves each time they let someone off."

"Ah," she said, backing up as Jake squeezed in until she felt her bum hit the back wall of the elevator. They were squashed inside, the four of them. The doors slid shut. Jake took another step back toward her, close enough that his elbow brushed her forearm. He looked down and smiled at her, stuffing his hands in the pockets of his jeans.

He smelled the same. The thought hit her as she gripped the stroller with one hand, holding it steady. Even through the filtered air, she could breathe in his scent of cedar and cinnamon. A smell of her past, the smell she'd fallen asleep to for so long. No, not so long . . . *so long ago*. She felt herself blush and ran another hand through her hair, sweeping it to one side.

"Wait, how did you know we were coming?" she asked.

"The museum has a schedule now since everyone has to book ahead," he said. "When I got your email, I knew you were coming, so I checked the system." He shrugged. "Is that okay?"

"Oh, right. Sure." She studied the toes of her shoes as the elevator dropped, her cheeks burning at being so awkwardly close to Jake. If she could smell him, could he smell her? God, what scent shampoo did she even use now? Certainly nothing expensive anymore. Not that it mattered anyway, right? She fiddled with her hair again.

The ride to the basement was only one floor down, twenty seconds at most, but it felt like they dropped in slow motion as if the elevator car itself thought it was hilarious to pin Marina inside a four-by-four-foot space with an ex-boyfriend. She suddenly decided her cardigan made her feel suffocatingly dull. She shed it, wrapping it around her buzzing cell phone, and stashed them both in the basket beneath the stroller.

THE DOORS POPPED and Marina pushed Sadie's stroller out of the elevator, toward The Time Stop Cafeteria, with the same gaudy orange sign it always had, and felt a rush of cold and undisturbed air wrap around her in the silent basement. Jake and Stella followed behind.

She'd remembered The Time Stop as a place overcrowded with families. Now, it had been reduced to a skeleton of vacant tables. The sandwich station and checkout counter had been replaced by vending machines that hummed against the wall. A green-and-yellow Subway machine that looked like it cost a fortune stood gleaming on the end closest to them. The entire space felt cold and unfamiliar.

"Go grab a seat by the window, Stella," Marina nodded toward the far wall. Stella darted ahead, ponytail flying behind her.

Technically the cafeteria was in the basement of the museum, but the building itself had been built on a hillside. Time Stop's back wall was all glass and offered a view of the museum's sloping rear lawn, the bridge that led toward Schenley Park and its four hundred acres of trees. Fall had well settled in, with the park looking like a patchwork quilt of yellow, brown, and orange.

"Now, *that* I miss." Marina nodded toward the window. "God, I loved studying back there."

"Not enough color in the islands?"

"Ha," she said, steering Sadie behind Jake. "We have different colors there. The girls have never seen autumn before now."

She followed Jake as he gave them a tour of their options. He paused before one labeled MEAT SANDWICHES that stocked a selection of generic white packets marked Hamburger, Hot Dog, Sloppy Joe.

"A Sloppy Joe from a vending machine?" She groaned. "Do people seriously eat this?"

"Oh, avoid that machine at all costs!" Jake frowned. "*All* costs! Here, pizza's probably safest." He stepped up to a machine labeled Zappo's. "The machine actually heats them up pretty decent before they dispense."

"Pizza's fine. How do we pay though?"

"They all use no-contact PALM." Jake stepped up to the machine and held his hand up, his palm inches away from the black payment panel. A digital sensor popped to life and a green beam of light blinked, scanning his hand. "Plain and pepperoni okay?"

"All pizza is okay."

"I'll get everything. Go get them settled."

Marina turned and steered the stroller back toward Stella, who'd taken a seat near the far glass wall.

"How about the iPad?" Marina asked, propping the stroller next to her. "We'll probably have a boring adult conversation."

"Then yes!" Stella nodded her chin into her chest. Her feet swung back and forth.

Marina dug out the old iPad they kept in the stroller bag, and Stella's plastic cat-ear headphones, and handed them over.

"Yes!" Stella flipped open the iPad and laid it on the table, hovering over it. She tapped the screen and opened a new fairy game she'd become obsessed with.

Sadie sleeping. Stella in her muted fairy world.

Satisfied, Marina slid into a seat at the table behind Stella and peered outside, soaking in as much of the fall colors as she could.

"Remember jogging there?"

Marina shifted in her seat, suddenly feeling awkward as Jake placed a stack of mini cardboard pizza boxes and cans of Coke on her table and sat down across from her. "I remember jogging in the snow there. The city buses flicking slush up on my sweatpants. But I never remembered fall looking so beautiful."

She looked back at him. She'd known that Jake was still the museum's head paleontologist, but he loved to dig, not sit in a museum. He was just like her father in that way. Months ago, after she'd received the invite to DINOSAURS IN THEIR ERA!, one of her late-night Googling sessions, fueled by panic for her girls, had led her to email

Jake a question about the Anthropocene Extinction that she couldn't find online, no matter what words she chose or rearranged to search again. Now that they sat just feet away, both kids occupied, she wasn't sure she was ready for the answer.

A serious look swept across his face, which was nothing like Jake's personality at all. His eyes are the same, she found herself thinking, a startling aquamarine color that so many girls had missed back in college, when all college guys moved at a hundred miles an hour unless you really had their attention. And Marina had. The last two years of college, the two of them had been like two halves of the sun: they saw only each other, everything and everyone else was peripheral. The entire social world of the university felt like it orbited around them. Their fascination with one another drew everyone to them like magnets.

"So about your question—"

Her stomach lurched. She wasn't ready.

"Tell me, were you—" Marina busied herself tearing the cardboard strip off her pizza box and folded back the lid. "Were you here at the museum when it broke out?"

"No," Jake said, his tone relaxing a bit. He cracked open his Coke and took a sip. "I was up in Prince Creek in Northern Alaska."

"Alaska?"

Jake nodded, taking a bite. "We've been excavating a new sort of duckbilled dinosaur up there for a few summers now. It's very cool. It's one with more than a thousand teeth."

"A *thousand* teeth?" She pulled the cheese off of her pizza slice, her stomach protesting to the sight of food. She grabbed her Coke and popped it open, hoping it would help with the queasiness.

"Yeah, I got stuck up there for two years." He wiped his mouth with a napkin. "The virus didn't seem to be a big deal at first, until it was. When it hit the U.S., the Canadian borders closed, then airlines stopped, and I was stuck. Traveling in the winter from Northern Alaska is nearly impossible anyway, so I stayed. Then when the vaccine failed and all, I didn't want to rush back."

"And when you did?" Marina felt the Coke swirling in her stomach.

He paused his chewing. "The city was . . . a mess. When I got back, the university here had closed. *Our* university. Can you imagine?"

Jake glanced over at Sadie and Stella. "How about you all?"

"We were home, in St. Kitts. We have a small place there. I've been running a marine conservation research program there for ten years or so," she said. "It's done now, no fancy donors left. My husband, Will, was Coast Guard Medic, so . . ."

Jake nodded, studying her face. She shifted her attention to her pizza. He knew what happened. She didn't have to finish.

"How about you?" She took a bigger sip of Coke. "No family? That's surprising."

"Got close once," he shook his head. "Didn't work out. Turns out it's easier to find a dinosaur in Alaska than a girlfriend."

Just then something rattled in the stroller basket. Damned calls.

"Is that your phone?" Jake tilted his head, peering down into the basket. "I think that's the second time I heard it go off. Do you need to get it?"

"Later." Marina stared out the window and was quiet a moment. Outside, the sloping lawn that led down to the bridge was fading to yellow. Elm trees lined the far sidewalk. Trees, grass, sidewalks. Such simple things that *humans* had placed there outside the museum. Simple things that could easily outlast humans now. Things that didn't have lungs to ruin, eyes to blind.

She could sense Jake watching her.

"We tried to warn them, Mar," he said, softly. "The Anthropocene Extinction? Scientists, biologists, ecologists, conservationists—marine conservationists like you. They've tried to warn people, for decades. Hell, we've watched it happen our whole careers haven't we? Species going extinct and no one caring. Humans watched all this time and never thought it could happen to them."

"I just never thought we'd see the end of it. Not in our lifetimes, I mean." Marina slid her drink in the circle of condensation it'd formed on the table. "Not this way. Human life ending through human stupidity." She was quiet a minute. "I'd never wish him gone, but I'm almost glad my father's not here to see this."

That's how life felt now. Divided. Marina's father had died in the *Before*—two years before the virus—from a heart attack while on a dig in Australia. Little Sadie, Marina and Will's surprise baby, knew only the *After*.

"What do you miss most?" she asked. "From before?"

Jake finished his slice, then started on a second. "Sports."

She raised her eyebrows. "You hate sports!"

"Okay, that's kind of true, I don't really care if we win," he said. "But I do miss being in a packed sports bar, watching a game with the guys. Quarter wings, cheese fries, Bud Light on draft, the noise, all of that."

Marina nodded. "Each one of you talking shit louder than the other."

"Probably." He smiled.

"You really haven't changed, have you?"

"Probably not. How about you? What do you miss?"

She thought for a minute. "Little kids' birthday parties."

"Really?"

Marina nodded. "It's weird, I know. Piles of balloons, a house full of shrieking children, bounce houses, parents who would get drunk and try the bounce house and fall on their ass. Really sugary cake."

They were silent a minute.

Jake crumpled up a napkin and tossed it in his pizza box. "The question you emailed me—"

"Jake, I changed my mind," she said, yanking her pizza into pieces. There's no way she could eat. She'd save it for Sadie when she woke up. "I don't—"

Her cell phone buzzed again. She didn't move.

Jake was silent for a minute.

"Marina, what's happening? Who are you avoiding?"

Suddenly Stella yanked off her headphones and stood up behind Jake, peering at something outside the window.

"What's wrong?" Marina said.

Stella stepped over to the window and looked at something down at the bottom of the sloping lawn. She turned back to them, forehead wrinkled.

"Who are they?"

Marina turned in her chair to look in the direction of Stella's gaze. "Who's who?"

But Stella only nodded out the window. "Them. Down there."

Marina stood and followed her daughter's gaze toward the bottom of the hill. A stream of people dressed in translucent-white raincoats, faces painted white, were trudging silently over the bridge and up the hill toward the museum. Fifty at least. She felt the brick of anxiety drop in her stomach again.

"They're protestors, honey," Marina said, softly, as she watched as the group moved closer. "We've seen them before. On the news. Remember?"

"The ones who protest the vaccine?" Stella asked, staring.

"Yes."

"The vaccine that didn't work?"

Marina swallowed. "Yes." Pockets of protestors, enraged over the failed CVIV vaccine, still popped up in big cities to rally in front of hospitals. ER doctors and first responders had been the first inoculated with CVIV, which politicians had rammed through FDA approvals while the viral strain spreading in the real world had silently mutated. The uselessness of the vaccine was recognized too late. Thousands of doctors had died. Then hundreds of thousands of their patients. From here, the protestors had to be heading, no doubt, to either Presbyterian Medical Centre, Pittsburgh Psychiatric, or—

Marina glanced at Jake.

"Children's," he mouthed.

She gripped the back of her chair, feeling dizzy where she stood. St. Benedict's Children's Hospital. Jesus, was there no end to this?

"Why do they wear those raincoats?" Stella asked.

They represent body bags.

Marina heard the words in her head and squeezed her eyes shut, wishing her own brain silent, as if Stella could hear her thoughts. Marina took her by the hand and pulled her back from the window, unable to say more.

"Hey listen, we've eaten enough," Jake interrupted, quickly gathering the torn pizza boxes up into a messy stack. "I have a few minutes before my meeting. Why don't I give you a paleontologist's tour of the exhibit, Stella?"

"Okay," she said, brightening a bit.

"You're ready, too, right Mar?"

"Right." Marina nodded. "Take her? I'll clean up real quick. I'll meet you upstairs."

"Okay." Jake nodded. "Ready?"

Marina watched Stella follow him back out through the tables to the elevator, then turned and stared back out the window. The first protestors were halfway up the hill now. Her eyes trailed to the far back end of the line. One protestor that she could tell was a woman, as her long brown hair spilled out of the dies of her raincoat's hood, shifted as she moved up the hill, walking slower than the others. Within a few steps, she pivoted and Marina could see why—she was holding the hand of a young child, maybe five years old, who obviously didn't understand what they were doing. Or why. Anger washed over her. Marina had been led up the same hill so many times as a child to go to the museum, to the park, to the Pittsburgh Floral Gardens—places that were now banned, closed, or so limited in capacity it felt as if you were the only people left on earth. She watched as the child tried to march along like the others, unaware that he could be next. Unaware that he was on his way to watch the world die.

The woman in the raincoat looked up at Marina, startling her enough to back away from the window. Could they see inside? She tried to remember what the museum looked like from the back lawn.

Marina watched the woman and her child climb the hill. Just behind them, to the far right, so far right that Marina had to lean to see it, was a fountain. *Their* fountain. Her and Jake's. A three-tiered fountain in the back corner of the museum's ground, sprinkled with yellow leaves from two half-shed elms that grew around it. The two of them, on one very drunken night, had run out of alcohol. All the bars were closed, but they weren't ready to end the night. Somehow, she could never remember who—but one of them had had the brilliant idea to go skinny dipping in that fountain at four a.m.

Behind her, Sadie let out a snore-whimper.

Marina cracked. A sob shook her shoulders. She turned and knelt down next to Sadie's stroller and stroked one of her perfect little pink-sweatpants legs.

"I'm sorry," she whispered. She said those words so many times in the last few years, but had felt those words move through her whole being even more often. The apologies ran like a flurry.

I'm sorry you can't have a birthday party with friends.

I'm sorry you don't have any friends, other than your sister.

I'm sorry you won't have a silly summer job, like working in an ice cream shop. Because there aren't any.

I'm sorry you won't get in trouble for texting in class because schools no longer exist.

I'm sorry you won't have a big wedding.

I'm sorry. I'm sorry.

That's what life felt like now, floating in a dualistic existence that straddled the *Before* and the *After*, one that felt the agony of the difference between the two, the loss: her husband, the life she'd thought she'd give to her kids, stupid simple things like ice cream shops and school. And falling in love and getting drunk and going skinny-dipping.

Beneath her, the phone buzzed again.

Marina pulled her bundled-up cardigan out of the basket and got to her feet. Outside, the white-hooded horde of protestors had realized cutting through the museum lawn offered a shorter path to the hospital, which meant they'd walk right by her window in a few seconds. She backed up, pulling Sadie back with her. As they drew closer, a dull noise rattled the glass.

They were chanting.

She tried to pick out the words but didn't dare move closer to the glass. Most protestors weren't dangerous, but grieving people could be. So were groups. The mutated VI spread so quickly through air and lingered so long that the only safe environments now were air-disinfected ones, like the inside of the museum, in the hotel where they stayed—even the Uber Clean car they'd taken to the museum—

offered sealed environments in which expensive filters purified every breath of air. Crowds outdoors were completely risky. A group over five could be deadly. She watched them, a living group of ghosts, as they chanted and hiked up the hill, to risk their lives as a reminder of the already-dead.

One mustached man shook free from the crowd and slammed his balled-up fists into the glass. Marina jumped back past the next set of tables away from the window.

"Join us!" he yelled, staring blindly over Marina's head—he couldn't see her. "Join us!" he repeated, then turned back, the white of him disappearing into the group like a cloud.

Marina backed away, snatched up the iPad and headphones from Stella's table and the lone pizza box with Sadie's torn-up bites inside. She dropped everything on the stroller's tray and headed toward the elevator doors. When she got to it, she wiped her eyes, then waved a hand in front of the touch-free digital elevator call panel. While she waited for it, she unrolled the cardigan, grabbed her phone, and looked at the screen. Ten texts. Two missed calls.

Within a minute, Marina steered Sadie, who was groggily trying to sit up, back through DINOSAURS IN THEIR ERA!, searching the exhibit for Jake and Stella. She could hear Stella talking excitedly from deeper inside, her high-pitched voice echoing through the cavernous room, but couldn't see them with the foliage and fossils in the way.

"Sadie, I think they're down here," Marina said. Her heart pounded as she gripped the phone tighter.

She rolled past the brontosaurus, continued underneath the swooping pterosaur, and passed the raptors. As she turned the corner at the end of the first room, she spotted two T-Rex on her right. They were poised as if ready to fight over some prey that lay in a pile of bones at their feet. One T-Rex stood on its back legs, jaws open wide, its teeny forearms clawed and grasping. A smaller one ducked down, ready to lunge at the larger one's feet. She paused. She'd seen the large T-Rex before—from the original exhibit on the second floor. Its head was tilted only slightly to the right, showing off teeth. She stopped.

"Mama out!" Sadie demanded, hearing the sound of her sister's voice promised that fun lay deeper in. She pounded her fists on the stroller tray, trying in vain to move it.

"Okay, okay." Marina unclipped her and wiped her curly hair off her forehead, then set her down on the ground. "Go find Stella for me."

"Stell-wa!" Sadie called in her little voice, toddling off.

Marina waited until Sadie was a few steps away, then grabbed her phone, and stepped up to the rock wall that separated her from the T-Rex. She stared at its mouth full of teeth, its pitiful forearms and scratching claws. Most people thought dinosaurs were positioned to look ferocious, but Marina knew the truth. Their bones were found frozen in the position in which they'd died. Open jaws weren't snarls. They were last gasps of breath, a mourning howl for a lost one. The terror of the last extinction, frozen in time and put on display.

Marina sighed. Her eyes fell to the T-Rex's hip sockets, its caramel-brown femur holding up the sizable pelvis, the power center that gave the carnivore its power to chase, to hunt.

"What's the difference between a dinosaur and a lizard?" She'd asked her father once. She must've been Stella's age at the time. They'd been touring the old exhibit on a rainy day one weekend, examining this exact T-Rex upstairs.

"Dinosaurs and lizards are both reptiles," her father had answered, "but dinosaurs are different than lizards because of their pelvis, see?" He'd pointed to this very T-Rex. "Dinosaurs' rear legs plug into their hip sockets. That enables them to walk upright, like us. A lizard skeleton is structured differently, which is why they slither or use all four feet."

"So T-Rex stands upright, like us?" Marina had asked.

"Right. Like us."

"HEY LADY, DON'T knock it down."

Jake's voice shook her from her thoughts. He was back walking down the path toward her.

She smiled weakly, put her hands up, and took a step back. "I'll try not to."

It was a long-running joke between the two of them. People always assumed dinosaur bones were as fragile as an eggshell, but in reality, sixty-six million years in mineral-rich dirt fossilized bone, making it as strong as stone.

"We did it one year, you know." Jake grinned a little, walking closer and staring up at the T-Rex. "For April Fool's Day. We picked a family on the way out the door. Told them one of their kids had run back for one last look, then handed the dad a bill for five million dollars."

"You did what? That was my idea! I always wanted to do that! I can't believe you did it!"

"You should've seen his face!" Jake smirked, stopping next to her. "Got me into a bit of trouble with your father, but it was so worth it."

Just then, Stella and Sadie's happy shrieks issued from the other side of the T-Rex.

"The girls—" Marina ducked down, trying to see them through foliage.

"They're fine," he said. "Stella was lowering your little one into a replica triceratops egg to see if she can fit inside."

"What?!"

Jake waved his hand. "It's an interactive part of the exhibit."

"Ah."

Marina crossed her arms over her chest and looked back at the T-Rex, the phone clutched facedown against her chest.

The awkwardness was back.

"Marina, you're strong as hell, you know that?"

"What do you mean?"

"You are." He stepped in front of her and sat down on the faux rock work. "Anyone raising kids in the middle of this . . . shit . . . well, you are. You always were."

Don't cry. She bit her lip to keep it from shaking.

"What's wrong?" he said, quietly.

"Everything," she said finally, staring at the T-Rex. "I'm tired. Of being strong, I mean. I'm tired of this shit. I'm tired of losing people, normalcy . . ."

He nodded, quietly. He glanced at the phone Marina held and got to his feet. He slowly pulled it from her hand.

"And this?" He turned it over in his hand. "Why are you ignoring it?"

She took a step back, drawing in a breath to power her words. "Test results. The thermal scanner at the airport flagged us when we landed. None of us are showing symptoms, but—" She put a hand on her chest, the words catching in her throat. "We had to get vaccines to get back in the country. Sadie, she gets fevers after shots. I think that's what it was. They gave us a rapid test at the airport, but they took blood to make sure. Jake, I wouldn't have let us come here if I thought it was anything other than—"

He nodded. "But if Sadie has it—"

"Then the three of us have it." She stopped, unable to find the words. She glanced at the air purifiers that lined the far wall over Jake's shoulder, the machines that stopped the person-to-person spread. "It has to be the flu vaccine. It has to be. But what if I'm wrong? I can't lose her. Either of them. They can't lose me. Not after losing their dad. I'd have to take her to a hospital, Jake." The thought horrified her. Hospitals weren't where people went to get better, they did that in the *Before*. In the *After*, the infected went there to die alone. No loved ones allowed.

The tears had started again. Hot and fast and angry, and she was angry at each one as they trailed down her cheeks. She wiped them away with her wrist.

"The question in my email—" her voice cracked. "—about the Anthropocene Extinction."

"Yeah."

She looked back at him, at his clear aquamarine eyes. So clear. St. Kitts clear.

"How long do we have?" She nodded up to the dinosaurs. "How long did it take them? Once the asteroid hit. How long did it take them to die?"

"No one knows." Jake stepped closer, still holding her phone. "We know from fossil dating that all plants died at once, likely within days because of the eternal night. But the dinosaurs? Could've been days. Weeks. Starvation. Suffocation. But this is different. This is a virus no one can control, not an environmental disaster."

She searched his face. "What if we have it, Jake? What will we do?"

"You'll stay," Jake said.

"Where? Here?"

"Yes. Stay with me."

"What?"

"Yeah, it's insane." He shrugged. "And we broke up a long time ago and it was messy and I handled it badly and I'm not asking you to, to, whatever . . . but listen. Your Father picked me to take care of all this."

He glanced around the exhibit. "This was his work, his love. This was part of *your* life. And he entrusted me with it. Let me take care of you, too. And your girls." He handed her the phone. "But first, you gotta know. Answer the phone."

"If I'm positive, they'll come look for me. They'll know exactly where I am." Marina studied Jake's face and took the phone. She took a breath, then held the phone up to her face. It illuminated, reading her facial ID. The home screen flickered to life.

She scrolled through the texts, her brow furrowed. Six texts from her Mom in Florida, one from her best friend Kim in Tampa, another from Mom. Then there they were: three from the CVI Response Team. The first ones were received just as they'd rolled into the exhibit forty minutes ago. Their CVI results were in, one text sent for each of them. Her thumb hovered over the blue link in the text.

In the *Before*, you'd have a sympathetic doctor deliver the bad news, time to say goodbye, you'd have the luxury of dying surrounded by loved ones holding your hand. But no more. In the *After*, this is how you learn if you're going to live or die. By text message.

Marina tapped open the first one from CVI, which said "Access your CVI results here," followed by a blue link.

She felt her stomach tighten within a centimeter of vomiting. She tapped.

Results for Sadie St. James. The report read.

Her arms shook as she struggled to hold the phone still. She covered her mouth, waiting for the page to load.

"I got you." Jake stepped closer to her and wrapped an arm around her back, his chin resting against her forehead.

Marina nodded and felt, for just a blink, that she might pass out. The screen flashed, loading before her.

Printed in bold: CVI Negative.

Marina let out an exhale so strong she felt like a deflated balloon. "She's negative."

"That's good, good. See?" Jake squeezed her shoulder.

Marina swapped back to her text screen and tapped on the next one, opening Stella's results.

CVI Negative.

She sighed. "Oh my God. She's safe, too." The corner of her eyes watered.

"Good. Keep going," he said.

She clicked back, tapping on the link to get the last results. Her results. She could feel Jake's chin tilt down against her forehead, looking at her screen. She tapped.

Marina St. James.

CVI Negative.

She exhaled and dropped the phone to her side. Jake pulled her into a hug. His long arms swallowed her. She breathed in his smell and buried her head into his chest.

"Thank God. Thank God. Thank God," she murmured. They stood there for a minute, frozen together, his hand on the back of her head. Her boyfriend from so long ago. Her *almost* family member. The embrace felt awkward and desperate and much needed, all in one. She grabbed the back of his shirt, pulling him tighter. Years be damned.

"It's okay, see?" he said.

"What's wrong?" A tiny voice called. The sound of the voice pulled them apart. It was Stella, holding Sadie's hand at the end of the path, looking back and forth at both of them. "Did something bad happen?"

"No, honey, everything is fine." Marina held her phone up. "Our test results came back from the airport. We're fine. We're okay."

Marina quickly glanced at her texts from her Mom and Kim, then shut the phone off.

"Kay." Stella shrugged. "There's a cool dinosaur egg over here. Sadie can fit inside. Can someone lift me up and drop me in too? We want to see if we can both fit inside!" Sadie turned and took off, darting back toward it.

Marina pivoted toward Jake, only then realizing his hand was still placed gently on the small of her back. She felt the warmth of his hand spread up her spine. He pulled it away. She shivered, just like she used to with him, and stepped away, surprised.

"I . . . I have to drop Stella in an egg," Marina stammered, wiping the tears from her face. She didn't dare mention the offer he'd made. "Thank you for—"

"It's fine," he said, quickly, smiling a little as she started to walk away.

She looked back at the T-Rex again. "No idea how long we have left?"

"Nope." He put his hands in his pockets. "Could be weeks. Could be years."

"Years," she repeated. If they could be so lucky. That's what it came down to, wasn't it? The luck, or fate, or blessing of living a life.

Marina glanced at Jake over her shoulder. "You coming?"

He caught up to her within two strides. "So what are you going to do now?"

Marina shrugged. "Well . . . it appears we have to stay. For a while at least."

"What I said back there, you don't have to feel obligated at all to—" Jake stammered as they turned the corner. Up ahead, Sadie peeped the top of her blonde head out of a dark brown egg the size of an end table. Stella danced back and forth next to it, her glittery shoelaces flapping.

"No," Marina said, holding up her cell. "We literally have to. Those other texts, the ones from my Mom and my friend? The state borders closed this morning. The governor of Pennsylvania declared another state of emergency. We're in lockdown again. We can't get out. We can't go—" she paused, the word *home* holding in her throat. She looked back at her girls, in her father's museum. In Jake's museum.

She reached back and, after a second, held her hand out toward Jake.

"Want to help me drop a little girl into an egg?"

Partners in Crime

Victoria Ferenbach

A SLIM YOUNG woman in black with a gold stud in the side of her nose steps into Natalie's line of sight offering a tray of drinks. Natalie points to a narrow glass of something bubbly.

"Prosecco," the woman says.

"Perfecto," Natalie says, smiling as she lifts the glass from the tray.

She takes a sip and moves toward the perimeter of the high-ceilinged space, maneuvering around the crush of people to the expanse of white wall on her left, stopping in front of a large, brilliantly colored canvas, one of twelve hanging around the gallery. She recognizes it from the front of the invitation, a giant portrait of a strange otherworldly creature, possibly half woman and half fish, although another person might see it differently.

The painting is quintessential Sam Field, celebrated artist of the evening and her favorite living painter, though not one she tries to emulate. Her own work is less extravagant, more mundane, the efforts of an amateur. She couldn't imagine ever creating something so dazzling and sensual, but it's a thrill to stand this close, taking in every brushstroke.

She sips the fizzy wine and moves toward the next painting, edging past a sleek blond woman in a pair of enormous horn-rimmed glasses who is in deep conversation with two bearded men. She gazes at the second painting, admiring the bold, assertive slashes of blues and purples and the ethereal floating imagery.

As she makes her way toward the third canvas, wondering if she is the one person there only for the art, she senses someone next to her and turns to see an exceptionally tall man in a dark business suit.

"Natalie," he says. "I thought it was you."

"Adam," she says after the split-second it takes to recognize him as the father of one of her son's high school classmates. "How are you?"

"Very well thank you. How's that boy of yours?"

"Happy as a clam at Middlebury. What about yours? Carlton, right?"

"Absolutely loves it," Adam says bending down as though to impart a secret. "Aren't we the lucky ones to have such well-adjusted kids?"

She gets a whiff of his aftershave, something spicy and darkly woody, and without thinking takes a step back.

"Where's David?" he asks resuming his full height.

"In Atlanta for a couple of days," she answers. "Ellen?"

"Oh God, she hates these things," he says waving his glass toward the crowd, splashing several drops of red wine onto the poured cement floor. "Even the lure of seeing Sam wasn't enough to get her out of the apartment."

"Sam," she says. "Sam Field. You know him?"

"We went to college together," Adam says. "A lifetime ago. Roommates and partners in crime for four years."

"Wow," she says. "What's he like?"

He looks around, craning his neck to see above the crowd. "Sam's over there," he says nodding toward the far wall. "You can see for yourself. Want to meet him?

"Are you kidding?"

"Follow me then," he says pivoting into the densely packed room.

She walks a few steps behind Adam as he forges a path through the stylish throng, noting his immaculately tailored pinstripe jacket and slicked back graying hair. The last time she remembers seeing him was at graduation in June. Now that the boys are off at college, the only parents she keeps up with are a few of the mothers, close friends that don't include his wife Ellen. Natalie recalls her as a quiet person, someone who kept to herself, not a joiner. An odd match for such a socially confident man as Adam.

She runs the fingers of her free hand through her short dark hair. For a moment she regrets not changing out of the leather jacket and jeans she's worn all day. She catches herself mid-thought, however, as she squeezes between two women, one in a clingy silver sleeveless dress, the other in a faded black T-shirt and floppy striped pants that look like pajama bottoms. Anything goes here tonight, so if he even notices, Sam Field is unlikely to care what she's wearing.

Once they reach the other side of the room, she has no trouble spotting the artist. She recognizes him from interviews in *Artforum* and from the picture on the back of the invitation stuffed in her jacket pocket. The shock of salt-and-pepper hair falling across his forehead and the dark eyes peering out from under thick brows are enough to identify him but it's his brilliant sapphire blue shirt and saffron tie that clinch it. Sam Field's brand is color.

He is standing opposite a short stocky woman in a leather skirt. She is leaning toward him speaking intensely, her face mere inches from his. Natalie watches him deftly move his head a few inches back without interrupting her or breaking eye contact.

When he does look up and catches sight of Adam, a grin spreads across his broad face. He says a few words to the woman, gives her a peck on the cheek, and moves past her toward them.

"Adam fucking Hyde," he says. "I was hoping you'd be here."

Adam chuckles and leans down to envelop Sam in a bear hug. "When have I ever missed one of your openings?" He unfolds his angular frame to its full height. "Good to see you, man. It's been a while." He turns to her. "Meet Natalie Ballard."

"Natalie Ballard," Sam says taking her hand. "Lovely name, lovely lady." He tilts his head toward Adam. "How the hell do you know this big ugly guy?"

She laughs. "Our sons went to school together."

"Aha," he says. "And you are an art lover?"

"Well, I love your work," she says. "And I paint a little too." She immediately wants to kick herself for blurting out such an inane personal detail.

"Good for you," Sam says, releasing her hand. "Great therapy, don't you think? I couldn't survive without it."

"I agree," she says, relaxing as his easy banter diffuses her nervousness. "It takes you out of yourself."

"Exactly," Sam says with a slight bow.

"I didn't know you were a painter," Adam says sipping his wine.

"Off and on," she says. "I've gotten back into it recently after a friend asked me to share a studio with her. We split the rent, but we worked out a schedule, so we aren't usually there at the same time."

"Good plan," Sam says. "You don't want another person around when you're working."

"Or not working," she says. "If you know what I mean."

"Hah," Sam says. "Indeed, I do. Waiting for the muse."

A young man with a ponytail and small round wire-framed glasses approaches them carrying a bottle in each hand. Adam holds out his now empty glass and the server pours a few inches of pinot noir. He lifts the glass, clinking it against the bottle. "Keep going."

Natalie notices Sam looking at Adam through narrowed eyes. "Easy pal," he says.

Adam ignores him, raising the glass to his lips as soon as it's full.

The young man turns to Sam. "Sir?"

"No thanks," Sam says. "Nothing for me."

"I'm fine, too," Natalie says.

The server switches the bottles to one hand, grabbing them by the necks. "I'll take that," he says reaching for Natalie's empty glass with his free hand.

As he turns away, she notices a clutch of people hovering behind Sam. "We should give your other admirers a chance," she says nodding to them. "It was such an honor to meet you. Congratulations on this gorgeous show."

"Thank you my dear," Sam says, resting his hand on her shoulder. "I'm always happy to meet a fellow painter, especially such a pretty one. Good luck to you, Natalie Ballard. I hope we'll meet again." He gives her shoulder a squeeze.

"And you, you big oaf," he says looking at Adam. "Behave yourself."

"Likewise," Adam says.

As Sam turns his attention to the people behind him, Adam moves over to the wall between two of the paintings and leans his shoulder against it. "What now?" he asks. "There's a little bistro down the block."

"I need to get home," she says, startled by his suggestion. "I'm just going to have a quick look at the rest of the paintings then head uptown." She begins to turn away. "Thanks so much for introducing me to Sam. Give my best to Ellen."

She walks toward a pair of large rectangular canvases hanging on the rear wall of the gallery, weaving her way among the clusters of chattering guests, excusing herself as she pushes past them. Glancing over her shoulder she is relieved to see that Adam is not behind her.

The two huge paintings are clearly the centerpiece of the show, mirror images of each other, one darkly intense, the other bright as sunlight. Both appear to represent birds soaring over a wide expanse of water, gulls maybe or possibly hawks, she isn't sure.

She continues to work her way around the edge of the room, stopping briefly at each of the remaining paintings. As she gets closer to the front of the gallery, she spots Adam talking to a woman in a leopard print dress. She moves quickly toward the door, pushes it open and steps out onto the sidewalk.

The relative silence and the cool evening air are a relief from the packed gallery. She zips her jacket and pulls her phone from her back pocket. Seven thirty. She'll be home by eight and in her pajamas five minutes later, ready to reheat last night's penne and hunker down in front of the television.

Two couples emerge through the gallery door behind her and she moves aside to let them pass.

"The guy's a fucking genius," a man with a shaved head says. "If I had an extra mil, I'd buy one of his paintings."

The other man snorts. "In your dreams."

"He may be a great artist," the woman on his arm says. "But I've heard he's a real dick."

Natalie watches them walk down the block to the left. She wonders if they are headed to the restaurant Adam mentioned and feels relieved to have dodged that bullet.

The gallery is on a side street between two avenues. She turns right and walks in the direction of the uptown avenue where she is more likely to find a taxi going her way. She passes several other galleries, all shut for the day, and a small secondhand shop with an eclectic assortment of objects in the window. A red lacquer box with a filigree brass clasp catches her eye. She imagines it in her studio, perhaps as a container for small brushes or even better as part of a still life. There's a closed sign on the door however, so she keeps walking.

At the corner she sees a number of cabs but none with their roof lights on. While she is debating whether or not to cross to the other side, she spots an available taxi and raises her hand to hail it. The car stops in front of her and she steps off the curb, reaching for the door handle.

"Allow me," a man's voice says.

She freezes for a moment, her heart sinking. Shit. Adam. He must have followed her. She takes a breath and turns to find Sam Field smiling at her from the sidewalk. He's wearing a short black nylon coat buttoned to the neck with the collar turned up. The bright shirt and tie she admired in the gallery are out of sight.

She frowns. "What are you doing here?"

He shrugs. "I had enough. Couldn't take any more boring small talk."

"Boring," she says. "Those people came to congratulate you. To admire your paintings."

He waves his hand in front of his face. "I couldn't care less about them. And the paintings, they'll sell whether I'm there or not."

She's confused, somewhat uneasy. She's still standing in the street. He's on the sidewalk a few inches above her giving him an advantage even though he's not much taller than she is. The taxi she hailed has driven off, leaving them alone.

"Well, Natalie Ballard," he says. "Since fate has brought us together on this deserted street corner, why not join me for dinner?"

Half an hour ago, the invitation would have been unexpected but flattering. Now something feels off. "My husband is waiting," she lies. "I need to get home."

"I have a car," he says. "I can drop you." He reaches into his coat pocket and pulls out his phone. "Jorge," he says. "Pick me up on the corner."

She tries to think what to do but within what feels like seconds, a black SUV pulls up next to them. Sam steps off the curb and takes her by the arm. "Hop in," he says opening the rear door.

"Thanks anyway," she says. "I'll just get a taxi."

"Don't be ridiculous," he says. "Get in."

She feels his hand pressing on her back. Maybe she's being silly. He's just offering her a ride.

"In you go," he says nudging her forward.

"No," she says pushing back against him. She twists away toward the sidewalk. A tiny, hunched woman in a threadbare coat pushes a grocery cart full of junk slowly past them, talking to herself. Natalie almost calls out to her. Traffic whizzes up the avenue.

"Be nice," Sam says pulling her back toward him "We're friends now, aren't we?"

His breath feels hot on her neck. "We just met and you're making me uncomfortable."

The driver gets out of the vehicle, leaving the engine running and walks in front of the headlights to where they're standing. He's a few inches taller than his employer, a wiry younger man with buzz-cut dark hair. In his black shirt and narrow pants, he reminds her of the waiters at the gallery.

"Problem, Mr. Field?" he asks.

"No problem, Jorge. Just trying to convince the lovely lady here to let us drive her home."

He's holding her arm again, tighter this time. She's afraid the two men are going to force her into the car, and she feels the panic rising.

She looks at Jorge. "I'd prefer to get a cab."

"Take her arm," Sam says.

Jorge's hand closes on her other arm, firmer and tighter than Sam's. She turns her head and sees a group of people spilling out of the gallery down the block. They walk off in the opposite direction and her heart sinks. *Somebody please come this way*, she prays.

"On three," Jorge says.

The hands squeeze her upper arms. "Let me go now or I'll scream."

"That would be foolish, Natalie."

"Let her go," a voice says. "Now."

Her arms are released, and she spins around. Adam glances at her before he grabs Sam by the coat collar and drags him onto the sidewalk. Jorge shrinks away toward the front of the vehicle.

"You son of a bitch," Adam says. "You're so fucking transparent. I was on to you as soon as you started spouting that 'painting is therapy' and 'waiting for the muse' bullshit."

"Let go of me," Sam says struggling to free himself.

Adam yanks him up hard by the collar. "Not before you apologize to the lady."

"I have nothing to apologize for," Sam says. "I was just offering her a ride home."

"Don't fuck with me, Field. I saw you and your sleezeball sidekick grab her." He raises his free hand, curling it into a fist in front of Sam's face. "Say you're sorry."

"Okay, okay," Sam says. "I'm sorry."

"Look at her when you say it."

Natalie has moved away from the men and the vehicle. She's standing in the middle of the sidewalk, shivering even though it's only late

October and not really cold yet. Sam, still restrained by Adam, looks over at her.

"Sorry," he says without meeting her eyes.

She's about to respond but realizes there is nothing to say.

Adam lets go of Sam's coat and shoves him toward the car. "Get the fuck out of here."

Sam stumbles, trying to regain his footing. He coughs and brushes his hair off his forehead, smooths his coat, and walks toward the car. Jorge is back behind the wheel.

"Next time you're on your own," Adam calls after him. "I'm done saving you from yourself."

Sam turns around, his eyes blazing. "Look who's talking. How many times have I scraped your boney ass off the floor?"

"I'll give you that," Adam says. "Sometimes I drink too much. But it's my ass. I've never hurt anyone."

Natalie is standing several feet from the men, listening to their angry words fly back and forth across the sidewalk in the night air. Sam looks shrunken and powerless against the gleaming bulk of the SUV. He starts to say something else to Adam then clamps his mouth shut, turns away, and climbs into the back seat.

She flinches at the sound of the door slamming then holds her breath until the vehicle pulls away and merges into the traffic. Once it is out of sight, she turns to Adam.

"Thank you for rescuing me."

"No thanks required."

"How did you know?"

"I saw you leaving the gallery. Sam left right after, which seemed strange. Too early for him to abandon his own party. It dawned on me what he might be up to, so I followed him."

"But I never saw you."

"I stayed behind the bus stop, watching. When the driver grabbed your arm, I knew you were in trouble."

She looks over at the bus shelter. A garish color photo full of shooting stars and helmeted figures advertising some outer space movie fills the rear wall. The waiting bench is empty, as it was since she arrived at the corner. Hours ago, it seems, although she knows it was only minutes.

"I guess you know him pretty well.

"Too well. We went to college together."

"You mentioned that."

Adam gazes up at the cloudy night sky for a moment. "I don't know," he says shaking his head. "I just don't know."

Several people have arrived at the corner. When she looks back down the block, there are others on the sidewalk in front of the gallery.

"I'm sticking my neck out here," he says. "But maybe you'll change your mind about dinner. I could use the company."

"I don't think so," she says. "I really need to get home."

"Understood," he says. "I'll get you a taxi."

He steps into the street and raises a long arm. A yellow cab stops in front of them and he opens the rear door. She slides in, pulls the door closed, and rolls down the window.

"Take care of yourself, Adam."

He nods. "You too, Natalie"

She gives the driver her address. The traffic light is red, so she leans back against the vinyl upholstery, breathing deeply, collecting herself. Out the window she watches Adam stride off down the block, his pinstripe jacket flapping behind him. When the light turns green, the taxi accelerates up the avenue.

Sins of Our Fathers: Part 1
J.L. Price

Virginia 1848

HATTIE MAE STOOD on the front porch watching the storm roll in over the fields, large gray clouds ringed in dark outlines with flashes of light searing through them at irregular intervals. It hadn't yet started raining, but she could smell the moisture in the air. It wouldn't be long before those clouds moved overhead and let loose their sheets of water. Normally, particularly this time of year, she welcomed the storms. In late May, there was still enough spring lingering and enough summer yet to come that a big storm would take the heat out of the air without making it too cold, or too oppressively humid. When she could get away with it, like today, she liked to take a minute and watch them come in. She liked the power big storms held and the reminder they gave that there was something mightier than men, and it had a will all its own. But today as she watched, she didn't feel her usual peace. Instead, the storm reflected the unease that had been swirling through her insides for a good long while now. Today, the storm wasn't the usual welcome sight, but an omen confirming what she'd been knowing for a while. Something bad was headed their way, and like the storm, she feared there'd be nothing she could do to stop it.

The door banging open behind her made her jump, as she instinctively clamped down her mouth to keep from crying out in fright.

"Didn't mean to startle you, Hattie Mae."

Hattie Mae lowered her eyes to the wooden planks of the porch, cutting them sideways just enough to see JC, the master's son, who'd come out to stand next to her. She said nothing.

"What you doin' out here anyway?"

"Nothin', sir," Hattie Mae replied. "Just watchin' the storm roll in, tryin' to figure out how much time I got before I got to get the washin' off the line."

"Sure does look like it's gonna be a good one, don't it?"

"Yes, sir."

Hattie let the silence settle between them. Having spent her whole life as a slave, she'd learned early on to only speak when spoken to, and then only as much as necessary to keep folks moving on and not noticing you.

"You seen Phoebe around here?"

Hattie's gut clenched and her palms began to sweat as the uneasy feeling that had been churning in her stomach started making its way up her spine. She kept her eyes down, fighting the urge to wipe her hands on her apron, as she lied, "No, sir."

She could feel JC's eyes on her as if he knew she was lying and was looking for telltale signs of proof. She didn't give him any.

"Well, you know where she is then?"

Hattie shrugged, picking up the basket by her feet, "I reckon she's still out in the fields, sir."

"Still? But I saw Percy and the others come back in a while ago."

"I don't know, sir," Hattie said, just as a spear of lighting shot across the sky, followed by a loud crack of thunder. Thankful for the distraction and the excuse, Hattie continued, "I best be gittin' this laundry off the line, 'fore it gits wet and the missus gits mad, if it ain't done 'fore she gits home."

JC nodded absentmindedly to her, his eyes scanning the fields in front of the house, presumably looking for Phoebe. Hattie took that as permission to leave and scurried to the right toward the clothesline over on the side of the farmhouse. The wind picked up as she rounded the corner of the large, two-story structure. The sheets and clothes whipped and cracked on the air, flying sideways like flags as the wind blew harder. She worked quickly unhooking the sheets and the master's clothes from the line, all the while straining to hear whether JC had decided to go to the fields looking for Phoebe, or whether he'd headed back into the house to wait. She hoped to God he'd decided to go back into the house.

After what seemed like forever, she heard him swear into the wind, and slam the door going back into the house. Hattie let go the breath she'd been holding, quickly unhooked the last of the master's pants off the line, stashed the basket under a bush, below the overhang covering the cellar, and quickly ran across the yard, thankful there were no windows on this side of the house. She ran past the barn that held most of the animals used on the plantation, and then past the shacks that housed the slaves, until she reached the far side of the north fields, the ones that ran adjacent to Mr. Johnson's land. Just as she expected, she saw Phoebe standing by the big white oak tree, talking to Mr. Johnson's negro boy, Will. Hattie slid behind a smaller oak, just out of ear shot, trying to catch her breath. She looked back toward the house, thankful she hadn't been followed. Her heart thudded against her chest. She had to move quickly in case JC changed his mind and decided to come out looking for Phoebe. Hattie took a deep breath and then approached the couple.

As she drew closer she saw Will reach out and brush the hair back from Phoebe's face as he hooked the stem of a bloodroot blossom behind her ear, its white petals and yellow center a pretty contrast to Phoebe's caramel-colored skin. The affection crackled between the two like the lightning in the clouds as Will leaned his head close in to Phoebe's. Hattie wished she could give them more time to enjoy the stolen moment, but the thought that JC might soon be coming behind her let her know she couldn't wait, or they'd all pay.

"Phoebe!" Hattie yelled across the ten feet separating her from the couple. Her voice sounding harsher than she intended. Phoebe and Will jumped apart as though bit by a snake.

"Jeez, Hattie! You about scared me half to death." Phoebe said, clutching at her heart.

"Hi Miss Hattie Mae," Will said, giving her a smile and an acknowledging nod of his head.

"Will," she replied without returning the smile. Her heart twisted to see the disappointment in his innocent face at her curt reply, but much as she wanted to, she knew better than to encourage whatever was going on between these two. It would only lead to heartache for them both, or worse.

"Best be coming along now, Phoebe. Storm's rollin' in and master JC's been looking for ya."

Phoebe cast a longing look back toward Will, giving him a delicate wave, as she started walking slowly toward Hattie. Will gave her an exaggerated bow, and then tipped an imaginary hat her way, his broad smile again lighting his face. Phoebe giggled in return, a slight blush rising in her cheeks. Hattie grabbed Phoebe's wrist, pulling her along.

"Jeez, Hattie," Phoebe said, wrenching her wrist free of Hattie's grasp. "You could at least say goodbye to him."

"I told you about hanging out here following after him."

"I ain't hurtin' nothin'. We been done workin' for a while now. He an' I just talkin' anyhow." Phoebe twisted her hair around her finger as she walked with Hattie back toward the house and the slave quarters, a wistful look playing across her features. To Hattie's knowledge, both of Phoebe's parents had been slaves, but Phoebe's lighter skin and wavy hair showed there was some mixture in there somewhere.

"Besides," Phoebe continued, "he said he wants to jump the broom with me and that in about a year, maybe more, he'd earn enough workin' for Mr. Johnson that he could buy my freedom."

Hattie stopped short, as the uneasiness that had been swirling around inside her congealed into a lump of dread that fell heavy in her gut. Unlike her and Phoebe, Will wasn't a slave, being born into one of the few free black families in this part of Virginia. From what she knew, his family had a place in town, and Will hired out to old man Johnson, who owned the small plot of land adjacent to the Carter plantation.

"You need to stop this foolishness now, right now, you hear me?"

Phoebe's head snapped back as though Hattie had slapped her. Hattie felt horrible as she saw tears well in Phoebe's eyes, but there was no hope for it.

"I know you think he loves you, Phoebe, and maybe he does. But you know it don't work like that for people like us. You just can't be havin' those kinds of dreams. Phoebe, you only goin' to end up hurt in the end."

Phoebe gave Hattie a look that made Hattie's heart ache. "You just don't want me to be happy," Phoebe spat at her. "You're just afraid that

I will leave you here, and go be happy and free, and have a real family of my own." Phoebe wiped away a tear that escaped from her eye.

The last part stung Hattie, but she didn't let it show. "Phoebe, you know that ain't true. That's not true at all. I love you like my own. Raised you like you was my own. And I'd want nothin' more than for you to leave me. To go far away from here and be free. That's just not the way."

Phoebe laughed without humor. "Really, then what is the way? You tell me Miss Hattie Mae how I'm supposed to get up off this plantation any other way? How I'm gonna get me my own house and my own family if I can't be with Will? You tell me Hattie, how that gonna happen?"

Hattie stood, twisting her fists in her apron, all the thoughts colliding in her head tying up her tongue. She didn't dare tell Phoebe that she'd been working on another way, another way for both of them. She didn't know how to tell Phoebe about JC and what he might do if he ever saw Phoebe with Will. Phoebe still saw JC as the kid she grew up next to, but Hattie had been watching, watching close. JC no longer looked at Phoebe like a playmate or even a sibling. Lately he'd had a different look about him, whenever he looked at Phoebe. A look filled with lust, possessiveness, and jealousy. Hattie had lived long enough in her thirty years to know that look was dangerous to any woman it fixated on.

"Just go 'bout your business and leave me alone, Hattie," Phoebe turned and headed off to the slave quarters, her arms clutched around her, warding off the wind that blew her hair in all four directions. Hattie watched her go, but didn't try to stop her or chase after her as she felt the first drops of rain pelt her nose. She had to get back to the laundry before the clouds let loose and she still had dinner to finish too.

"I THOUGHT YOU said you didn't know where Phoebe was, Hattie Mae."

The voice behind her back made Hattie Mae jump so bad she almost dropped the spoon she'd been stirring the beans with. She glanced back and to the side without turning her head, enough that she could see JC propped up against the doorway that separated the kitchen from the dining room. He'd spent most of his life in and around the kitchen with her, but in the last several months his presence had made her increasingly uncomfortable. For one, since last summer he'd shot up and filled out. He'd always been kinda tall, but over the last year as he came up on eighteen, he'd filled out and muscled up. Up until now Hattie had always been sure she could take him in a fight if it came to that, she not being a small woman and on the sturdy side herself, but she knew that was no longer the case. For two, he was starting to learn his place and her place in the world, and inevitably and surely the nature of their relationship was changing. He came to her less and less for comfort and advice, like a son would a mother, and had more and more started telling her what to do, his voice gaining more authority each time he gave a command. He'd soon be taking over this place from his Pa, who was around less and less these days, and JC knew it. Just like he knew he owned her and everything on it.

"You hungry?" Hattie asked, taking a plate from the shelf above the stove.

"Hattie look at me."

Hattie steeled her features into her best imitation of innocence and slowly turned to face JC.

Jacob James Carter the third, or JC as everyone called him to distinguish him from his daddy, stood about three inches taller than her five-foot-eight-inch frame. His sandy blonde hair framed a face that still had some of the boy in it, but not much. He stood, leaning to the side with his left shoulder propped against the doorjamb, his shirt sleeves rolled to his elbows, his hands shoved into the pockets of his trousers, kept up by the suspenders hooked over his shoulders. His right boot-clad foot crossed casually over his left. His relaxed appearance belied the tension she could feel coming off him in waves. His white shirt still had spots of rain splatter. He must have been standing outside watching her and Phoebe walk back in from the north field. She silently cursed herself for not noticing and taking a different route back.

Hattie turned back to the stove and began shoveling beans onto the plate. She always found it much easier to lie when she wasn't looking a person dead in their eyes.

"I didn't know, not for sure. I just know that these days when she done workin' she like to go out in the yonder field where the pretty wild flowers grow. Since you was askin' after her, I went to go see if I could find her." Hattie sat the plate on top of the stove and bent over to pull the corn bread out of the coals, hoping her lie held enough truth that JC wouldn't question it.

For the moment JC seemed satisfied and pushed himself away from the door, stepped fully into the kitchen, and pulled up a chair at the small round table. Hattie added the pork she'd been frying to his plate and set it in front of him. She grabbed a fork and a knife from the sideboard and set those in front of him also. Normally, JC would have eaten in the dining room with his parents, but they were currently away visiting the missus's sister. Hattie would have preferred for JC to still sit in the dining room, but he'd always been a lonely sort who wasn't good at keeping his own company, which meant that when his parents were away, JC always found himself in the kitchen with her.

"Food not to your likin'?" Hattie asked as she ladled some water out of the barrel into a cup and set it beside his plate.

"I'm sure it's fine like always, Hattie," JC replied, making no move to touch his food as he twirled his fork through the fingers of his right hand and watched the rain pelt the small window that sat above the kitchen table.

Hattie let him sit, content to let the sound of the rain pounding the roof fill in for talk, as she finished making dinner for the other slaves. After a while, JC spoke, "You ever wish things could be different than how they are Hattie? Like way different?"

Hattie let out a snort before she could stop herself but didn't say anything in reply.

JC looked a little sheepish as he took a sip of water, "Yea, I guess you being a slave and all that was a stupid question."

Hattie didn't respond, turning her back toward JC as she pretended to get more flour, so he wouldn't see her smiling.

"Can I be honest with you, Hattie?"

Hattie stopped what she was doing and turned to look at JC. It had been a long while since she'd heard that kind of earnest pleading in his voice.

"Of course," she replied, wiping her hands on her apron, crossing her arms across her chest as she prepared to listen.

"I miss how things used to be, Hattie," JC continued, his voice so low she had to strain to hear him over the rain.

"How you mean?"

"How they used to be. When it was just you, takin' care of me and Phoebe. When me and Phoebe used to spend all our time together." JC sat, looking at the food he still hadn't touched, his hands balled into fists on the table. Hattie hugged her arms tighter around herself as she fought the urge to go wipe back the hair that had fallen across his eyes and give him a hug like she used to do when he was little and upset about something.

"I know Mom and Dad left right after plantin' time to see how I could handle things. Now I'm grown I know he wants me to take over. They've even been talkin' about movin' into town. Pa never much liked runnin' the plantation."

JC stopped, swallowing hard, then looked back at Hattie, his eyes filled with anguish, "I can do the farmin' fine, Hattie. I was born to that. I know that like I know how to breathe. It's the other I don't know if I can do . . . At least not with you, and not with Phoebe."

Hattie's breath caught on the last, as a trickle of dread and fear ran down her spine.

"I know where Phoebe was, Hattie," JC said, his blue eyes burning holes through her, his tone sharp.

"I know you knew it too, and I know you lied to me."

The trickle turned into full-on fear. Hattie dug her nails into her forearms to keep from trembling, bracing herself for whatever might come next. JC had never spoken to her like this.

"Hattie don't look at me like that," JC said, his tone softening. "I'm not gonna hurt you. I could never hurt you. That's the problem."

Hattie let go the breath she'd been holding but still stood with her arms clutched around her, on edge, like a cat that had been cornered waiting to make its escape.

"I know, by rights, I should take a switch to you for lyin' to me like that and for coverin' for Phoebe, and to her for goin' over to Old Man Johnson's property and carryin' on with that boy Will even when I told her not to."

He knew. Oh God, he knew. Another wave of fear hit Hattie. It was all she could do to stay upright on her wobbly knees.

"The problem is, Hattie," JC continued, "I know I shouldn't but I think of you like my own momma. You was the one that raised me.

You was the one that was always there for me. I know I need to, but I could no sooner take a switch to you than I could my own momma."

Hattie turned back to the sizzling pork that was starting to burn, swallowing the lump in her throat, rapidly blinking her eyes. All the emotions tearing around inside her, choking off any words she might say. A memory of JC flashed unbidden in her mind, before she could force it away. Him toddling into the kitchen on his three-year-old wobbly legs, his arms outstretched to her, tears streaming down his face. He'd fallen or something. There was a scrape on his elbow and his knee. He'd been crying so hard he gave himself hiccups. Instinctively, she'd bent down and picked him up, hugging him, wiping away the tears. She'd turned in time to see his own momma watching them from the doorway. Hattie froze, then tried to hand JC to her, but his own momma had shook her head and walked away. Hattie had sat JC down in the chair in which he now sat, tended his cuts, and given him a chicken bone to gnaw on.

Hattie stabbed at the meat in the pan, removing it to a plate, blinking hard to clear away the blur that swam in her eyes. She took a deep breath to steel herself, and found her voice.

"You know I ain't your momma, JC. It was my job to see you grown, and I done did that." She took another deep breath, fortifying herself against the hurt she saw in his eyes. "Probably best we both be movin' on."

"That's just it, Hattie. I don't want to move on. I don't know if I can move on. Not if it means I can't come to you. We can't sit and talk like this. Not if it means I have to sit and watch Phoebe take up with some other man."

And there it was, out in the open, the confirmation of what Hattie had known but had been hoping wasn't true. The bad feeling that had been nagging at her heels for weeks now had a source.

"What you tryin' to say, JC?" Hattie knew if anyone else, particularly his daddy, heard her talk to him like that she'd be slapped or worse, but she didn't care. Any fear she had being overridden by her need to protect Phoebe. Her need to stop this train in its tracks before they all got ran over.

JC gave her a sheepish look before turning away. "You know what I'm trying to say, Hattie Mae."

And she did. "You know that won't work, JC, that will never work. You need to just be puttin' that outta your mind right now, or you gonna ruin both your life and hers." Hattie pulled the rest of the corn bread from the coals and started cutting it into small squares. But for the rain, which was coming down hard and heavy now, someone would have probably already come up from the quarters asking about dinner. She needed to hurry.

"Don't you think I know that? Don't you think I've tried? I want to hate her, Hattie Mae. Or even better, feel nothing at all for her, but I can't. I miss her too much when she's not around. I spend all day just waitin' to get a glimpse of her. Thinkin' of ways to get her to smile at me, to make her happy. Why did Dad put her out in the fields anyway? Why ain't she workin' in here with you?"

Hattie knew the answer to that question, but kept her mouth shut. Hattie hadn't been the only person noticing how JC had been looking at Phoebe. How he'd been treating her. Helping her carry water from the pump. Talking to her almost like he was courting her. His daddy had noticed to, and so as much as she hated to do it, Hattie had mentioned to the master that it was likely about time for Phoebe to learn how to work in the fields. He'd objected at first, until Hattie had explained to him that Phoebe would be even more valuable if she could do both field work and house work. And he had understood her hint when she told him there might be other good reasons to get Phoebe away from the house. She had thought that separating them might cause JC to start seeing Phoebe as she was—a slave he owned. But her plan had clearly backfired.

"I know," JC said, answering his own question, leaning back in his chair, crossing his arms, as a look of understanding settled into his features. "He knows, doesn't he?"

Hattie was saved from answering by a soft knock on the back door. She opened it to see Percy standing in the yard, rain running off his hat, like the side of a roof.

"Just checkin' to see if you needed some help gittin' the food out to everybody in the rain," Percy said, shaking off water like a dog.

"That's mighty kind of you, Percy," Hattie said, handing him the big pot of beans. "Go on, I'll be right behind you with the pork and the bread."

Percy took the pot, looking past her to where JC sat, the look of concern in his eyes communicating the question he dared not ask out loud. Hattie shook her head slightly in answer.

"Thank you, Miss Hattie," Percy said, loud enough that JC could hear. "You need me to come back and help you bring the rest?"

"No, Percy, I'm fine. I'm gonna be right behind you. Go on ahead."

Percy gave one more wary look to JC, nodded, and then headed back toward the quarters. Hattie watched him walk away, his path lit by intermittent flashes of lightning shooting out of the darkening sky.

"I don't care what he knows, Hattie." JC's voice was low and laced with steel.

Hattie turned back to face him, the look of determination on his face unnerving, as he rocked back and forth on the back legs of his chair. Hattie could see the wheels turning in his mind.

"You know as well as I do that this place and everyone and every-thing in it will be mine soon. I don't care if it's wrong, Hattie." JC rocked forward, the front legs of his chair hitting the floor hard, as he slammed his palms on the table, causing her to jump. "I can't see her go off with Will, or anyone else for that matter. I can't and I won't."

Hattie felt her fear and dread turn to anger as she watched him. If he really loved Phoebe, he'd let her go be with Will. If he really thought of her like his momma, he wouldn't keep her here like this. She had spent his whole life trying to keep an emotional wall between the two of them, knowing from the beginning that eventually this day would come. As she watched him now, knowing the kind of pain his feelings were going to inflict on Phoebe—Phoebe who she'd raised since she was a baby. Phoebe, who couldn't be more her own daughter had she birthed her herself—she felt that wall around her heart thicken and grow strong, pushing out whatever tender feelings she ever had for this man. He was no longer the boy who'd toddled around pulling at her skirts, who'd freely given her hugs and kisses, and whose laughter always made her smile. He was the master's son, with the same power, the same meanness, and the same awfulness as all the rest. But master's son or not, she wasn't going to let him hurt Phoebe. Whatever she had to do, no matter what, she was going to find a way to protect her, even if it meant giving up her own life.

With that thought, Hattie grabbed the two platters laden with pork and corn bread and headed out the door into the rain, leaving the master's son with his head in his hands wallowing in his own misery.

The Box

Lynn Bemiller

"ONE MORE THING before you go, Minkler." Dr. Fulton W. Forrest, III, my boss, leaned over my shoulder as I sat at my laboratory workbench and scowled at the neat row of postcard-sized plastic trays that I'd spent the last two hours meticulously pipetting reagents into.

I set the multi-pipet down on the bench top and looked up. He hung over me like a vulture, giving me an oblique view of his acid-yellow-print bow tie and his luxurious black nose hairs. "Sure thing," I said, and added, "It's Winkler."

Kristin Winkler. Very junior postdoc in cell physiology, in search of fame, publication, and grant money. True to form, I was the only one of our team left in the cramped, windowless space at this hour, as befit my status. Not that the glaring overhead fluorescents allowed any indication of the actual time of day, but the other three postdocs had left hours ago, and the lab director's blue blazer and brown brief bag suggested around his usual departure time of seven p.m.

"The data from that last set of experiments is not clean enough to include in our R-01 grant application, Minkler."

"Right" I nodded, rubbing my nose through my mask with the back of a gloved hand. "I'm running a set of control experiments now, with increasing titers of the neutralizing agent. Hopefully the data will be cleaner."

He shoved his glasses up onto his forehead and picked up one of the trays with a spider-like thumb and forefinger. He peered at the tray, tilting it from side to side before plunking it back on the bench. I winced in spite of myself, hoping he hadn't slopped the contents of any of the milliliter-sized wells from one to the other.

"Hmmf. Well. Let's hope so. We haven't got forever." He flipped his glasses down and was readjusting his blazer when the massive minus-seventy-degree freezer on the wall behind him emitted an ear-splitting shriek.

"What was that?" I jumped up, nearly knocking a large Erlenmeyer flask of buffer solution off the stirring plate at the back of the bench.

"Temperature alarm." He turned and squatted to read the digital display at the bottom of the unit, all pointed elbows and bony backside in baggy slacks. I heard a small click, then nothing but the ringing in my ears as he paused the alarm.

"You better move all the samples in here to another freezer before they thaw and ruin a year of work." He stood up, gave a cursory sideways glance at me and then strode out of the lab and into the dim hallway without waiting for an answer.

The automatic lock on the door clicked shut behind him, leaving me in stillness. I sighed with relief, knowing I could finally get some work done. Between the constant white noise prattle of Jeremy, our lab tech surfer dude, endless banter between the Italian fellow Lucca, and the Australian one, Gareth, and lobs of derisive commentary from the proper English one, Anwen (all glad for American grant support and California weather, but otherwise contemptuous of our "Yank" ways), there was no way to concentrate on science during most of the workday.

I pulled off my mask and gloves, and stepped down to the floor from the high metal lab stool. I arched my back, pushing out the kinks with both hands. A small timer sitting on the bench-top showed thirty-one minutes and counting, indicating when my trays would be ready to be read by the hulking countertop Becton-Dickinson plate reader on the bench beside me. I set the plates into position on the reader, pondered what to do with thirty-one minutes and counting, and then remembered the freezer.

I went out to the hall to find our backup freezer among the freezers and refrigerators of varied sizes and vintages lining both sides of the linoleum-tiled hall of our decades-old lab building. Just to the left of our door sat a chest-style freezer, with a sign taped to it that read "Forrest Lab Only," with a biohazard label pasted below it. I opened the latch and let a cloud of water vapor boil up and out, and then looked in. Lucky for me, it was empty; plenty of space to accommodate the stuff I needed to move. I closed the freezer back up and returned to the lab.

After donning a pair of giant thermal mitts and picking up a long pair of tongs from the counter near the freezer, I plucked twenty identical white boxes — each about seven inches long, four inches wide and two inches deep — from the shelves inside and stacked them together on a small rolling cart. When the shelves were empty I closed the freezer door and switched the unit off. Maintenance would deal with the problem in the morning.

I checked my stack of twenty boxes against the freezer's inventory list, rolled them out to the hallway freezer, loaded them in, and shut the door.

When the timer chimed, I fed my plates into the reader, and watched as the instrument printed out cash-register-like paper ribbons of numbers that corresponded with the strength of the reaction.

All the results looked good on first review, so I tucked the paper strips into my notebook, thinking that whatever it was that we were testing seemed to be doing whatever it was it was supposed to be doing, and made a note to analyze the data in depth in the morning.

LUCCA, WHO HAD a PhD in biochemistry and advanced degrees in skiing and flirting was already in the lab when I arrived at eight the next morning, Friday. He was weighing out salts for a new batch of buffer and humming along to a Verdi opera he had on in the background. Near him on the bench, his four-cup espresso pot steamed atop a Bunsen burner ring.

I sniffed the air as I walked past Lucca's workstation. "What's that smell?"

Lucca gaped in feigned horror and clutched his chest. "How do you not know the aroma of espresso? Barbarian!"

"No, not that smell." I rolled my eyes and smiled. "Something else, like rotten socks or something."

"Ah, that." He propped a leg on the bench, pulled one foot from its well-worn Birkenstock and waggled his naked toes. "I think it's—*come si dice*—sportsman toe?" He reached under the desk, pulled out a spray can, and vigorously sprayed the exposed digits.

"You mean athlete's foot?" I grimaced at the little cloud of spray that arose. "Are you sure you should be doing that in the lab?"

He winked, and then smiled. "Will be our secret, *sì*?"

I smiled and shook my head as I walked past him to my own workbench in the next row.

I spent the first few minutes of the day entering yesterday's data into a program on my laptop that—bingo!—created just the sort of reaction patterns I'd been looking for. Feeling pleased with the outcome, I flipped to a clean page in my notebook, wrote a summary of the previous day's experiments, stapled in the printout strips, and tabulated my conclusions.

Shortly after nine, the main door from the outside hall swung open and let Anwen in. She dumped her heavy laptop bag onto the other half of the bench she shared with Lucca. She adjusted her huge horn-rims and finger-combed her flaming red hair, then gave me a little wave. Behind her, congratulating themselves for having ripped the morning's glassy sets, came Jeremy and Gareth. Both broad-shouldered, blond, and sunburned, the two exuded the scent of Old Spice body wash. I looked up, nodded a greeting as they settled into their spaces, and then popped on noise-cancelling headphones so I could try to concentrate on work.

It was after two p.m. when I heard shuffling and banging from the freezer maintenance man. The rear end of his navy blue coveralls filled the narrow passage between the broken freezer and the end of my bench. I pulled off my headphones and looked around. Through a windowed door, I could see Anwen in the "clean" room, swathed in gown, gloves, and mask, working on something under the fume hood. Gareth, Jeremy, and Lucca had vanished, undoubtedly getting a jump-start on their weekend. Forrest was still here, though. I could hear his voice coming from the direction of his inner office.

I looked back at my computer screen, pushed save, and then print. In a moment, I heard the printer in Forrest's outer office whir. I got up, inched carefully behind the freezer repair guy, and walked into Forrest's outer office to pick up the pages.

The tiny room looked like the scene of a midwestern tornado. A small cluttered desk guarded the door to Forrest's inner office. The other walls were lined with tall filing cabinets. File boxes littered the floor, and stacks of journal article reprints, chemical supply catalogues, instrument repair manuals, and unopened mail occupied every available surface. I could see through the half-open door into Forrest's office, spacious and immaculate in an Ivy-Leaguish way. His polished, dark wood desk filled half of the room. Behind it stood built-in bookcases filled with bound journal collections, tasteful *objets d'art*, and all of his diplomas, degrees, and awards in silver-colored metal frames. The wall to the right of the desk was floor-to-ceiling windows, with a view of the ocean. He stood behind the desk, talking into his cell phone. When he saw me, he waved me into the room. I stood in front of the desk, looking around in a way I hoped was unobtrusive as I pictured myself as the future owner of an office like this one.

He switched the phone to his left hand, and gestured briskly with his right for the papers I was holding. "Well," he said into the phone, his voice cold, "you may think you have found it, but I can assure you . . ." He looked at the top page, nodded vigorously to me, and then gestured me out of the room. "No," I heard him say into the phone as I turned, "I wouldn't pursue publication if I were you. It would be a huge mistake."

I pulled the door closed behind me, glad that I wasn't the person on the other end of the phone. When I returned to my bench, the repair guy had disappeared. I ambled over to the freezer and looked at the maintenance log taped to the front. The tech had signed it off, and the temperature display now read negative seventy-two degrees.

I could still hear the rumble of Forrest's voice from inside his office. Eager to seem indispensable, I retrieved the sample boxes from the hall freezer to restock the repaired one. I took the rolling cart, tongs, and thermal mitts out into the hall, and counted out the boxes as I pulled them out of the vapor. There were twenty-one.

"Crap," I said out loud. I peered down into the freezer and fished around with the tongs, verifying that the unit was empty. Then I closed the lid, and recounted the boxes on the cart. Ten stacks of two and one left over. I picked up the twenty-first box in my mitted hands and turned it over. It was identical to the others, except that instead of a box number and date, someone had inked "F.W.F. Research Samples, Box 1" in angled, all-cap printing resembling Forrest's own.

"Huh," I said. I wondered how long it had been since Forrest had actually sat at the bench and analyzed his own samples. Might have been when I was in kindergarten, for all of that.

I rolled the cart back inside the lab, checked twenty boxes against the inventory list, and arranged them numerically in stacks of four. Then, I opened the newly repaired freezer and reloaded it, one stack at a time. When I picked up the final stack, the bottom box slipped, toppling the whole pile. I fumbled them in my clumsy mitted hands and managed to straighten the stack, but not before my right elbow caught on the twenty-first box, still on top of the cart, and sent it skidding over the edge and onto the floor. It landed top-down, emitting a faint sound, like the crack of melting ice.

I winced at the sound and then bent over to inspect the damage. I fancied I could still hear Forrest's voice saying ". . . a huge mistake" as I picked the stray box up from the floor and set it gingerly on the cart. It looked fine, I thought. The lid still fit snugly, with no cracks. I turned it over and checked the bottom and sides; they looked okay too. Relieved, I reopened the freezer, stowed the final stack of boxes, tucked the mystery box in the back corner of a shelf at about eye-level, and slammed the door.

I WAS ALREADY hard at work when Gareth appeared on Monday morning. He occupied the bench closest to the door, across from Lucca.

"Where's Jeremy?" he said. "Anyone seen him? He wasn't out at the point break this morning." I looked around, and shook my head.

"Spent the weekend here didn't he?" Anwen said. Her gaze was fixed in front of her, and very steady voice suggested she was doing something else, very carefully, while she talked. "He had gobs to do before Forrest flies off to that big funding meeting of his."

"Right. So I was sure he'd be out at the beach this morning. Guess I'm on my own today then with this latest experiment." Gareth came around to the freezer at the end of my bay and pulled it open. He grabbed the tongs and rummaged noisily for a few moments before pulling out a box. He turned to me, leaving the door hanging open. "Kris. Didn't we just have this thing serviced?"

I nodded without looking up from what I was doing. "Last week. Why?"

"What's that smell, then? And this purple mist? Has Jeremy been storing some shit of his in here again?" When I looked over, he had his head stuck as far into the freezer as seemed possible without incurring frostbite, and was sniffing in a way that made his head bob up and down like a beagle dog on the scent. "Anybody else smell that? Lucca?"

Lucca got up from his bench and walked over to the freezer. When I looked up, he was standing behind Gareth. "Smells fine to me," he said.

"Huh," Gareth replied. "Don't know how you smell a thing above the smell of your feet, mate. Maybe it's your socks in here?"

"I've heard that works," I said, "freezing your workout gear before you wash it, to get rid of the funk."

Lucca laughed. "You Americans! You need to always smell good. But, since you mention it, I must try!" He pulled off his sandals and lifted them toward an open shelf.

"Good God, not here," said Anwen. "Do it in your freezer at home!"

I heard the freezer door slam as I turned back to my work. I pulled two tiny tubes from the ice bucket in front of me, popped the lid off the first one and pipetted less than a drop of its contents into each well of the rectangular plastic plate on the counter. As I watched, the contents of the wells began to fluoresce a shade of green that was almost invisible in the wells closest to me, but got progressively more intense in the farther ones, suggesting that the right reaction was occurring. I smiled with relief. One step closer to filing that grant application.

ON THURSDAY MORNING Forrest, who for reasons known only to him had beat us all to work, emerged from his inner sanctum at eight a.m. sharp. He was impeccable, of course, in a blue blazer, blue-and-white oxford shirt and khakis creased to a knifelike edge. He sported his trademark yellow bow tie, and smelled of expensive French cologne. He looked around the lab, blinking, his thick lenses magnifying his eyes. "Do I hear the hum of brilliant discourse from busily engaged minds?"

"No, that's me venting steam," Gareth said. "Big experiment today, and here's Jeremy off on some unscheduled holiday. We've not seen him all week."

Forrest sounded as though his mind was elsewhere. "Well, never mind. I'm off to talk up funding with some very important parties from back east, very hush-hush. Back on Monday." For a moment, he assumed his vulture pose behind me as I typed data into my laptop. I smelled coffee breath and Altoids. "Your work is improving, Minkler. Your diligence will certainly pay off."

"Thanks, Dr. F," I murmured. "Safe trip."

As soon as the door closed behind Forrest, I heard the sound of slamming cupboards and drawers coming from Jeremy's workstation.

"Does the man not keep records of the work he does? No notebooks, nothing?" Gareth's frustration level was rising.

"Try his work laptop," said Lucca

"It's with him, apparently, wherever that is." Gareth gave a long snorting sigh, followed by the sloshing sound of ice and water being thrown into the deep sink at his bench. "This has gone far enough. I'm of a mind to go to his place and . . ."

Lucca stood up and put a hand on Gareth's shoulder. "Relax, my friend. I'll go with you. Probably he just partied too much. Or met somebody, maybe. Yes, that must be it." Lucca's eyes lit up and he smiled broadly as he held the hall door open for Gareth.

"Lucky little bastard," I heard Gareth reply, just before the door banged closed behind them.

More than an hour passed in blissful silence. I was in the "clean" room, dressed head-to-toe in personal protective gear, and setting up a new set of samples for testing when Anwen opened the door and popped her head in. "They're not back yet. But when they show, I think it's time we ladies took an afternoon's mental health break." She shoved her glasses up, and gave me a sly smile.

"I don't know," I said, blinking at her from behind my face shield, "seems we're under a bit of a time crunch. And what with Jeremy slacking off . . ."

"Trust me, the work will still be here tomorrow."

"Speaking of trust," I set down the pipet, "why do you suppose Forrest thinks we need funding from hush-hush sources? Is that typical in antibiotics research?"

Anwen gave me an opaque look. "Competition, intellectual property rights and all that. I suppose." Before she could go on, the door banged open, and Lucca and Gareth entered. I followed Anwen out into the main room of the lab. "Any luck?" she asked.

Gareth shook his head and flopped down on his lab stool. "No sign of his arse. But," he bent over and pulled Lucca's work laptop from his knapsack, "we did find this, at least." He set it on the counter and flipped it open.

"That's not the strange thing, though," Lucca said. He flashed us a conspiratorial smile and lowered his voice. "There was absolutely no sign of life. We used a spare key from under the mat to get in. Everything inside looked like he just stepped out for a minute, not like he packed and went away or anything. And then, we found this." He held up a Ziploc sandwich bag filled with something that looked like fine, deep purple sand.

I squinted at the bag and took half a step back. It had a faint iridescent shimmer to it, like the sheen on the surface of rotting meat, that repelled me. "What *is* that?"

Lucca shrugged. "Some new party drug maybe? We thought to analyze it later."

Gareth looked up. "I've not seen anything quite like it. Got a snootful of it, though, when I swept this little pile of it off his sofa. Smells pretty disgusting."

Anwen put out her hand to take the bag from Lucca, but I stepped in between them. "Wait, don't touch it. I don't like the look of it," I said. "I'm going to put it in the biohazard locker until we decide what to do with it." I took the bag over to the fume hood, rolled it into a tight little cylinder, stuffed it into an airtight specimen tube, and deposited it into an adjacent countertop refrigerator covered in red biohazard stickers.

Lucca caught my eye and gave a little eye roll. "Well, that should contain anything."

I carefully removed the gown, gloves, and face shield, and deposited them in the biohazard trash. "Can't be too careful, you know." I looked over at Anwen, who adjusted her glasses, gave me a *we should talk* look, and then bent and picked up her gear bag. "Don't know about you, Kristin, but I'm ready for lunch."

"Great by me," I said. I grabbed my own bag from the knee hole under my workstation and followed her out the door.

THERE AREN'T TOO many ills that can't be vanquished by a juicy burger followed by an afternoon at the beach. Once I sat down at the bench next morning, though, I had to admit that I felt just a little guilty about having blown off the previous afternoon. So I didn't waste any time: I mixed up a fresh batch of buffer solution, put on a clean gown, gloves, and visor, and settled in the clean room to set up my experiments. It was another new set of samples today, something Anwen—admittedly after three craft beers and too much sun—said was "top secret stuff." I was disinclined to believe her; not just because of the beer and the sun, but because as a foreign national on a student visa, I doubted she'd be in on such sensitive things.

When I emerged from my protected retreat at lunchtime, Anwen and Lucca were hard at work.

"Where's Gareth?" I asked, looking around. I could see the back of Lucca's head as he bent over the gas chromatograph, feeding it a sample from a reagent tube.

"He was still here when I left at midnight," he said without turning around.

I strolled over to Gareth's workstation by the door. Both his and Jeremy's laptops sat open on the bench top. An ice bucket sat to one side. The ice inside had melted and two plastic tubes with green screw-top lids floated forlornly in ten centimeters of water. "Funny he didn't clean up after himself," I said. "He's usually so meticulous." As I turned to go, I bumped the lab stool that he'd left sticking out into the aisle between benches. A rivulet of purple sand slipped off the seat, barely missing my shoe as it made a tiny pile on the beige floor tiles. "Uh oh," I said, "more of that purple stuff. What's *with* that, anyway?"

Lucca leaned around the end of the bench to look. "Just like we found at Jeremy's place. It's a big mystery, girls," he said in a meant-to-be-funny voice. But I caught a little crease between his dark eyebrows. "All this drama is making me itch," he said. He pulled a spray can out from under his desk and sprayed it vigorously over his bare toes.

Being the only one in protective gear, not to mention still being the low person on the research totem pole, I fell to cleaning up the stuff on the floor. I collected some airtight tubes, a bottle brush, and a small plastic dish for weighing out chemicals, and proceeded to sweep the purple sandpile from the seat of Gareth's lab stool and decant it into the sealable tubes. That finished, I bent to do the same with the stuff on the floor. The pile looked much smaller than it had just a minute ago, seemed to bubble slightly around the edges—or was it just the light down here?—and was outlined in a rim of lavender foam. I turned my head to the left and found myself looking directly at Lucca's Birkenstocked toes.

"Lucca," I projected my voice upward like a diva from the Italian opera, "did you step in some of this stuff?"

His face, tilted at a 270-degree angle, popped into the kneehole connecting the two desks.

He looked at the bottoms of his sandals, and then at me. "Appears not. Why?"

"I guess less spilled than I thought," I said, still eyeing the rim of foam. I shrugged, and bent to sweep the floor.

Before I could seal the specimen tube, the phone on the wall rang with one of those obnoxious Bell telephone jangles from the building's original days. I flinched, whacking the back of my head on the underside of the bench as I unfolded myself.

"Anwen can you get that? You're closest!" Lucca called.

Anwen snorted, but answered it anyway. A moment later, she said, "It's Forrest. He wants Gareth."

Lucca and I were now face-to-face. We looked at each other and shrugged. "Put him on speaker," I suggested.

"Hello?" Forrest's distorted voice filled the room.

"We're here. Lucca, Anwen, and Kristen," Lucca said, apparently feeling an uncharacteristic need to take charge.

"Where the hell is Gareth? He's supposed to be the senior fellow in this lab. We need to talk right away."

"He worked very late last night testing the new samples that arrived from the university," Lucca said, sounding unconcerned. "He'll be along any time."

Forrest exhaled loudly, and tutted. "Damned inconvenient, but it can't wait. You're all fired."

No one said a word.

"Did you hear what I said? It has come to my attention that a research team here in New England—I won't say where—is already light years ahead of us, and has a high-level customer salivating—SALIVATING!—to commercialize my discovery. So, you're obviously no longer needed." He stopped, and we let the pronouncement sink in. Anwen was frozen in place, expressionless. Lucca scowled, red-faced, looking like Vesuvius about to blow.

"First thing in the morning, two top scientists from their team will come by to personally collect your samples and ship them here. Please have them ready. Oh, and fill out your time sheets. The institute will send your final paycheck at the end of the current pay period. That's all." The line went dead.

We listened to the dial tone for a few seconds before Anwen hung up the handset. Lucca jumped to his feet. He gave his stool a kick that sent it clattering to the floor. He stared at it for a couple of seconds before picking up his laptop and stomping out the door.

After a moment, I walked over and righted the stool. "Good thing my CV is still up to date. Maybe I can get my old position at the biotech company back. If this is what academia is like, I'm out."

Anwen wrinkled her nose at me, which pushed the tops of her owlish lenses up over her eyebrows. "Something is just not right."

I raised my eyebrows. "What, you mean besides us being fired and Jeremy disappearing? Maybe Gareth knew what was coming and decided to split."

She frowned, shook her head, then pulled her cell phone from her pocket. She punched a number, and then turned the speaker on so I could hear it. After several rings, voicemail picked up.

"Gareth here. Leave a message."

She dialed another number and a woman's voice answered. She muted the speaker, and walked out into the hallway, talking softly as she closed the door behind her. I grabbed my notebook and carried it into Forrest's outer office. If I had really been fired, I wasn't about to leave all my work behind. Starting at page one, I made a copy of each notebook entry using the boss's fax machine, so that each page came out with a neat date and time stamp at the bottom. I was just finishing when Anwen appeared in the doorway. Her face looked like a thundercloud.

"What's up?"

"When you mentioned old bosses, it got me thinking. Forrest got his start at a private research institute in London. Catriona, my old boss, was there at the same time he was. She knew Forrest came here after he left her lab, so when I couldn't get funding, she wrote a letter to him recommending he take me on."

It was a common enough story after all. I waited, sensing there was more.

"Turns out, though, she wasn't entirely up front with me. Forrest left there under a cloud, after one of his techs died of an illness that might have been connected with the project they were working on."

"Oof," I said, making a face. "Not good."

She folded her arms and slouched against the door frame. "No."

My mind whirred, making connections. "Wait. Do you think Jeremy . . . No, that's crazy. Isn't it?"

Anwen took off her glasses and stared at something in the distance. "Is it?"

I pulled the last page out of the fax and tapped the pile of papers into a neat stack. I looked from the top page over to Anwen, who was still standing in the doorway. Our eyes met. "Anwen. What is it we're really working on?"

"Antibiotics. Really." Her eyes were steady, but she twisted her lips and chewed the inside of her cheek.

I folded my arms. "Antibiotics, but for just what indication? What is the pathogen?"

She sighed, slowly, ending in a sort of snort. "I've heard all kinds of rumors, but the fact is I don't know for sure. I asked Catriona the same question. She just says what she's said before: 'Ask the Yanks. It's classified.' "

I nodded slowly, staring at the papers in my hands. "If it's actually classified then Lucca and Gareth won't know, either." I set my notes down, circled around behind the cluttered desk, and pulled the center desk drawer. It resisted the first couple of tugs and then came free, practically exploding with Post-it pads, paper napkins, plastic forks, boxes of push pins, pencils in a rainbow assortment of colors, and a pair of boxer shorts covered in graphics of hot dogs with mustard. I dug my hand under a collection of soy sauce packets and felt around for the large paper clip with three keys dangling from it that Forrest's admin assistant kept in there somewhere. I fished them out and jingled them at Anwen. "We're going to find out."

I walked over to Forrest's door and jabbed one of the larger keys into the keyhole on the doorknob. It turned easily. I opened the door, pushed a box of printer paper against it as a door stop, and flicked on the lights.

Anwen hurried over to the "I-love-me" bookcase display behind the desk. "With his ego, I'm sure he keeps anything important in plain sight so he can admire it." We stood for a moment, perusing the shelves.

Shelves in the corner farthest from the door were covered in bound editions of major journals. Their spines read *Cell*, *Journal of Immunology*, and *Proceedings* in gold lettering, with the volume numbers beneath. The last four volumes on the bottom shelf had dark green bindings to match the others, but were unmarked. I pulled one out and opened it up.

"Look," I said, poking Anwen with my elbow, "his notebooks."

Our eyes met, and she gave me a slow smile. "Gotcha, Forrest!"

I stacked the books, lugged them to the outer office, then locked everything up, and pocketed the keys, just in case. When I returned to the lab, Anwen had opened a cupboard marked "Poison: Organic Solvents" and was pulling out a bottle of Bombay Sapphire gin and another of Schweppes tonic. On the counter were two clean beakers half-filled with crushed ice. I watched as she poured equal measures of gin and tonic into each, and handed me one.

"Now then," she said. "Let's hunt."

IT WAS HOURS—and three gin-and-tonics—later when I closed the last notebook and looked across at Anwen. She was leaning back on her tall metal-backed lab stool, with her feet up on the bench, and her glasses on top of her head.

"So, if I'm reading this right," I said, "we weren't working on an antibiotic at all. It's an antidote. To a weaponizable pathogen . . ."

". . . and Forrest was perfecting the pathogen." She stared up at the ceiling as she finished my sentence for me. "My hunch? It was a rogue project. There's nothing here," she shoved one of the notebooks in the pile in front of her, "to say that he was working for, say, your government or some legitimate weapons manufacturer."

"My hunch?" I said, "Whatever it is, it's purple."

She swung her feet to the floor and turned to look at me. We locked eyes as though attempting to read each other's minds, then she suddenly smiled and stood up. "I know someone who might be able to analyze what we've got. An old boyfriend, as it happens. I'll pack up the stuff from Jeremy's place and Gareth's bench." She paused and thought for a moment. "Did he say someone was coming tomorrow to pick up our antidote samples?"

"They're not getting them," I said, pulling on a gown, mask, gloves, and face shield. When I opened the door to the negative-seventy freezer, a lavender mist boiled out. I waved it away and peered deeper in. The mist rolled gently down from a shelf at eye level, accompanied by the funk of old socks. I stood on tiptoe for a better look. Purple ice covered the entire shelf, but the only box I could see was the one I'd put there myself. I pulled the box out, and carried it over to the fume hood, holding my breath and hoping that in spite of the mask and face shield the trail of lavender mist didn't seep into my lungs. In my mind's eye, I could still see Gareth with his head in the freezer sniffing vigorously. I shuddered and turned the ventilation on full blast. The lid came off the box when I tugged, revealing one-milliliter-sized plastic sample vials, forty all together. One sitting near the wall of the box had shattered, and was now nearly empty. Purple frost coated the inside of the box. I pulled each tiny vial from the box, put all but four into an airtight plastic bag, and zipped it shut. For good measure I added two more bags around the vials. The extras I wiped with disinfectant, and then carried everything out to the hall, where I hid the bag in the depths of the backup freezer. On the way back I set two of the vials on my bench, and handed Anwen the remaining two. "Better take these, too. Part of his original collection." She grabbed a marker and put black dots on the top of each one, smiling grimly as she packed them into a dry-ice shipping container—a sort of high-tech Playmate cooler—along with the carefully packaged sweepings from Jeremy's apartment and Gareth's bench. When she was done, she looked at her watch. "Nine p.m.. I can get the next flight to San Francisco. My friend says he can run the samples for us overnight, so I can be back here in La Jolla on the first flight tomorrow." Clutching the cooler in both hands, she headed for the door. "Wish me luck!" she called as she disappeared down the hall.

When Anwen was gone, I stripped off my protective gear and went down the main corridor to the communal supply room. Neat stainless-steel racks lined both walls from floor to ceiling. Cardboard cartons held all of the dry goods it takes to run a lab. In a box on the floor I found the white plastic freezer boxes I was looking for. I counted out twenty and toted them back to the lab.

Back at my bench, I carefully racked one-milliliter plastic sample tubes into each of the twenty boxes, and filled them all with a buffer solution, completely inert, but looking just like the antidote samples. By the time I was done, my thumb was sore from pushing the plunger on the calibrated pipet, but the array of tubes and boxes on my bench looked identical to the real ones in the freezer. For good measure, I took down the inventory list and neatly labeled and dated each of these dummy boxes to match the real ones.

Sometime after midnight I stopped and stretched. The buzz from the gin-and-tonics had worn off. A tired dull feeling settled behind my eyes and made me irritable. The lab was dead quiet except for the faint humming of the old-fashioned fluorescent tube lights that made the small room brighter than daylight.

I stifled a yawn, rubbed my eyes, and looked around. On Anwen's bench sat an ice bucket of half-melted slush. I picked it up, stuck my head in the sink, and poured the contents over the back of my neck. The cold made my chest constrict—next best thing to a plunge in the ocean—and I shook myself awake, wet puppy style.

I gowned up again, and fished all the boxes of our real antidote samples from the purple-iced freezer, wiped them with disinfecting solution, and stashed them in the hall freezer, with the samples of the purple stuff. The decoy boxes went right into the negative-seventy machine. I retrieved the broken box and sample tube from the biohazard trash and tucked them back on their shelf. I smiled when the cold air hit them, triggering a swirl of purple mist. Then, I locked both freezers and went home.

TWO GUYS HOLDING a dry-ice shipper were standing outside the lab door when I arrived the next morning. I opened up the lab with my copy of the master key, and then paused with my hand on the knob. "Can I help you?" I asked.

A thin round-shouldered guy with greasy side-parted dark hair and a receding chin nodded. "We're postdocs from the University of New England." He pointed back and forth between himself and a small South Asian-looking guy with coke bottle glasses who stood next to him. "Dr. Forrest sent us to pick up some important research samples, for a project of his that we are taking over. Said one of you'd know about it." He made a very brief smiling motion with his mouth.

"Of course," I said. "He called yesterday. Let me show you where they are." I held the door open for them, and then brushed past and unlocked the freezer door. I pulled the inventory out of the document holder magneted to the freezer door. "Here's a list of the contents. Help yourselves."

I picked up all of Forrest's files and notebooks from my bench, and carried them to his office, as far from the freezer as I could get. "I'll be in the office," I called over my shoulder. "Let me know if you need anything." I left both the outer and inner office doors open just a crack so I could hear what they were doing. Then I flipped on the copy machine and opened the first notebook to a page I had bookmarked.

"What stinks in here?" I heard one slightly muffled voice say. "Here, come smell this. It reminds me of something."

I heard sniffing sounds, and pictured them inhaling that purple mist. "Reminds me of your feet," the tall guy's voice replied, "it stinks like fermented sweat socks."

"Yeah, that's it. Sweat socks," said the first voice.

After a few minutes of scuffling noises and rattling boxes, I heard the freezer door slam. I looked out from behind the office door. "All done?" I said.

The small guy waved the hand that wasn't holding his end of the cooler. "Got them all. Thanks."

I waved as they turned to go.

"Now I can't get that damn stink out of my nose," I heard him say to his partner.

I got back to work, determined to get copies made of anything incriminating before Anwen returned. I was so focused on the clunk and whir of the copier that I didn't hear the outer door open. The first clue to Forrest's presence was his indignant bark.

"What the hell are you still doing here? I thought I made clear that you're fired." He stood in the doorway, fists on his narrow hips, hairy nostrils flaring. The overhead light winked off his glasses so I couldn't see his eyes.

"Dr. Forrest," I said, startled. "We weren't expecting you until Monday." I stacked the pile of copies neatly and closed the last of the notebooks before I turned to face him. "I came in to make sure the samples got picked up by your new team, as you requested."

He hesitated. "Ah, yes. The samples. Much appreciated, Minkler. I hardly think the others could have been trusted." He opened the door to the inner office and set his brief bag on the university side chair. When he turned back, his eyes caught on the stack of notebooks next to the copier.

"What are you doing with my notebooks?" he asked, his voice cold and crisp.

"I'm collecting evidence," I replied, in as calm a tone as I could manage.

He stared at the stack of notebooks, then at me, and then back at the notebooks. "What do you mean, evidence?" He peered at me as though I were a bug on the floor. "You have no idea what we do here, do you?"

"No, I don't. But I do know there's a box in the freezer containing samples of something that turns purple and smells like old socks when exposed to the air," I said. I shuffled down through a few of the pages in my hands as I inched backward toward the door. "And I'm betting it's the same lethal stuff used in these experiments—" I waved the papers at him—"on small mammals. And it just might have been exposure to the same stuff that killed your lab assistant some years back."

His face flushed a deep red. His eyes bugged, magnified weirdly by his glasses, and his Adam's apple bobbed as he swallowed. He took one long step toward me, lunging for the papers.

I whipped the pages behind my back and out of his reach, as I edged through the doorway and into the outer office. Out of the corner of my eye, I could see the wall clock. If Anwen had taken the 6:15 flight from SFO like she'd planned, she could be coming through the door any time now.

"Just wait a minute." He took a deep breath and straightened his bow tie. He went on in a more reasonable tone. "Look, Minkler. You have shown some real promise in your time here. Ambitious young scientist that you are, I'm sure we can find a way to make this worth your while."

I walked briskly out into the lab and over to my bench. Keeping one eye on him, I stuffed the papers into my backpack, and then turned to face him, stalling for time. "Well. I suppose there's no harm in talking things over. What did you have in mind?"

He studied me for a moment, and then made a forced sort of grimace that passed for a smile. "Perhaps I was a bit hasty before, firing you. I'm sure we could find a—an appropriate role for a collaborator with your skills."

"A collaborator?" I asked.

"Certainly. It would, of course, mean preserving the confidentiality of some aspects of the program. But—the opportunity to be a coauthor on the paper we're writing more than compensates, don't you think?"

"Confidentiality? Meaning, I suppose that we'd just sweep Jeremy and Gareth under the rug and let it be our little secret? No, no. For that, I'd need to be a partner in any commercial enterprise that results from—" I patted my backpack—"all of this."

"Sweep? Gareth?" He turned a bilious shade of green that clashed with his blue shirt. "What do you mean?"

I picked up the vials of purple dust and held them up to the light. "I mean this."

Before he could say anything, the hall door banged open and Anwen appeared. "We were right, Kristin," she called as she came through the door, "this is no ordinary pathogen. It's a flesh-eating fungus, capable of rapidly reducing human DNA to a pile of purple spores."

"Yes," Forrest hissed, walking slowly toward us. "The perfect biological weapon. I happened upon its properties by accident. I couldn't believe my luck when that snooping fool at the lab in London provided me the perfect proof-of-concept in humans." He glared from one of us to the other. "Just a few more experiments, and I'll own both the weapon and its only known antidote. I'll be sitting on a fortune!"

He stopped, eyes glittering with excitement, and looked at us as though he expected applause. For a long moment, no one moved. The only sound was the slow tick of the wall clock. Then, in a sudden frenzy of impatience, Forrest shouted, "I will not be defeated by a stupid pair of twits like you," and lunged at me.

Startled, I clutched the vials, but not quickly enough to prevent him knocking one of them to the floor, where it shattered. When the air hit the contents, a thin shimmer of purple dust started a slow swirl upward. I dove out of the way, my shoulder plowing into Forrest as I fell. The momentum skidded us up against the kneehole under Lucca's desk.

"Hang on to him," Anwen shouted. "I'm calling security!"

I scrambled to put a knee into his chest to hold him down, but he flopped around like a beached fish, and toppled me over. My arm knocked into Lucca's can of foot spray. Forrest got to his hands and knees, but before he could scuttle away, I grabbed him by the belt with one hand, and with the other, I sprayed him full in the face, then climbed on his back and kept spraying. As the spray hit the purple mist, it fizzed briefly, and then both dust and foam disappeared.

Six months later

"MY COLLABORATOR AND I just couldn't be happier with your respective offers," I said. "And knowing that commercial-scale production will begin immediately, well . . ." I raised a heavy cut-crystal flute and caught Anwen's eye across the table. She winked at me through her owlish glasses, which gave a delightfully quirky touch to her black silk dress and very English opera-length pearls.

The pharmaceutical company rep sitting to my right looked from one of us to the other and beamed. He had the perfect smile of a toothpaste ad, which complemented his perfectly tousled blond hair, snow-white shirt, and slightly loosened striped tie. "Our firm is absolutely delighted to be doing business with such a promising and—may I say—dynamic team." He took a large mouthful of champagne before continuing, "You know, we had a call late last year from another lab that was just about to publish similar results. We were eager to get a piece of the action—but they never came through."

"Well," Anwen smiled, leaning back in her chair with an air of satisfaction, "science is a fiercely competitive business, as you know. One minute you make a breakthrough, the next minute the competition is sweeping you up off the floor."

The defense contractor's rep, the one with the ex-Marine physique and eyes the color of espresso, ran a hand through his close-clipped curls, and leaned toward us. "The word on the street is that two of their researchers absconded with the goods, and haven't been heard from since." He gave a little shrug. "It looks like you left them in the dust."

I paused, picturing the exact color of that dust. "I'm just sorry that Gareth and Jeremy aren't here with us. Their contribution to the project early on was invaluable."

The blond rep shook his head and looked sorry. "Such a tragic accident, losing those two. And frightening too. I mean, if we can't trust our elite scientific community, then who can we trust?"

"Oh, I agree absolutely," Anwen said, rolling her eyes most sincerely.

"Well, thank goodness Forrest is behind bars." I smiled over at Anwen, who tilted her glass in my direction. "He put up a good fight, though. It took both of us to keep him pinned to the ground until the police came and carted him away."

"Wait," the ex-Marine said, "wasn't there someone else on the original team with you? How did he manage to escape getting infected?"

"You mean Lucca," I said thoughtfully. "You know, without him we'd never have known the weapon's big vulnerability."

"Athlete's foot spray! Who'd have thought?" he replied.

"Now you have a better weapon, and we have an even better antidote," the blond said. "Two companies, two patents." The two men clinked champagne glasses, and then drained them.

Anwen smiled. "Don't worry about Lucca. With the proceeds from our shares in both patents, Kristin and I will make sure he gets enough to live like a prince on the surf beach of his choice."

"Right," I said, "let's toast Lucca and his stinky feet!" I reached behind me for the bottle of Veuve Clicquot and refilled each glass. Then I lifted mine. "To a long and happy collaboration."

Melissa's House

Jeannie Hua

I'M SITTING ON the pink shag carpet of Melissa's bedroom. Stuffed animals sit on rows of shelves along her wall. More fabric denizens sit on her bed. The mute inhabitants, bedspread, pillows, carpet, everything in her room reeks of boiled hotdogs and shares a similar shade. John, Melissa's older brother, walks to her door and says something to her in English. I look down and hug my legs. I can't understand him and I pinch clumps of the carpet between my toes to keep busy. Melissa says something to him then looks at me. I nod because I don't know what else to do.

John shares the same blue eyes and blond feathered hair as his little sister, but his hair is darker. He says something to Melissa again. His voice sounds lower than the last time I was at their house. I look up and see fuzz on his upper lip. Dressed in a T-shirt and basketball shorts with bare feet, I see him gazing back at me.

John points with his stubbled chin at the back of Melissa's room. The corners of Melissa's lips turn downward. She says something to John. She stands up and stomps her feet. He smiles and looks toward me. He strides into the room, grabs my arm, and pulls me up. I'm confused; he usually isn't very nice to me. Whenever he'd see me, he'd pull on the outer corners of his eyes and make them narrow and slanty. The sounds that'd come out of his mouth didn't sound friendly. But now he's cupping my hand in his and pulling me toward the door. I follow with fear and curiosity.

From Melissa's bedroom, we walk down the stairs. We cross the faded linoleum floor of the empty kitchen to the basement door. He lets go of my hand and places a hand on the doorknob. He turns to me and puts his finger to his lips with his other hand. He pulls the doorknob and the door squeaks as it opens, revealing wooden steps with gray chipped paint. I peer down the narrow steps that lead down to the darkness below. I'm scared of basements even when well lit. But now Melissa's brother wants me to go down and I don't want to disappoint him or embarrass myself. Besides, I wouldn't be by myself, John is with me.

John looks at me, says something, and tilts his head at the stairs. I step behind him.

The stairs creak with the weight of our steps as we walk into the cool and damp darkness. The air conditioner rumbles in the background. The smell of boiled hotdogs has even conquered down here. John holds me by my wrist now. I can feel the sweat from his hand around my wrist. The darkness shelters us from the bright summer heat outside. The only light streams through two tiny windows several inches from the ceiling. Pipes and beams line the walls and ceiling. We tiptoe across the cement floor as we make our way to the other side of the room

I hear Melissa, still on the second floor, loudly and laboriously counting to a hundred. I make out the outline of their oldest brother's unmade bed.

He gets on the bed. I stop by the edge, unsure of what to do. Leaning on his knees, he grabs me by my upper arm and pulls me onto the bed. A faded sheet covers the mattress and an unzipped sleeping bag lies rumpled over the sheet. He pushes me down on the bed by my shoulders so I'm lying down. He throws the sleeping bag over us and pulls me close to him. The bed smells like old socks and pizza.

He adjusts my body so I rest on my side. Then he props himself on his side and faces me. He pulls me against his body and pushes on the top of my head so my face is level with his chest. He takes my hand and puts it in his basketball shorts. He's not wearing underwear. He wraps my hand around a long hard object. It's soft on the outside but hard at the same time. I know it's a part of him but I don't know what it is.

"*Shi ma?*" I squeak.

"Shhhhhh . . ." He puts his index finger to his lips and mumbles something out the corner of his mouth. My face is pressed against his chest and I can feel it rise and lower rapidly. I'm not getting any air under the sleeping bag.

He whispers to me. I'm silent and still. He puts his hand over mine, the one still holding the object, squeezes and makes an up and down motion. I squeeze the object once. He responds by bucking his hips a couple of times. Whatever game this is, I'm not enjoying it. I feel like I have a stone in my heart.

Melissa says something from upstairs.

John answers back, his voice cracking in the middle of his sentence. When he speaks, his chin hits the top of my head.

Melissa's voice gets louder and there's a pounding from the ceiling. My hand is still on the object but I don't squeeze and I don't rub up and down. I wiggle my body upward to try to get some air. The stubble of his chin rubs against my forehead as he presses down on my shoulder. He wraps his hand around mine and makes my hand rub the object in an up and down motion. I feel his body tense and shake.

The blanket is too warm. I start to wiggle my head out from under the sleeping bag. The flannel underside of the sleeping bag is making my face itch.

Melissa's voice sounds even closer. He pulls down my yellow cotton shorts and puts his hand in my underwear. My underwear is light blue and has Cinderella and her mice friends on the front. I feel the tip of his finger in my *jiji*. As he turns his finger to and fro, I feel his nail cut into my skin.

"*Aiya!*" I cry. He puts his hand over my mouth to shush me. His other hand cups my *jiji*.

Melissa stomps down the basement stairs. She shouts something and pulls the sleeping bag off of us as John whips his hand out of my underwear. I pull up my shorts, crawl off the bed, run toward the stairs and up the basement steps.

Melissa hollers something behind me. I tug my stringy black hair out of my eyes as I stride through the kitchen, down the unlit hallway to the front door. I find my yellow flip flops by the door, hook them on my toes as Melissa calls my name.

Her voice fades behind me as I scramble out of her house. The afternoon sun follows me home, casting a shadow before me. My flip flops slap against the sidewalk flanked by well-mowed, lush green lawns. I pass a neighbor watering his roses in the front yard. He raises his head up and looks toward me. I half raise my hand to wave and he turns his back to me and aims his water hose to another section of roses.

Nearing my house, a flip flop falls off my foot. I put it back on while hopping on the other foot. A German Shepherd barks at me from behind the picket fence of another yard. With flip flop in hand, I limp to the fence. I stick my hand between the wooden posts to pet him but he turns and plods away. I tread back to the sidewalk and keep my gaze on my shadow until I reach our driveway. I ring the doorbell. My mom answers the door to our one-story, rust red, ranch. I kick off my flip flops and follow her down the hallway. The linoleum floor cools my sore feet.

My mom enters the kitchen. She's making my favorite dish: soy sauce pork, stir fried cabbage, and rice. I head into the family room and gravitate to the TV, pushing the on switch and twisting the channel knob to nineteen. I walk around the coffee table and plop down on our gray clothed couch. The couch's rough fabric rubs against the back of my legs as I rest my feet on the table. I can't see the TV clearly. My face is wet. I grab the bottom of my shirt and rub my face. Within the safe confines of my couch, I stare silently at the screen. Skipper smacks Gilligan on the head with his captain's hat. I let the laugh track fill my head and push out thoughts of what came before.

Road Closed

Nell Porter Brown

OUTSIDE THE CITY, beyond the tidy suburbs, the road finally narrowed to one lane. Leafless oaks and pines heavy with snow raced by as I focused on the driving. We thought we had escaped the worst of the storm in Boston. But now the windshield wipers barely cleared a wedge of glass with each rhythmic whack. I ducked my head to catch sight of the icy asphalt, squinting to stay on track.

"Just look how magnificent the trees are!" my mother said, bundled in her parka beside me. "Like cakes topped with crystal icing."

Freezing air swooped in as she opened the passenger window for a better view. "It's such a beautiful world we're destroying. It's so sad I can't stand it. Why must we kill this mother earth? Is Saran wrap and eating meat that goddamned important?"

A gravelly cough doubled her over. Covering her mouth with the crook of her arm, she tried to talk through the spasms—"I hate—" she rasped—"that nobody—"

"Water?" I pulled a plastic bottle from the cup holder, my eyes glued to the road, wary of weasels and skunks darting out and getting crushed under my wheels.

"No," she waved her mittened hand at me, "I'll be fine."

I gripped the wheel. Her phlegmy hacking reverberated through the compact car. Like she was wracking my own body. I chugged icy water as snow bits whirled around us. "Can you please close the window?"

She took a shuddering breath. "It's something I can't bring up. It hurts. Everything just sits in my chest."

"Mom, window?"

"The respiratory nurse at the hospital said she didn't hear any wheezing, the X-rays seemed clear." She shivered. "Oh, it's so cold in here—"

"Shut the window!"

She glared ahead, but glass rose up against the elements. "Dahlia, you don't need to yell at me. Please, I've been through a lot this week. I missed my Thanksgiving for God's sake."

She dipped into the plastic bag at her feet and rummaged through brown pill bottles, extra socks, her inhalers, scraps of paper hastily penned with instructions. "They gave me this," she stuck it up to my eye, "to help with the cough. But we don't have any water."

"We do. Here." I passed the bottle again.

"Oh, thank you, sweetheart."

She touched my arm and drank like she'd never before tasted this stuff, this holy balm. "Remember?" I chirped. "They said your bronchial tubes were irritated and that's what was causing the coughing. Not anything else."

"I *know* that. I was a nurse before I found my calling in the theater."

She took off her red knit cap. Her hair was still coal-black like her father's except for stark strands of white. I saw it suddenly as the inverse of the bleak scene outside, where skeletal trees stood black and lonely against the snow.

"I'll have to talk with my pulmonologist when I get back. And my cardiologist, and oncologist, the gastroenterologist—blah, blah, blah. All I ever do anymore is call doctors, take pills. Go to appointments." She sighed, looked out the flurry-dappled window. "The chemo makes me sleep—then it does not *let* me sleep. Insomnia! Do you know that at your house I was up for thirty-seven hours straight? Do you know what that's like? It's awful."

"I know. I'm sorry." My hands tightened on the wheel. Progress was slow along the old road. It followed woodland paths forged by Native Americans, who had trailed the forest animals, who had evolved through a million years through the ice ages.

"Didn't mastodons once roam New England?"

"Yes," she trilled, "I fondly recall riding them as a child."

We laughed. But the road had not yet been plowed, and the snow was thickening. Up ahead red taillights glowed on what quickly emerged as a logging truck. I imagined the ropes and chains breaking free and the massive felled trunks hurtling across our path. Jerking the wheel, I'd swerve away, but then I'd smash through the guard rail and we'd free fall, end to end, bumping and crunching down the rocky incline into the rushing river.

Would crashing there be better than a side-long plunge into the truck? What if a log simply fell off the back, bounced up, and shattered the windshield? That thing would kill us in a nanosecond. I slowed to let the taillight embers fade into the snowy distance.

If this were my film, that's how I'd end the scene: two tenacious broads battling the elements against all odds. A mother and daughter trudging toward the bright lights of an assisted-living complex after a failed Thanksgiving. But, really, I didn't quite know where we were.

"Where *are* we?" she croaked, as if she'd heard me. "Hills and trees. Not a single human being since Boston. No houses, even. Hey! I thought we were going to find that place I saw on Zillow. That darling old English-style farmhouse, right out of *Chitty Chitty Bang Bang*? It's not too far out of the way—you said that."

I'd hoped she'd forgotten. But Zillow house-porn was one thing that still made her giddy.

"I would guess we're near Athol, about a third of the way back to your place."

"Athol?" She laughed. "Never heard of it—at all!" Then squawky coughing tripped her up again. When it stopped, she unfolded the paper map I'd given her at the start of the trip. "I don't even see Route 2 on here."

"Keep looking, it's—" I darted my eyes to her veined hands, finding the blue-lined route snaking across the paper—"around there."

The car careened onto the rutted shoulder. Pine trees lunged at the windshield.

"Watch out!"

I slammed the brakes and skittered front-end sideways back onto the road.

"Got it! Just a little bump," and I patted her knobby knee dressed fashionably in black leggings. "We're fine."

"I don't like journeying through the Siberian hinterlands like this."

"What? Before we left you were looking forward to a 'drive in the country.' Go see your dream house."

In Boston, the snow had been raging. Sheets of white specks flew across the condo's lovely windows overlooking the South End. But Peter and the girls were snuggled in front of *Little Miss Sunshine,* with cocoa and banana pancakes. We kissed them goodbye, closed the front door, and made our doddering way along the corridor. The soundless elevator whooshed us seven flights to the underground parking lot. I rolled my mother's bulky suitcase and walked stiffly, trying to keep her heavy shopping bags, their plastic handles cutting into my palm, from banging my shins. The bags held European wines, cheeses, jams, and chocolates from her favorite gourmet store: "Life's little luxuries that I cannot find in the *Hee Haw* sticks."

But she'd been atypically anxious to get back to those sticks, back to her unit at Eden Woods. The compound of beige townhouses, connected through indoor carpeted hallways to what was cozily called the "lodge," was conveniently close to my sister's house. In the three months since my mother had relocated from her Manhattan apartment, however, she'd mounted a one-woman show of sarcastic soliloquies. "Eden Woods. As in End of the Woods: next door to End of the Line?"

Institutional grub on plastic plates. Hideous watercolors of sunsets and seashells. The sugar-padded staff quips, which she hilariously imitated: "Okay, Diana? You want your ass-a-wiped? Wouldn't that be nice?" But what really got her pissed were the white-haired "dolts" who'd sneakily excluded her from the Movie Selection Committee and ignored her requests for less Bing Crosby and more Ingmar Bergman.

But perhaps her stint in the hospital unit had softened her outlook. Peter and I had taken turns visiting, armed with crosswords and British detective novels. We read Ibsen and Chekhov out loud until she fell asleep. Few could ask for more courtly entertainment and consolation. But as soon as she was discharged, the haughty queen had flapped her crow wings and ordered her trunks packed for departure.

"Remember? You wanted to get going, even with the snow," I told her now. "Why not sit back and enjoy the scenery?"

"The scenery! Did I ever tell you about my time in the Swiss Alps? Now *those* are mountains. Wagnerian, symphonic peaks," she chorused, quoting some play. " *'Dark abysses of mystery and danger: time-traveling lands of sirens and centaurs, medieval magicians,'* not the piddly stuff you have here."

She sniffed. "But, yes, the snow is pretty. New England is quaint. Although it's strange that we've come to see Puritanical white churches and box houses, where people were tormented, tortured, and these dung-heaped sheep commons, as beguiling. *The Crucible*—what a horrific play!"

Packed into her parka, she was smaller than she used to be. Her face still shown with those majestic cheekbones and lips tinged a signature crimson. That face, of which I knew every cocked brow, wince, pout, and blazing smile. That face of leading lady Diana Darling had once lit up stages, albeit small ones, across the country and in Europe. She'd be gone performing for months in shows we'd hear about from the aspiring opera divas and punk rockers in charge at our Westchester County home. The failed clown had actually been the best because she took us on subways to her sprawling Italian family gatherings in Queens, where people hugged and argued, screeched and laughed, and ate pasta and cannolis all day long.

Our father usually loomed up late; after work and whatever else he did in Midtown Manhattan. He could be sweet, but was distant. It took me years to realize that his special Daddy smell stemmed from a bottle of Jameson Irish Whiskey. After the divorce, my mother moved us to her parents' raised ranch near Boston. From there, my sister Natasha and I were mostly on our own.

I glanced at my mother now. Her head poked out of her coat and she blinked around like a groundhog coming up for air. "Try to relax. Scan your body for tension. Breathe. Count five on inhales, seven on exhales. You know—'Be here now.' Did you even listen to the CD I gave you?"

"Don't start with your meditation stuff. I know I should do it—you've told me that." Her head bobbed toward the windshield. "Yes, I do love these trees!" She gave a wheezy, stagey sigh. "Dahlia, dear, I know I don't do all the things you think I should be doing."

"This is one tiny thing that would really help—it helps with anxiety, and everything, I've found—"

"Where's the heat knob?" She jabbed at the console lights. "It's freezing in here!"

"You said before you were hot!"

I cranked the knob, blasting heat in our eyes.

"That's too hot and dry!"

I turned it down.

"My body doesn't regulate. If you ever get sick like this, then you'll know."

She settled back and looked at the map. "I think this place is not far from here." She ran her crooked, manicured finger along the lines. "Remember when you were little, I read your palm? Told you how many children you were going to have? How strong your lifeline was?"

"Mm-hmm."

She looked at her palms, running her oxblood-colored nail from her wrist around to her thumb. "That's the heart line. Least that's what the palm reader told me at that fair when I was little. I've always loved those psychic women, with their probing looks." She loomed into my sideview, radiating creepy intensity.

"Oh, a lot of them dressed for the part," she allowed: "Black eyeliner, scarves, and bangles. But the real ones? They were spectacular, otherworldly creatures. Burrowed in their dens with bones, dirt, and rocks, diving their hands into your ancestral soul. Conjuring your stories of who you were, who you could be. Such incredible theater!"

She'd gone into a smoky-eyed reverie. "Oh my—all the beauty, all the things you believe are real . . ."

Snowflakes rained across the road. In that snow-globe realm, everything was beautiful and clean and good; a faraway storybook place my mother adored. But clean and good was her Clorox-mopped hospital room where nurses and aides padded in and out, checking her pulse, watching her exhale into a tube to chart her lung capacity. IV fluids pumped up her old body, like it was an air mattress, and returned faint color to her face—which had always been pale. She never tanned. Only burned.

Years ago, melanomas were removed from her forearms. But she had sewed "sun sleeves," and still safety-pinned these Miss Havisham accoutrements to the shoulders of her silky summer dresses, winding other lacy strips around her head, making it all look exotic and elegant instead of insane. Last August at her bimonthly Dana Farber visit, she'd worn that get-up, explaining that she stay out of the sun or she'd get cancer. Natasha and I looked at the doctor, a beatific Senegalese man.

"Does she need to worry about that now?" Natasha asked.

"Not anymore," he answered, and smiled softly at our mother, who'd become enraptured by the framed wall poster illustrating fire-exit protocols.

"You can spend the whole day at the beach, all you want. Good vitamin D."

"I have to say"—she turned to him with a stony, bug-eyed gaze—"I've never loved the beach."

The move was pitch-perfect, her best Barbara Stanwyck, and I had to laugh. She did, too. And for a moment we were hysterical.

That happened again on Thanksgiving Day at Mass General.

When the special turkey dinner arrived on a tray, she sat up gleefully, bouncing like the fat kid in Willy Wonka's candy land. "Goody-goody. Rehydrated potatoes and paste-board poultry with MSG gravy! How delightful!" We erupted in giggles, wiping our eyes together.

Those three days at the hospital were prompted by shortness of breath and gulping panic in the middle of the night at our house. But doctors had found nothing new seriously awry. Snapping out of her fortune-telling realm in the car, she clapped her hands. "Yes—yes— let's see the house. Mountain views. English cottage. Barn out back you could use that as your studio, right?"

"I suppose so."

"All right!" She crinkled the map on her lap. "I see it now, Route 2. Hmm. Athol, Warren, Wendell. Looks like we take a little offshoot, Russell? Worcester? It's too small to read."

"Here, just plug the address into my phone."

"I have my own phone. I can do it."

She futzed with the device. "Why isn't it loading? This damn phone."

"Are you on Google maps? Or Apple maps?"

"The one I always use! What do you mean? It usually works fine." She flicked the screen, jabbing the keyboard. "No signal. These things are useless! The digital age—it sucks! I say just drive north, not too many ways to go around here, it's the country! We'll find it, I'm sure. We can ask someone."

I stared at the white woods and drain-water sky. The logging truck was long gone. But then, like a mirage, a sign appeared, The Old Caboose, and there it was. A revamped metal-clad train car attached to a shiny Art Deco diner with a giant hand-drawn See You Next Spring! poster in the window.

I pulled into the empty parking lot, took the map, and pinpointed Wendell, where the house was, approximately seven miles from where I guessed we were. We'd detour off Route 2, rejoin it further east, then jet down the interstate to her unit. Simple.

"I want to get there. I'm getting tired now." She laid her head on my shoulder.

I flicked up the map on my own phone and typed in the Zillow address. 19 Plum Lane. Miraculously, the directions loaded: a fifteen-minute drive. "Here, just hold this phone and tell me where it says to go." She didn't move.

"I like leaning on you. I like it when you're nice to me."

"What are you talking about? I do everything, I—"

"Remember in high school, for your graduation we took that trip to England?" She sat up and patted my arm. "We saw Stonehenge and Tintern Abbey. Dylan Thomas's house in Wales?"

"Yes." I looked at her. Her dark eyes and hair clear evidence of her own Welsh heritage. "That was a good trip. Those were good times, right?"

"Mm hmm."

"Remember how I had to drive the car on the wrong side of the road?"

"And you got into an accident because you were marveling at Stonehenge and sideswiped that car coming the opposite way?" I wheeled back onto the road, the tires straining for traction. "The police came, we got towed to a garage, and then we spent the whole day at the pub next door waiting for a new rental car."

I wanted to laugh, make it a funny story. "And remember how then you'd had a few pints with the bartender, we ended up staying at the pub's 'rooms to let'? And how the next morning you were not in our room, but in someone else's room, so hung over we spent a second day at that dingy pub playing cards with the skinheads and octogenarian alkies?"

"They were a lot of fun!"

"Really?"

"You always pick out the bad parts—why do you do that? There are plenty of good parts. We loved staying at that manor house with the pool; we went skinny-dipping at night, with that magnificent full moon. Those stars! And then the manager came screeching at us to get out?"

I laughed, surprised by it. Surprised by how she looked like a little hurt girl, by what a little girl she always was. But then, in a blink, she'd morph into a rebellious, warring vamp.

"You loved it. In London we got the back-stage tour of *Cats*, on the West End?" Her eyes popped wide. "Who knew a whimsical poem by a dead man and humans prancing in feline leotards would become one of the greatest shows in history? And we went to that party, met Judi Dench! And the very young, and oh *so talented* Ken Branagh? You certainly enjoyed yourself *that* night—I didn't see you 'til the next afternoon!" She clucked her tongue, her eyes flirty-bright.

"I couldn't get into our room. The door was locked."

"No it wasn't, the desk had another key."

"They closed at 8 p.m. You were out cavorting. I didn't even know where you were. I got the last $15 bed at that fleabag hostel in Piccadilly Square."

"I thought you were out at one of those fun underground punk clubs and danced the night away? Found a purple mohawk-haired cutie."

"Ah, no. I like my eardrums, thanks."

"But it was something novel, an adventure! Life experience!" she sang out. "You need to have more fun. You and Peter—you don't go anywhere—office, condo, grocery store, kids' school. Following your little goat paths. What kind of life is that?" she squawked, flabbergasted by the silliness of my choices. "You should get out there, put on a backpack and—and just go!"

Her arm flared in a grand gesture across the blank horizon of central Massachusetts.

"This house! I think it would be a wonderful place for you and Peter and the girls—let's just go look at it. I can call the realtor right now, they'll meet us there."

"Yes, they will scurry over in this blizzard and give us the royal treatment."

"Stop that—there you go again, being sour."

When the phone told us to, I turned off the main drag, going slowly so the tires wouldn't lose traction. She left a voice mail message in her charming old-gal voice.

"I know it's a snowy day—so beautiful out here! My daughter and her husband, Boston executives, have been searching and searching for just the right home—and this is it! I'm just out of the hospital. Stage IV cancer. So this is the best time. Please. We're in town, on our way over there now." She pressed the end call circle and raised a pale jazz hand. "Ta-dah!"

"Applause, applause!"

She beamed.

"Cancer really gets people to do things for you! Way to go!"

"Oh honey, don't be mean."

"Sorry." I stopped. "I am sorry."

We went down one empty country stretch after another, passing no more than a dozen worn-out trailers and modest homes. Smoke curled from their chimneys into the white sky. The only color anywhere blazed from orange-lettered posted signs. No Trespassing. Private Property. Road Closed in Winter. Fifteen minutes was morphing into thirty.

We inched along a narrow hilly ridge. I hunched toward the windshield, the wipers wiping their hearts out.

She looked out the window. "A ravine! We slide down there, it's the end of us."

The car skidded a bit. She screamed.

"Mom! I can't concentrate if you're getting hysterical—"

"Whose idiotic idea was this anyway?"

She burst out laughing. I cracked a smile. We were in it now, no point in not plowing ahead.

"It should be up here somewhere, maybe take one more road, then it's off that," she waved vaguely, "the signal's gone again. But *I think* that's what the directions said."

A couple more squirrelly minutes of zig-zagging along, and we finally saw the sign for Plum Lane. It had apparently been plowed, but hours earlier. We turned in and crept forward, the car crunching new-fallen snow. Down a hillock, then across a twenty-foot simple wooden bridge.

"Stop. It's a stream!" She opened her window. "I want to hear the water."

Craning her neck outside, her skin was saggy and yellow in the raw winter light. "A faint trickle—under the ice." She closed her eyes and breathed in the sight.

We plodded forward. Around the next bend, at the end of a tree-lined drive, we saw it. The main house was a stucco English cottage replica, probably built in the 1930s, with a thick cobblestone base, sloping rooflines, and a turret. The house stood in a field blanketed with snow and faced sweeping views of the Vermont mountains far to the north. A second structure, the guest house, was just as charming. It was clear nobody was there.

"Drive up to the front," my mother gestured impatiently. "I want to get out."

Exiting the car, she tightened her coat around her small body, and set her beret at a jaunty angle. Her lips were dark red against the colorless winter, and she winked saucily, like the last of those black-and-white movie stars. The wind blew wisps of her hair, whatever had dug in against the onslaught of chemo. And despite everything, that stage twinkle became a real one, the real Diana Darling was radiant with joy; smiling in a way I had not noticed in years.

She slammed the car door and faced the house, the blue mountains spread forever behind her. Then her parka-hooded head appeared at the closed window. "Aren't you coming with me?"

When she'd first lighted on this place, hunched over her phone in the hospital bed, she'd said it had been professionally staged, the owners likely long gone since it had been on the market since last spring.

I eased down the window. "I don't think we really need to walk around. It's freezing. You just got out of the hospital."

"What? After all your hard work getting us here? No. Come on. Just take a peek." She turned around and began wobbling through the snow toward the home's front windows.

My ski cap on, I pulled the coat zipper to my chin, and stepped outside, where the cold whipped my bare face. She turned around, waiting. I traipsed over and she hooked her arm in mine, nudging me forward.

We dusted snow off the front windows and peered in. There was a mudroom hung with slickers and Wellingtons cutely lined up. Plenty of storage, and a central entrance anchored by a curving staircase. We crunched around to the side, arm-in-arm to French doors that opened onto a patio, according to my mother, who brushed the snow away to reveal blue slate. Through the paned doors, we spied the expansive living room with deep, soft sofas around the cobblestone fireplace.

Past that, was a glimpse of the kitchen. We rounded the side of the house, and looked in there: off-white, farmhouse-style with an old soapstone sink, loads of cupboards and counterspace and a round red-oak kitchen table. Adjacent to that was a formal dining room; the table was set with gold-rimmed white plates and cloth napkins, silverware, and gleaming candlesticks, as if dinner guests were arriving any minute.

"Isn't this glorious? What a dream!" She gripped my arm as she pushed her nose to the glass for a closer look.

"Mom, we're trying to de-clutter. Peter actually wants a tiny house, for God's sake. And what about maintenance? We do nothing at our condo, and we like it that way."

"This is wonderful. Seats ten, easily, for Thanksgiving!" Her eyes shone, looking at me with what had always been, before the cancer, an irresistible, infuriating beckoning seduction. I looked back. Really looked at her face, so close to mine. As close as mothers get to their little girls during those early years of intimate acts of washing, dressing, feeding. And loving.

She did not blink or move. She took me in, her eyes welling up. "Dahlia . . . my darling daughter . . ." I caught myself thinking she was playing a touching scene. *Act III: Mother and Daughter Reunite.* But then I felt it. I saw it. I thought it was actually love.

"Yes, Mom?"

She stepped away. The moment was gone.

"Look at this view!" She cried out, pointing to the snow-capped mountains. "You can sit here on the patio with cocktails, or whatever you drink, your protein shakes, and be *mesmerized* by this. Look! These 123 acres are all part of your property."

"A nice fantasy, but—"

"Let me show you the pool."

She shambled away, rattling her hand at me.

We stopped by the pool house, a beautiful fieldstone building likely leftover from the original farmstead. Caked with snow, the tastefully curved pool deck was banked by old-growth rhododendrons and blue spruce. "And the barn?" She nodded behind the pool to the red-clapboard building with a weather vane weaving in the wind. "It's in excellent condition, has heat and plumbing—perfect for, what do they call it, telecommuting? You're high enough up the food chain to do that, and the city's only ninety minutes away."

Snowflakes darted at my eyes. I blinked the sting away. She looked so happy. And I wanted her to be happy. I really did.

"You've always wanted a big garden, chickens, a sheep or goats. Right? Isn't that your dream? One of them, at least?"

"I guess—"

"No. From when you were very little, you've always said you wanted a farm. It's true—"

"Mom."

"You can do this. Yes!"

"Mom!"

"Yes?"

I didn't know what I wanted to say. I wanted a magical moment to just happen. For us to turn to each other and embrace, and cry. For her to say how much she never, ever wanted to leave me.

The chill crept through my jacket. She shivered and moved on toward the barn. I followed. We rolled open the door and the sweet, grassy smell of hay filled my head. High broad beams still held the place together. The old wood notched by hand with axes had been refurbished, and the horse stalls remade into rooms with built-in bookshelves and chic European wall heaters. I sidled along the hardwood floors, buffed bright, to get out of the cold.

The center of the barn was a huge, empty open space. She stepped into it and twirled around, her arms flying out. "You can do anything here. Put on plays! Concerts! Dances! There's so much potential—I would've died to have—" She stopped.

She looked toward me, her eyes warm. "See?"

She stepped over against the wall, then slid to the hardwood floor, her legs curled to the side. I sat, too, and she leaned into me. I put my arm around her slight shoulders.

"You know, we live thinking there's no last act," she said, taking off her mittens to hold my cold hand. "Scenes, they play out every moment of every day, and they just go on. The breakfast scene. Driving to the office scene. Then the tech crew cuts the lights because we're going to sleep. There's no thinking that any of that, the simple glory of living and breathing, seeing the gorgeous sky and the snowy trees, will end."

She wiped her face of melted snowflakes. "Dahlia. I want you to know—truly know, understand—how short, how frighteningly fleeting, it is."

I felt her pressure my hand, and I returned it, gently, her bones like spun glass. She raised her head toward the icy sunlight slanting through the old paned windows.

"*We shall see heaven shining like a jewel. We shall see all evil and all our pain sink away in the great compassion that shall enfold the world. Our life—*"

"*—will be as peaceful and tender as a caress. We shall rest.*" I knew these last lines of *Uncle Vanya* from her.

"Yes. *We* shall *rest*." She sighed. "Ahhh, my dear, you have been listening. I'm so glad."

She laid her cheek on my arm, and then nestled down like a furry creature, putting her head in my lap. I reached across the side of her body, landing my hand on her hip.

The barn doors were still open. Air rushed in with snowy flecks that evaporated before my eyes. The light through old paned windows above the heavy beams was a cold yellow stare. I don't know how long we sat there, entwined. The sky outside the door slipped slowly toward dusk as her breathing shifted. Shallow soundless inhales were cut with coarse wet wheezing.

She frowned in her sleep, her dry lips moved with urgency. A message I couldn't hear. A minute later I thought she'd crack open from a spate of coughs that shook her frame. But nothing woke her; her cheek was still warm.

I imagined her lungs strung out, overstretched from long runs of belting out all she had to give night after night. These lungs tired of diving headfirst into life, even when the pond was shallow. These lungs now infested with cancer that would eventually, probably quite soon I was afraid, choke her. Until then, she had a few songs left. She'd take her cues, graciously, or not, and I would no doubt be standing by in the wings for every single note.

When it got dark I carried her back to the car, careful not to wake her. It was so rare that she slept deeply anymore, so rare she got the chance to dream. Standing in the snow, her form folded in my arms, I saw the silhouette of the mountains receding, blurring with the dark. The snowy woods and meadow were already gone. I searched the vast night sky, the frozen air, but it was too cloudy for moons and stars, and way too cold for skinny-dipping.

a continuation of "The Harrow" from *Ground Fiction Vol. 1* and
an excerpt from a forthcoming paranormal fantasy novel

A Hex on Hallowed Ground
Kate M. Colby

AS I WALKED along the streets of downtown Salem, Massachusetts, a gray haze hung in the air, the remnant of early morning fog rolling in from the harbor. Despite being Halloween week, by far the city's busiest tourist holiday, the streets remained relatively empty. Then again, it was only seven o'clock. If I was on vacation, I wouldn't roll out of bed until the brunch restaurants started pouring bottomless mimosas either.

I scoffed and shook my head. After growing up in a family of paranormal investigators and facing a new supernatural threat with each case my parents took, I couldn't even imagine living in such blissful cluelessness. The tourists and locals alike had no idea what had truly happened last night, or they would have all fled town. A witch had attacked—harrowed, to use the magical term—the *Bewitched* sculpture. Poor Samantha Stephens sat headless on her flying broom, and the news reporters simply called it a sordid Halloween prank. Maybe the witch had had its fun with the sculpture and would leave Salem alone now. But even if it didn't, I wouldn't get involved. Let some other hunter pursue the witch. I, Lorena Rivera, knew the price of tangling with supernatural creatures, and I wasn't about to pay it again.

Shivering against the thought, and the chilly autumn breeze, I tugged my leather jacket closer to me and hurried on toward Witch City Psychic. After Halloween, business would slow down until spring, so I wanted to open my shop early and catch every curious tourist I could. As I turned east onto Essex Street, just a couple blocks away from the shop, a warmth spread across my chest. I unzipped my jacket to see that my aventurine crystal necklace had started to glow against my cream, cable-knit sweater. Instinctively, I covered the crystal with my palm. Its smooth, pale green surface was hot to the touch.

"What the hell?"

Like all crystals, aventurine had special properties. It was supposed to offer protection and luck, which was why I had chosen to wear the necklace in the wake of the witch's attack. Some crystals, perhaps this aventurine too, could conduct psychic energy and act as tools for practices like scrying or divination. But in all my years of psychic work, I'd never had a crystal glow or heat up.

I glanced around to make sure no one else noticed my necklace, but Essex Street remained deserted. Slowly, I lifted my hand away from the crystal, and it floated into the air. My fingers trembled as I pulled at the silver chain, trying to bring the crystal back down, but it stayed hovering a few inches above my chest. The crystal's sharp end turned southwest, and its light intensified. It was pointing me toward something . . . but what?

"No, I don't do paranormal anymore." I yanked on the chain again. The crystal didn't move. Instead, it grew brighter and hotter, its heat radiating up the chain to warm my neck. I brushed my auburn curls aside and tried to unfasten the necklace's clasp, but it was clamped shut. "You've got to be kidding me."

Footsteps and chatter echoed from down the street as a family approached. I couldn't let them see the necklace. If one lesson from my parents had stuck with me, it was to never reveal elements of the supernatural world to innocent people. I tried again to remove the necklace, but it wouldn't budge. The family was already between me and Witch City Psychic, so I couldn't make it to my shop to hide either. That left me with one option—following the crystal's lead.

With a huff that rolled cloudlike into the crisp morning air, I turned and marched west. When Essex Street intersected a pedestrian walkway between buildings, the crystal pointed south, and I followed the path. I emerged onto Charter Street, where I walked a short way west, until the crystal directed me south down a narrow street.

As I stepped onto the uneven asphalt, the crystal's illumination intensified again, and I slowed down to scan the area for signs of whatever the crystal might be leading me to. On the left side of the street was a long brick building that housed a few different businesses. It cast a shadow onto the pavement, blocking out the few rays of sunshine that were trying to burn through the haze. On the right side was the Salem Witch Trials Memorial. The grassy enclave was surrounded on three sides by shoulder-height stone walls. Rough-hewn stone benches extended out from the walls, each one inscribed with the name and execution date of a victim from the 1692 witch trials. Someone had scattered red rose petals across the benches. It was probably meant as a tribute, but it created the effect of splattered blood.

The crystal sent another wave of heat up its chain, so I continued past the memorial to the small parking lot belonging to the Salem Wax Museum. At the back of the lot stood a fake pillory, the wooden punishment device that bound its victim's head and hands, and a guide booth for some walking tour. Behind them rested Old Burying Point, one of the town's original cemeteries. It didn't take psychic skill to understand that the crystal had led me to the graveyard. The only question was why.

As I crossed the parking lot, the crystal released the tension on its chain and dropped to lie against my sweater. Even through the thick fabric, its heat irritated my skin, and I had to squint to see past its green light into Old Burying Point. A black iron fence surrounded the cemetery, its gate not far from the fake pillory. The gate was closed and, I assumed, locked, as Old Burying Point didn't open to the public until nine. Most of the tombstones were concentrated near the gate and arranged in crooked rows. Dirt trails snaked between them, worn down by the feet of hundreds of tourists. Toward the back of the cemetery, the graves thinned out, with seemingly no logic to their placement. There were trees back there too. Some were planted within the graveyard, but most lined the back border, failing to obscure the modern office building on the other side of the fence.

Before I could reach the fence, two figures emerged from behind one of the large trees at the back of the cemetery. Had the aventurine crystal brought me here to find these trespassers? Since I didn't know who—or what—they might be, I ducked down and hid behind the waist-high tour guide booth. Then, I zipped up my jacked to conceal the aventurine's glow. Trapping the crystal beneath the leather made its heat feel even hotter, but I clenched my jaw against the discomfort and peeked over the edge of the booth.

The figures had turned in my direction and were walking toward the front of the cemetery. They were still several yards away, but they seemed the size and shape of regular humans—one tall and lanky, one curvy and petite. Of course, that didn't mean much. The witch would appear normal too, given that it was once human. The figures strolled along the thin Puritan headstones, occasionally pausing and bending over, presumably to read the inscriptions. After a couple of minutes, they stopped at a grave not far from the gate and my hiding spot.

The tightness in my chest relaxed as details about the pair came into view—angular, dyed black bangs peeking out from beneath a stocking cap on the tall person and frizzy brown hair framing round, rosy cheeks on the petite person. It was the mother and teenage boy from the ghost tour, who I'd spoken to the night before. The boy had his cell phone out, his painted black nails visible as dark spots against his white phone case, and he angled it toward the tombstone. They must have come back to the cemetery in search of more spectral evidence. They were technically breaking the law, but that wasn't my business. And they sure as hell weren't a danger to anyone. So, why did my protection crystal suddenly start acting like a homing beacon? And why would it have led me here? It didn't make any sense.

As I started to push myself up—no longer concerned about being spotted—the crystal's heat spiked so intensely, I gasped and sat back down. The hairs on the back of my neck raised as an unmistakable crackle of magical energy rolled through the air, coming from the east and heading straight for Old Burying Point. The energy pricked at my skin like static electricity, exactly as the witness to the witch's attack on the *Bewitched* sculpture had described. That's what the crystal was trying to tell me. The witch's second harrow was happening. Right here, right now. With me and two innocent tourists in the middle of it.

I stood, my legs tensing with the urge to run, but I forced myself to wait. I wasn't about to risk my life by staying around for the witch's attack, but I couldn't abandon the mother and son without a warning. I waved my arms at them and yelled, "Get out of there!"

The pair looked up at me in alarm. The mother tugged on her son's sleeve, while the teenager stuffed his phone in his back pocket as though I meant to confiscate it.

"Sorry!" the mother called out, raising her gloved hands as if I were a police officer. "My son just wanted to—"

A deep rumbling sounded from beneath the cemetery. The mother yelped, and the son startled, shifting from foot to foot as if he could get away from the earth. Then, the ground began to shake, causing the headstones to tremble and the pair to lurch unsteadily. The earthquake, or whatever the harrow was creating, didn't extend to the parking lot. The iron fence seemed to act as a barrier, standing stiff and firm as everything within it, down to the brittle yellow grass, tremored.

I backed away from the cemetery, still waving at the mother and son. "This way! It's not safe!"

The pair crouched down and grabbed onto the nearest headstone. The mother raised her hand and shouted over the rumbling. "We're okay!" Then, she gripped her son's shoulder. "Just hold still until it passes."

I stood at the edge of the parking lot. My legs remained tensed, and I imagined I could feel the blood pulsing beneath the denim of my skinny jeans. The aventurine crystal's heat undulated against my chest, burning and cooling in rhythm with the rumbles from the earth. Maybe the tourists could ride out the witch's attack. The mother seemed experienced with—or at least not afraid of—earthquakes. And the witch hadn't harmed anyone when it harrowed the *Bewitched* sculpture. If it wanted to hurt people now, surely it would have waited until Old Burying Point was open and full of tourists.

As I moved to turn around, the ground shook more violently in the far corner of the cemetery. There weren't any headstones back there, but the grass swelled upward, like a blister preparing to pop. A cannon-like boom sounded—making me jump—and clumps of earth shot into the air. The mother shrieked, and she and her son turned to face the explosion. Dirt and rocks scattered into the air, hovering for a breath longer than gravity should allow before raining to the ground.

"This can't be happening." The mother gripped her son tighter.

The son clutched her back, trembling so intensely that his knees buckled. "What the . . ."

"Damn it," I cursed. Would these stupid people listen to me now? I ran the few yards over to the fence and wrapped my hands around the iron pickets. The vibrations from the earthquake reverberated through the metal, prickling my skin with the same static sensation the air had held. If it had been five years ago, and this was a routine paranormal investigation gone bad, I would have run into the cemetery and dragged the tourists out. But I wasn't a hunter anymore, and these strangers weren't my responsibility. I'd try to get through to them one last time, then they'd be on their own.

I banged my palms against the fence. "Hurry! Get out!"

Leaning against each other for support, the mother and son stood up. As a shockwave rolled through the ground beneath them, the pair stumbled and the tombstones around them rocked up and down. Then the earth began to give way. Starting at the base of the headstone, the dirt crumbled and fell into a widening hole. With each passing second, the hole grew, stretching outward in the shape of a freshly dug grave.

As the hole gaped toward the tourists, their eyes widened in disbelief and they screamed. The mother shoved her son away from the hole. He fell backward into another headstone, out of the widening hole's path. But the mother couldn't run away in time. The ground opened up beneath her. Her hands grabbed uselessly at the air, and she cried out as she fell from my sight.

"Screw this." I turned away from the cemetery, intent on running to safety. An earthquake was one thing—the ground erupting and swallowing people whole was another.

"Mom!" The teenager's wail cut through the rumbling air. "Help!"

My heart leapt as I realized he was yelling at me.

"Please help! Help my mom!"

I froze. For a split-second, a vision passed before my second sight. I saw myself, five years before, kneeling alone in the middle of a supernatural attack. I screamed for my own mom, over and over again, and she never answered me. I turned around and locked eyes with the teenager. Even from several yards away, I could see his face paled with fear. How could I leave him to brave the same pain I had? Especially when he didn't even understand what was happening.

Before I could reason my way out of it, I ran back to the waist-high fence and hauled myself over it. When my feet hit the trembling ground, I crouched to lower my center of gravity then scurried toward the teenager. He'd lifted himself onto all fours and was scrambling toward the hole.

I grabbed the sleeve of his hoodie and pulled him away. "Stay back. You don't want to fall in too."

"My mom!" The teenager yanked his arm, but I didn't release him. "What the fuck is going on?"

"We're gonna save her. I promise." I nodded and waited until he did the same. "What's your name?"

After a few panicked gulps, he said, "Pete."

"Okay, Pete. Do like me." I laid down and army-crawled toward the hole. "If you feel loose dirt, stop and go back."

Pete nodded again and followed me.

As we approached the hole, I noticed whose tombstone they'd stopped to see, and a lump swelled in my throat. Judge Hathorne, the most infamous judge of the Salem Witch Trials. Heat flared anew from my necklace, and I gasped. Though the crystal was pressed between my body and the ground, I felt a magnetic energy emanating from it toward the headstone. A small linen bag rested at the stone's base, precariously perched on the edge of the hole. If the crystal brought my attention to it, maybe it had something to do with the witch's attack.

Though the earth still trembled, the hole remained fixed in shape. It formed a near-perfect rectangle, roughly seven feet long and three feet wide. When I reached the edge, I slammed my fist against the dirt. It was as hard packed as the rest of the cemetery's dry ground. Dust hovered in the air, and I coughed as I peered over the edge. The hole was about six feet deep, and the quake's rumbling echoed within it. Pete's mom lay on her back in the bare dirt—Judge Hathorne's simple wooden coffin would have disintegrated centuries ago—and grasped her right shoulder. Her eyes were clenched shut—in fear or pain or both—but she was alive.

Pete's shoulder brushed mine as he reached the edge. "Mom!"

"Petey?" The woman coughed and squinted up at us. "Are you okay? What's happening?"

Pete scratched at the hole. "It's not an earthquake. It's a . . . I don't fuc—"

"He's fine." I elbowed Pete in the ribs to refocus him. "What's your mom's name?"

Pete winced. "Kim."

The neighboring headstone toppled over, and I flinched. We had to get out of there fast. We couldn't trust the ground. "Kim, I'm Lorena. I'm here to help." I brushed my bangs out of my eyes. "Are you injured?"

"I landed on my shoulder." Kim rolled onto her back, aided by the earth's trembling. "It hurts."

"Can you stand?"

Before Kim could reply, a loud crack sounded in front of me. I looked up as a fissure emerged in Judge Hathorne's headstone. The fissure started at the top and sliced through the stone, ending right where the strange bag rested at its base. As the headstone broke apart, pieces tumbled into the hole.

"Watch out!" I cried.

Kim curled into a ball and covered her head with her good arm. She groaned as the stones showered down on her. They would leave bruises, but they weren't big enough to break bones or knock her out. Pete tried to push himself forward into the hole, but I held him in place.

Dust particles hung thick in the air. Kim brushed the stones off herself and choked out a ragged breath.

Pete leaned further over the edge and held out his hands. "C'mon, Mom. We'll pull you up."

Kim shook her head. "I need a minute."

Another deep rumbling erupted a few yards to our left. I rose to my knees to look toward the source. As the noise grew louder, a crevice about a foot wide formed in the dry dirt next to an aboveground sandstone vault. The crevice began to lengthen, snaking its way around the tomb.

"There's another hole." I laid back down and reached out my hands as well. "Kim, you gotta get up. Now."

Kim rolled onto her good side and started to push herself up. As her hand connected with the ground beneath her, she screamed and scrambled to her feet. When Kim stepped toward us, I saw what had startled her and grimaced. Protruding from the earth was Judge Hathorne's bleached white skull.

Kim extended her good arm upward, but her injured arm hung limp. "I can't raise it."

"Let's try this." I leaned farther into the hole and grabbed the shoulder of Kim's coat. Pete clasped her good arm. "On three. One, two, three."

As we pulled, Kim shrieked. "Ah! I can't!"

The shockwaves intensified, and I glanced toward the crevice again. It had completed its circle around the burial vault. The ground beneath the vault began to crumble as a second hole formed. As the vault tilted into the widening hole, I noticed another linen bag. It slid off the vault's lid and disappeared beneath the earth. Then, the tomb itself started to sink. How many more graves would the witch drag into the earth?

I clasped Pete's bony shoulder. "I'm gonna jump down there and boost your mom. You lift her out then help me."

Pete nodded.

"Pardon me, Your Honor." I swung my legs over the side of the hole and lowered myself into Judge Hathorne's grave. As I landed, Kim clasped my arm to help steady me. I nodded my thanks to her. The ground trembled more violently beneath us, and Judge Hathorne's skull sank into the ground. Kim had her back to the head of the grave, so she couldn't see that the ground was starting to give again. I bit down on my lip to keep from crying out and braced myself against the side of the hole in a squatted position. I interlaced my fingers and held my palms open between my legs. "Put your foot here, and I'll hoist you up." Then I yelled toward the top of the hole. "Pete, you grab under her arms."

I couldn't see his reaction, but Kim set her jaw in determination. "Ready?" she asked.

"Let's go."

Kim stepped onto my palms, the treads of her tennis shoes biting into my skin through my gloves. Gritting my teeth, I pressed my hands upward to lift her out of the hole. A few seconds later, her foot sailed out of my hand as Pete yanked her to safety. The earth continued to crumble at the head of the grave, and I felt the dirt beneath my feet begin to loosen. I jumped and clutched onto the shaking ground at the top of the hole. As I pulled myself up, Pete leaned over me and gripped my waist, helping haul my lower body aboveground.

The earth's trembling had grown so violent that I couldn't get my balance enough to stand upright. I inclined my head toward the cemetery fence, and the three of us crouch-walked toward it. Pete had wrapped his mom's good arm around his shoulders, supporting her so she wouldn't fall and have to catch herself with her injured arm. I followed close behind them, arms outstretched in case they stumbled backward.

As we approached the fence, another rumbling erupted. Two more headstones, located to the side of the gate, shattered and crumbled to the earth. Dirt pushed upward, bursting out of the ground in thick clumps and settling in a ring around the two graves.

Kim and Pete slowed down to stare.

"Don't stop!" I pushed them forward. "Move!"

When we reached the fence, Pete leaped over it first, his scarf whipping behind him. Then, he and I helped Kim climb over it. Once she made it, I hoisted myself over the fence and led them to the center of the parking lot. My legs felt weak and shaky on the steady asphalt.

Kim leaned over to catch her breath. She hacked and spat brown saliva on the pavement.

Pete stomped his Converse sneaker against the asphalt, as though to test that it was solid. Then, he looked over at the cemetery, where the ground still quaked. His eyes widened. "This isn't fuc—"

"Language." Kim cradled her injured arm.

"Seriously, look." Pete pointed toward the cemetery. "The earthquake is only over there. How is that possible?"

I put my hands on my hips, focusing on slowing my own breathing and the frantic beating of my heart. What could I tell Pete that would seem believable and make him let it go? I couldn't tip him off about the witch. Besides the fact that I shouldn't break my family rule, Pete already believed in ghosts—with my luck, he'd start snooping around to find the witch and piss it off even worse. "That must be the edge of the quake radius."

"But look over there." Pete took out his phone again and started a video. He zoomed in on the shaking headstones then directed the camera toward the trees surrounding the cemetery. They remained still, save for the gentle rustle and fall of their leaves in the morning breeze. "It's only the cemetery. Nothing else."

I shrugged. "Must be a sinkhole then."

Another rumble sounded, the loudest one yet, near the gate. About a foot back from the fence, the dirt crumbled and caved into the ground. It created a ditch at the front of the cemetery, stretching from one end of the fence to the other. As the dust settled, the quake stopped. The aventurine crystal went cool beneath my jacket.

Pete raised his pierced eyebrow at me. "Have you ever seen a sinkhole do that?"

I ignored him and touched Kim's good arm. "How's your shoulder?"

"I don't know." She winced as she craned her neck to look. "It hurts pretty badly, and I can't move it."

"You probably dislocated it." I snapped my fingers to get Pete's attention. "Your mom's hurt. Give me your scarf and call 911."

Pete took off his scarf and handed it to me. His attention stayed, thankfully, on his injured mother.

"I'm not paying for an ambulance." Kim's frizzy hair stuck to her forehead where she'd started to sweat from the pain. "Get an Uber to take us to an urgent care."

Pete took one more suspicious glance at the cemetery before turning his back to it and opening the app.

I tied the scarf around Kim to make a sling. "Try not to jostle it too much. If they make you wait to see a doctor, ask for an ice pack and some ibuprofen. That'll help with the swelling and the pain."

Kim nodded. "Are you a nurse?"

I scoffed, remembering all the bumps and bites and bullet wounds I'd tended when my parents came back from a rough paranormal investigation. "Not quite."

"Thank you for all your help." Kim extended her left hand to me, and I shook it awkwardly.

"Don't mention it." If my cheeks hadn't already been flushed, I might have blushed. Since I'd been living in Salem, I'd only remembered the bad parts of facing supernatural creatures. I'd forgotten what it was like to help someone—to save someone—from an evil they could never know about. It felt strange, but also, right.

"Speaking of . . ." Pete shifted his weight from foot to foot. "You're not going to tell . . . that we snuck into . . . ?"

"God, no." I wrinkled my nose. "Were you trying to get more ghost photos?"

"Yeah. I wanted a video with Judge Hathorne's grave." Pete rubbed the back of his neck. "It was stupid."

"Oh, honey, you couldn't have known anything bad would happen." Kim's forehead creased, and she turned back to me. "We should notify the authorities, though. Pete's right. That wasn't a normal earthquake. Whatever happened here caused a lot of damage, and we don't know if it'll happen again."

"I'll take care of it." I waved my hand to dismiss any discussion. "The cops don't need to know about your trespassing, and you should get medical help right away."

Pete inclined his head toward the cemetery. "Do you need me to send you the photos? So, you can show the cops or whoever?"

For the love of God, drop it, kid. "That's okay. I'll describe it to them."

Pete's phone buzzed, and he put his hand on Kim's back. "Our Uber's almost here. Thanks again, Lorena."

Kim smiled at me, but I couldn't force myself to return it. Then, the pair turned and headed toward Derby Street to catch their Uber. Once they were safely out of sight, I checked the immediate area to make sure no one else was around. I wanted to get a better look at what the witch had done to Old Burying Point, and I didn't want to leave its magical bags around for an innocent person to find. I'd take them back to my apartment for safekeeping, as I'd done with the poppet, the Puritan version of a voodoo doll that the witch had used to destroy the *Bewitched* sculpture, and figure out what to do with them later.

When I was satisfied the street was still empty, I headed back over to the cemetery and hopped the fence again. After jumping across the narrow, newly formed ditch, I hurried to Judge Hathorne's grave. The small linen bag still rested at the base of the cracked headstone, less than an inch from the open hole. I took out my phone and snapped a photo of the scene. Then, I reached down and picked up the linen bag. As I did, the aventurine crystal hummed a warm warning against my chest. My suspicion must have been correct—the bag had something to do with the witch's attack. I tucked it into my jacket pocket, and the crystal cooled, but not completely.

Next, I examined the burial vault that had sunk. Though the sandstone slab was broken, I could make out enough to learn that a few members of the Gedney family had been interred within it. The linen bag I'd seen had disappeared into the earth. Digging for it would take too much time, and I wasn't about to chance falling in the hole. I'd have to hope that the authorities wouldn't uncover it when they came to inspect and repair the grave.

After taking photos of the tomb, I moved to the back of the cemetery, where the first hole had been created. The hole didn't have a head-stone, but the bones at the bottom told me it was an unmarked grave. Its linen bag had landed among the clumps of dirt. I took a photo then picked up the bag.

Finally, I jogged toward the cemetery gate, detouring at the two graves that had been destroyed near it. The headstones had shattered into too few pieces to read, but two linen bags remained intact among the rubble. That meant every grave that was attacked had been marked with the strange bags. I photographed the damage, grabbed the bags, and hoisted myself over the fence.

As I headed back toward my shop, I kept my gaze fixed on the sidewalk, trying not to draw attention to myself. I placed a hand over my full jacket pockets, as if the witch's bags might claw their way out. And maybe they would—I barely had an idea how that kind of dark magic worked, and yet I'd jumped right into the middle of the witch's harrow. But what choice did I have? Pete couldn't have rescued Kim by himself. If I hadn't helped, she would have been swallowed up and buried among Salem's oldest dead. I couldn't stand by and watch a kid lose his mom to a monster—I knew firsthand that was something you could never recover from.

Next time around . . . my heartbeat spiked at the thought. One harrow might have been a fluke, but two meant business. There *would* be a next time. The witch wasn't done yet. And, as far as I knew, I was the only one who could protect Salem.

The Night the Wall Came Crumbling Down

Alyce Werdel

November 9, 1989
East Berlin, German Democratic Republic (GDR)
5:45 pm

JENS STRODE DOWN the center aisle of the windowless auditorium. The International Press Center on Mohrenstrasse was quickly filling. News correspondents from across Europe and even the United States squeezed past each other to claim a chair, each upholstered in the deep red favored by the Communist German Democratic Republic. As usual, Jens held himself perfectly upright with his shoulders back. His tall frame was smartly dressed in a tailored, gray-green military uniform. He enjoyed the jingle his medals made each time his foot hit the floor. He especially enjoyed the look of fear his violet collar patch instilled in those around him. No one wanted to be on the wrong side of a lieutenant colonel in the Stasi. Westerners included. He allowed himself a small, satisfied smile. The East German secret police were well-known for silencing their enemies, even those outside their walls.

He climbed the row of steps fronting the stage and walked toward the dais table, backed with four chairs. Günter, spokesman for the Communist Party that had ruled the country with an iron fist since the end of the Second World War, sat slumped in his seat next to three colleagues. He looked like a typical East German bureaucrat—middle aged, receding hairline, and fleshy faced. He was wearing his usual gray suit, gray striped tie, and disinterested look. Jens tilted his chin up. His sharp features reflected none of the softness he detected in the older spokesman.

Jens took a seat at the left end of the table, next to Günter, and switched off his microphone. He had no intention of speaking. He was there to observe East German journalists who lately had become a little too bold for his taste. Officially, however, he represented the Politburo, the tight circle of Party members who ran the government. Those seated to Günter's right were members of the Central Committee, charged with carrying out Politburo mandates.

With Günter's recent promotion to the Party's second-in-command, Jens supposed he should be polite. So he leaned toward him and asked, "How was your holiday? Bulgaria was it?"

Günter rolled his head toward his left shoulder. "Wonderful. We stayed in a small village on the north coast, where the Balkans border the Black Sea. Breathtaking views." He tilted his face up toward Jens. "Why do our citizens want permission to travel outside the Soviet Bloc? We have everything the West has—beaches, mountains, beautiful capitals. Prague and Budapest, those are great cities. What more could they want?"

Jens smiled, a tight tug at the corners of his mouth. "I agree completely. So, what's on tonight's agenda?"

"Oh, the Party conference that came to a close today. The new members of the Politburo, the speakers, their topics, and so on." Günter opened his mouth wide and let out a vocal yawn.

Jens winced. As Party spokesman, could Günter at least sit up straight and look somewhat alert? It was embarrassing.

"I did not see you today at the meetings," Jens said. In truth, failing to attend a meeting had no bearing on whether Günter could summarize it. Nothing meaningful was ever communicated at these press events. It was always the same old government propaganda.

Günter shrugged. "I was dealing with an urgent matter. But I stopped by on my way here. The General Secretary handed me the press release. And a copy of the new travel law." He tapped a folder on the table in front of him.

"So you spoke with Egon?"

"Um, not much. He seemed a bit harried. He has been in office what, two weeks, and he already has to run a Party conference in these difficult times? He started to say something about the new travel law—that it is namely what we have been discussing these past few days—but he was pulled away midsentence."

"But you have read the materials?" Jens asked.

"Why would I? I can read aloud." Günter chuckled at his own joke.

Jens looked up at the room filled with foreign media representatives. A twinge of concern flashed through him. The written law had little bearing on how things actually worked. It was drafted to appease certain vocal groups both inside and outside the country. Usually plenty of caveats were included to give the government an out if challenged. He assumed this one did as well. Nevertheless, reading the text aloud could leave people with the wrong impression. The language may need finessing.

Jens leaned toward Günter. "A few minutes remain before the start. Perhaps you should skim—"

Günter held up his hand and said, "Excuse me a moment." Then he turned toward the woman on his right, who had asked him a question.

Jens glanced at the double doors at the rear of the room. A few stragglers pushed their way inside. Several hundred people had crammed onto the main level and the orchestra level above. Cameramen were stationed along the walls, adjusting their lenses and microphones. The din of competing tongues—ranging from soft and sensual Romance languages to harsh and guttural Germanic—echoed off the teak-paneled walls.

At 6:00 p.m. sharp, Günter picked up his half-moon, wire-framed glasses and set them on the tip of his nose. He tapped a fingertip against the mic, triggering an ear-piercing screech. Several in the audience cringed and covered their ears. At least it got their attention.

The room quieted, except for shuttering cameras. Günter began by introducing others at the table. When Jens' name was called, he stood, nodded curtly, and returned to his seat.

Günter then transitioned to the papers in front of him and proceeded to drone on about recent personnel changes to the Politburo and Central Committee, the topics discussed at the Party conference, and god knows what else. Jens stopped listening and shifted his focus to the spectators. His long-time informant and courier, a reporter for an international news organization, was seated in the middle of the room. A black tape recorder was propped up in his lap and his head tipped to the side, like he was about to nod off. Jens had always worried the man's height and film star looks would be a problem, but he took plenty of precautions and kept a low profile. Next to him sat the famous American news anchor, Tom Brokaw. His eyes were squeezed shut and his brow furrowed as he concentrated on the translator's voice coming through his earphones.

Good god, Jens thought as he scanned the room, Western men

and women have no self-respect. The women appeared downright frightening with their helmet-head hairstyles and oversized shoulder pads. And the men looked ridiculous in their pastel sweatshirts and block-patterned sweaters. Even the famous American, who was at least wearing a suit and tie, had on a *purple* shirt. His light brown hair was too long, covering the top half of his ears. Others, however, were far worse. Their manes reached their collars and their upper lips were carpeted in thick chevron moustaches. Were there no barbers on the other side of the border? Perhaps he should send the men home with razors and scissors.

Their GDR counterparts looked quite dignified by comparison, if not a little drab. They wore dark, conservative polyester suits and their hair was neatly kept. But when Jens caught sight of two pairs of brightly colored, smooth leather pumps in the front row—one cherry red and the other royal blue—his chest deflated a bit. Both had pointed toes and thin, stiletto heels. The type of shoes his wife kept pestering him for. But he could not justify spending hard currency on such impractical footwear. It was just bad luck that these Western reporters sat on either side of the female journalist from *Neues Deutschland*, the East German paper and Party news outlet. Her black, clunky shoes with a square toe and rubber soles looked like clodhoppers. He tapped his own against the wood floor. At least he had real leather soles.

After a while the audience began shifting in their seats, trying to stay awake in the overfilled, stuffy room. A few walked outside for fresh air. Others slid off their sweaters and loosened their collars. Nearly all fidgeted with their pens and pencils. Jens glanced over his right shoulder. Even Günter looked bored, slouched in his seat, speaking in a slow, flat monotone with an excessive amount of "uhs" and "uhms" mixed in.

Jens glimpsed the clock above the double doors. Only twenty more minutes of this mind-numbing, excruciating charade. He started thinking about the Jeagerschnitzel his wife, Helga, was preparing for dinner. His mouth watered at the thought of breaded and fried meat, boiled potatoes, and roasted cauliflower. She was unable to find veal or pork because of the shortages, but she had sausage. And she promised to take a precious banana from the freezer for dessert.

Günter slid off his glasses and set them on the table. "Questions?"

Jens perked up. Günter was a graduate of the journalism school at Leipzig's Karl Marx University. His was accustomed to dealing with Communist-era press, where a government spokesman announced the news, journalists jotted it down, and state newspapers and newscasters published it. Recently, under pressure from the international community, which the GDR desperately wanted to be a part of, the government had allowed Western press representatives to attend these conferences. And that meant following an entirely new format, where the Party spokesman took questions. Jens knew this was where things could go sideways.

Günter handled the first few inquiries without a hitch, skillfully providing long-winded, noncommittal answers. Then a hand shot up from a young man sitting on the steps fronting the stage, to the right of the table.

"Ja?" Günter said, pointing at the man.

The reporter stood along with his cameraman. In sing-song Italian-accented German, he said, "Ricardo Ricci, representing the Italian Press Agency. Sir, do you believe it was a mistake for the government to introduce the new travel law three days ago, given the reaction of the people?"

Jens leaned forward to get a good look at the reporter. How dare he pose such a question. It was disrespectful. But the damned travel law had been a mistake. That was for certain. It had been written to give the impression the government was loosening restrictions on travel outside the Soviet Bloc. But the troublemakers read the fine print, filled with caveats, and recognized it for what it was: more of the same. Mass demonstrations had erupted across the country. Film of the unrest was smuggled to West Berlin TV stations. It was mortifying. Jens committed the reporter's name and employer to memory. If this self-satisfied, condescending asshole thought he would be granted a visa for the next conference, he was mistaken.

Günter handled the upstart's question with his customary calm. "No, it was not a mistake," he said. He rambled on, stringing together a stream of positive sound bites that amounted to nothing concrete. "The government understands its citizens have this psychological need to travel. But first we must engage in a renewal of our society so that they can find what they are searching for here. That involves several steps . . ." Blah blah blah.

Jens relaxed his posture, just a touch. Günter reminded the audience that, after a temporary halt, GDR citizens could again receive permission to travel to its neighbor and ally, Czechoslovakia. He did not address why travel had been suspended in the first place—because tens of thousands of vacationing East Germans had taken refuge in the West German embassy in Prague and ultimately emigrated to the West. Nor did he acknowledge that this trend had resumed last week when the border was reopened. The thought of these events made Jens' body temperature rise, especially when he considered the ultimatum the Czech government delivered a few days ago: "We will close our side of the border if the GDR cannot control its citizens. Their actions are stirring up local opposition against the Czech governing Party."

Günter paused and picked up his glasses again. "Oh. I nearly forgot to mention a brand new travel law is being discussed at the Politburo level." He thumbed through his papers. "As a transition, the government today decided to implement one provision of this new law. Let me find it."

Jens furrowed his brow. Did Günter really need to read the text of the new law? Couldn't he simply spew more generalities? Jens coughed, trying to get Günter's attention. But Günter was completely absorbed in the file. One of his colleagues pointed him to the passage.

"Ah here . . . it seems today, as far as I know . . . uh . . ." Günter turned and looked over the rim of his glasses at Jens. His bushy eyebrows were raised, as though he wanted Jens to confirm his thoughts. But Jens had no idea what Günter was about to say. He shook his head, trying to communicate, *Shut your mouth! No one asked about this!* Instead Günter turned toward his colleagues on his right. They shrugged, too.

"Well," Günter muttered, returning to the stack in front of him, "as I was saying, the Politburo decided to implement one paragraph of the proposed law, as a transition. And . . . um . . . therefore, they have decided that . . . um . . . every GDR citizen may apply to emigrate and—" He stopped abruptly to scan the print below. Then, as though clarifying the law for himself, he read the text aloud so quickly that it came out as a rushed mumble. ". . . and for private trips abroad. Citizens may exit through any border crossing?"

The room erupted into a cacophony of low voices and shuttering cameras. If the reporters had been on the verge of dozing off moments ago, they were awake now. Even Günter slightly straightened as he took in the reaction.

Hands shot up across the room. A reporter sitting next to the middle aisle stood and asked, "Do they need passports? What about visas?"

Jens leaned toward Günter. "Yes," he hissed, "both."

But Günter could not hear him over the commotion. His fingers shook as he shuffled his papers. "You know comrades, I was just informed of this on my way here. I know only what is written." He arranged his glasses and read aloud: "The responsible departments in the district offices of the People's Police are instructed to promptly issue visas for permanent exit and private trips abroad without having to satisfy prerequisites." The words made it sound like the visa was essentially a rubber stamp.

No, no, no! Jens felt his face flush. That was what was written, *not* what was decided. He watched the reporters' reactions in horror. His informant sat with his arms across his chest, his lips pinched shut. His hard glare told Jens exactly what he thought of this announcement. The famous American's eyes had popped open. He was seeking clarification from the bilingual Associated Press reporter next to him.

Someone in the back called out, "When does this new regulation come into effect?"

Jens bent toward Günter again, this time whispering loudly, "The law is not operational yet. And it is subject to regulation by the Council of Ministers."

But again, Günter could not hear him. He rubbed his chin and scanned the page. "It is written here . . ." He shrugged and looked up. "Immediately, without delay."

Jens' vision clouded. The audience became a smear of color and movement. The provision allowing permanent exit was supposed to appease their Czech comrades. The agitators could quietly leave, eliminating the need to travel through the neighboring country. And the bastards would never be allowed back. Goodbye and good riddance. Of course, the "private travel" language was only to appease local demonstrators and those irritating Western human rights activists who kept waving the Helsinki Accords in their faces, demanding the GDR abide by the terms they agreed to. Which, thanks to the meddling

American Secretary of State, George Schulz, included the right to free travel. Jens had begged the General Secretary not to sign that agreement.

But being right was no consolation. Jens stared ahead. He felt sick to his stomach. With one slip of the tongue, Günter had basically said East Germans could travel abroad. And it had been recorded by news outlets. There was no taking it back.

Next to him Günter was visibly rattled. He stood abruptly, pushing his chair over behind him. "It has been brought to my attention that it is seven o'clock. So comrades, I must end this conference." And with that, he gathered his papers and hurried from the reporters rushing the stage.

Jens' peripheral vision shrank until he could see only a narrow circle. The surrounding clamor converged into a high-pitched ringing in his ears. He ran his fingers under his collar and tugged, trying to get air. He started processing how this could play out. The news footage could be used to demand exit. And if that happened, it would be curtains for the Party. And for him. He needed to do damage control. Quickly.

He stood and walked to the drapes backing the stage. He slid between them and found his informant there, pacing with his arms crossed tightly over a navy blazer.

The man spun toward Jens and threw his hands in the air. "What the fuck was that?" he said in a shrill voice, using his native American tongue. "Your government has screwed me!"

"Shh. Keep your voice low," Jens responded in English.

The informant's brown eyes narrowed. The usual warmth was gone. "Don't you dare tell me to keep my voice down!" He grabbed fistfuls of wavy hair. "Christ, I mean, what the hell?"

Jens held out his hands, his fingers spread wide. He spoke slowly, translating his thoughts to English. "Relax. Nothing changes. We get rid of the radicals. Permanently. On rare occasion, just for show, the government permits a personal trip abroad. But only to a trusted Party member and one who leaves behind a minor child or spouse."

The American dropped his hands to his waist and stared at Jens in disbelief. "Were we in the same meeting? Your spokesman said people can come and go. And you know as well as I, controlling movement is the Party's source of power."

Jens stiffened. "Nonsense. The Party retains control of the government, as always."

"You've been drinking your own Kool Aid. When people have 'free movement,' " he made quotation marks with his fingers, "they leave unless they have a right to vote."

"GDR citizens have a right to vote," Jens said tightly.

The American threw his head back and laughed without humor. "How do you even say that with a straight face? The Party wins by a ninety-nine-percent margin, yet people are shot trying to escape across the borders. You're delusional if you think anyone believes those results."

Jens pursed his lips. Americans were so high and mighty. It was particularly hard to swallow coming from this one, who had made a bundle violating the terms of his country's embargo by selling banned technology to the GDR. But Jens dared not insult the man. His access to information was second to none. So he clenched his jaw and let the man rant.

The American wagged his finger. "First comes the right to travel. Then real elections. Just look next door at Hungary! That means your guys won't always win. And this is where *I* come in." The American's breathing was coming in jagged bursts. He leaned into Jens' face. "The new guys will have access to all that information the secret police have squirreled away in their files over the last forty years."

Jens wiped the spit off his face. "Do not worry. Stasi files are secret."

The American scoffed. "Right. You tell Matthias, I no longer work for him. And let Hans know his source for pipeline technology has dried up." Then he jabbed his finger in Jens' chest. "Any files that contain my name must be destroyed. Tonight."

Jens took a few paces back. "It is not so easy. Our files are not always organized by name. And when this is the case, it can be the name of the target, the informant, or another involved person. Some are even organized by address. It takes weeks if not months to examine the registry and determine which files your name appears in."

"Then you'd better get going. Because so help me god, if you don't, I'll light that building on fire." He turned and stormed through the door at the back.

Jens stood in place, frozen. His informant was right. Holes were emerging in the Iron Curtain. There was talk of democratic elections in Warsaw Pact countries, something unthinkable even six months ago. All those years that he had overseen the roundup of East German dissidents and their imprisonment could come back to haunt him. Shit, people like him would be arrested and thrown in prison. At best.

He ran through the door, raced down the hall, and commandeered an administrator's office. After locking himself inside, he stood over the desk, gasping for air. Thank god no one was here to see him like this. Outside the streets were relatively quiet, although he could hear shouting in the distance. The news was leaking out.

His fingers trembled as he dialed the rotary phone. It took forever for the wheel to return to the home position. He fought the instinct to force it back faster. When he finally heard the tinny ring come over the line, he exhaled.

"Da?" said a male Russian voice.

"We have a problem. Günter gave the impression our citizens are permitted to cross the border."

"What . . . ? What do you mean 'cross the border'?" The Russian's German was fluent, but heavily accented.

"To the West. Switch on the television. The proposed travel regulation—the one that sounded good but would require passports and visas?" He took a deep breath. "Günter made it sound like East Germans could go through any border crossing. Effective immediately."

Silence filled the line. In the background Jens heard the Russian flip on the television and turn the dial. It stopped on the nightmarish clip from the press conference.

"Did your government get Soviet permission for this new law?" The Russian spoke in a slow, quiet voice.

"Does it matter? It is done. Now we must do damage control. I'll notify the head of passport control. Tell him no one is permitted to cross the border without a visa, which they cannot get. You notify Moscow. We need Russian tanks to reinforce the crossing points, especially in East Berlin."

"Right. Meet me at Karlshorst," the Russian said. "I will drive up from Dresden." The Karlshorst district of East Berlin was home to the KGB headquarters. The KGB and Stasi had worked together for decades, sharing foreign intelligence and suppressing dangerous Western ideology.

"You will phone the others?" Jens rubbed his hand across the back of his neck. "I must stop by headquarters."

"Yes." The Russian ended the call.

Jens jiggled the phone hook button and listened for a dial tone. His first call was to his subordinate, the head of Passport Control, ordering him to contact all checkpoints and communicate a clear message: no one may pass without a valid visa, regardless of what they had heard on the television.

Then he dialed Stasi headquarters. If the Party lost control, and he really should prepare for the worst, then the public would demand to see their files. The full extent of the Stasi's surveillance of their own people would be made public—the wiretaps and cameras installed in homes, the intercepted mail, the conversations with neighbors and co-workers, the in-person tracking, all of it. But that was nothing compared to the treatment of the anti-Communist dissidents—kidnapping, imprisonment, even death—all well-documented in the files. He had to take full advantage of his head start.

"Hallo. Herr Schroeder h—" a deep voice said.

"Jens Eberlee here. We have a national emergency. Shred the files. All men on deck. No one leaves until the job is finished."

"Sir? What . . . what national emergency?"

"A terrible miscommunication was broadcast on the news tonight. It concerns the borders. If we cannot set things straight, it is possible that—in hours or days—protestors will be at the doors, demanding to see the files."

"Have you spoken with Herr Mielke?"

"I have," Jens lied. There was no time to track down the head of the Stasi. "He is in agreement."

"But sir, there are millions of files. Where . . . where do we begin?"

"With the one closest to you," Jens quipped. Then he ran his hand along the side of his head and said slowly, with forced calm, "We must protect our informants. And our methods. I repeat, no one leaves until all files are destroyed. I will be there soon."

IT WAS AFTER midnight by the time Jens climbed the cement steps to the two-story, gray stucco house in Karlshorst. He was exhausted. He had come straight from Stasi headquarters, where papers were being shoved into the mouths of shredders as fast as they could swallow them. It would take months to finish the job. But he had found several mentioning the American. He just did not know if he had found them all.

He passed under the rectangular portico supported by squared-off pillars, an architectural detail that looked like an afterthought on an otherwise unremarkable building. He pressed the small black button on the wall next to the front door and heard a shrill, insistent ring scream through the interior.

When no one answered, he pounded his fist against the wood frame, rattling the frosted inset windows.

"I said I am coming!" a man barked in German.

Jens recognized the voice. Seconds later Matthias cracked the door ajar and stuck his round, ruddy face through the opening. He gazed at Jens with hazy eyes. Strips of stringy brown hair drooped over his forehead, like he hadn't bothered to comb it after getting out of bed.

"Vladimir is on the telephone. We are the only ones here," Matthias muttered, holding a low-ball glass of vodka. He swayed slightly when he let go of the door.

Matthias was in his mid-thirties, same age as Jens, but his body showed more wear and tear. Mostly because he lacked discipline, in Jens' view. And lately Matthias had taken to wearing knockoff Western-style clothes, which were not designed for his stature. Tonight his wide-striped orange, gray, and gold tie reached halfway down his protruding belly, as though he could not afford enough polyester to reach his waist.

Jens wiped his feet on the mat, came inside, and shut the door. He was careful to take off his shoes before stepping on the wool area rug covering the entry. "It is hot as hell in here." He dropped his shoes in the basket next to the door and took off his overcoat. "Can we open a window?"

"No. Damned Russians. They live in saunas." Matthias turned and staggered toward the sunken living room on the right, sloshing his drink over the sides as he went.

Jens opened the closet opposite the front door. While he hung his coat, he glanced at the obligatory portrait of Stalin. The leader's walrus mustache covered all but a thin sliver of his lower lip. His thick black hair was combed off his forehead, like the back of an ocean swell. As usual, he stared into the distance as though entranced by a futuristic vision.

Upstairs a loud voice bellowed in Russian, "We need troops. And tanks. Now! Thousands have descended on the border openings!"

Jens glanced toward the staircase on his left that led to upstairs offices, where Vladimir was obviously having a tense discussion. Jens sighed and shut the closet door. Since he had left the international press conference, which felt like a lifetime ago, his worst fears had been realized. The reporters that covered the press conference failed to mention the passport and visa requirements. Whether it was intentional or because they viewed them as purely administrative did not matter at this point. The message broadcast was clear: "East German citizens can pass through any border crossing, effective immediately."

Matthias called out, "Unlock the door, will you? I do not want to stand up again."

Jens twisted the button lock on the handle. Then he turned toward the large front room, divided into a seating area on the right and a dining area on the left. Each time he descended into the space, it struck him as a strange mishmash of traditional and modern. In the middle a crystal chandelier hung from an intricate ceiling medallion of carved roses and vines. Similarly ornate panels were carved into the walls. Yet the parquet floors were covered with an olive green shag rug and the furniture was upholstered in shades of orange and brown. Jens found the contrast disquieting.

He strode through the center toward the bar at the back, passing between the polished wood table that sat twelve, and Matthias slouched in a low-rise brown pleather sofa facing the entry. Jens knew Vladimir would lose his mind if he saw the German's feet resting on the modular wooden coffee table, but he was sick of anticipating and diffusing confrontation between the two.

At the back he opened the double doors to a wood cabinet. Inside the shelves held glasses tailored to every type of drink imaginable. He selected an etched tumbler and pulled a green labeled bottle of Moskovskaya pear vodka from the rack on the door. Using prongs, he dropped exactly one ice cube from the bucket into his glass. It crackled and popped as he drowned it in three fingers of Russian elixir.

"Can I get you something?" Jens asked, looking over his shoulder.

"Have what I need," Matthias responded, holding up his glass.

By the sound of things, Matthias already had a few under his belt. Jens swirled his drink and sauntered to an orange tweed armchair to the right of the couch. As he took a seat, a knock sounded on the door.

"It is unlocked," Matthias yelled.

Jens turned his head toward the cool air rushing in and took a long, deep inhale. A barrel-chested man entered. His thick cropped brown hair shot straight up, like a freshly mown lawn.

"Hallo, comrades." Hans waved and shut the door behind him.

Matthias glared while taking a swallow of his drink. Jens just scowled. He wasn't in the mood for Hans's relentless good cheer.

"Lock the door," Matthias barked.

Hans did so. Then he let his overcoat slide off his stocky frame, revealing brown wool slacks and a beige and forest green plaid jacket. "I see Stalin is still here to greet us. Wonder how long that will last." He hung his coat and took off his shoes.

"Longer than you, if you don't watch your mouth," Jens snarled.

Hans joined them in the living room. Like Jens, he walked straight to the bar. "After complete pandemonium earlier this evening, it is dead quiet out there."

"Where is everyone?" Jens asked, though he didn't really care. He just wanted to enjoy the vodka's burn as it slid down his throat, warmed his chest, and dulled his senses.

Ice cubes clinked against glass. "Either climbing the Wall or waiting in line at a checkpoint. Apparently they all want to go to the Ku'damm and have a beer."

The Ku'damm, short for Kufürstendamm, was the avenue running through the heart of West Berlin, known for its restaurants, bars, shops, and discos. Every young East Berliner had seen photos and wanted to experience it. And see if it was real. Now they could.

Hans sidestepped between Matthias and the coffee table, tapping Matthias's legs off the top. He dropped into a matching armchair opposite Jens and let out a loud exhale. "What a night. At one point the Stasi had regained control of some checkpoints, but not enough to stop the flow. Tens of thousands have crossed into West Berlin."

Matthias sipped his drink. "I turned off the television. The media is filming both sides of the Wall. It is impossible to reseal the border with the world watching." He groaned and slipped deeper into the cushions. "This is the end for people like us."

Jens knew Matthias was right. His chest felt heavy, like someone had hollowed it out. He did not even have the energy to speak. How could this have happened? Even the Party heads he had spoken with were confused. No one saw this coming.

"Probably so," Hans agreed, pushing his large wire-framed glasses onto the bridge of his nose. "But you must admit, we had a good run."

This was too much. Jens' lips curled into a sneer. "A good run? So you are satisfied then? We walk off into the sunset, and do what exactly?"

Matthias let his head fall back and stared at the ceiling. "All those years I spent creating the best spy network from Western Europe to the United States. No one had better contacts than I. What was the point?" he asked thickly. "It was all for shit."

Hans sipped his drink. "Come now, Matthias. You have banking experience. You will find a new position."

"Banking experience?" Matthias scoffed. "I don't think attending a Stasi training program on how to infiltrate the West German banking system will be viewed as a plus. I can hear the interviewer now: 'And what are your qualifications, Herr Werner?'

"Well, I ran a dozen informants inside the West Berlin office of Dresdner Bank. They handed over records for the bank's clients who worked in the defense industry. I determined who had financial problems and recruited them to steal military technology for the GDR. I paid them a fair price, of course. I know that is important to you capitalists." He paused to sip his drink. "And if that was unsuccessful, I collected kompromat and pressured them to spy for me. In case you are wondering, affairs, especially homosexual ones, were quite convincing." Matthias sighed. "Somehow, I don't think that's a winning sales pitch."

"I see the problem," Hans admitted. "But you and Jens have expert knowledge of Western technology." He wagged his finger in the air. "Do not underestimate the value of that. My god, Matthias, you were head of Department XV/3, responsible for stealing the West's latest and greatest. And Jens, you organized the effort at the Soviet level. Rocket science, aircraft technology—"

"Oh please," Matthias interrupted. "Just understanding it is of little value. Their progress is too rapid. The West is a generation ahead of us in everything—medicine, military, computers, auto mechanics, you name it. We have not invented anything new since *Grilleta*. And I don't care what you say, it does not hold a candle to a Western burger."

Hans pursed his lips. "Enough self-pity. All of us are in a difficult place."

Jens erupted. "*All* of us?" He jabbed his finger toward Hans. "All except you. Herr Gänzler, chief executive of the GDR's petroleum and gas industry—in charge of the pipelines that carry Russian gold to East and West Germany. Unlike the spy apparatus, pipelines will not disappear with the Party. If anything, you will be more in demand than ever. Imagine the Russian oil and gas that will travel through East Germany to Western Europe!" He sank back in his chair. "So you and your positive attitude can go to the devil, Hans."

Across the room the staircase creaked. The three men fell silent. Vladimir, their young Russian host, crossed the entry and dropped into the living room. His hands were shoved deep in the pockets of his fitted slacks. Jens resisted the urge to roll his eyes. The tailored button down shirt was surely intended to show off the Russian's muscular upper body. Probably trying to compensate for his thinning hair and protruding ears.

"What a royal screw up," Vladimir said as he passed them on his way to the bar. "That idiot spokesman of yours blew it. Did the new General Secretary even bother to read the press release beforehand?"

"There was a series of miscommunications," Jens said, miserably. "This morning Egon told the lawyers to come up with something that would satisfy both the Czech government and the protesters. When he received the draft at the end of the day, he was so busy putting out fires that he did not focus on the new language. Instead he skimmed it and thought there were enough caveats to control who left and when. He certainly never intended to open the border. If Günter had attended the meeting like he should have, he would have known that."

"Getting rid of Erich Honecker and replacing him with that clown Egon Krenz was your first mistake." The Russian filled a tall glass with still water from a pitcher.

"That was necessary," Hans said. "Honecker refused to follow Gorbachev's lead. He thought loosening the government's grip, even a little bit, was giving in to the West. Instead he did the opposite. He cracked down harder. And it backfired."

"It could have worked," Jens said, halfheartedly. He had supported the crackdown, but in hindsight, it did not look like the right choice.

Hans scrunched up his face. "What do you mean it could have worked? In the last week we had two protests drawing a half million people." He shook his head. "Erich had created a pressure cooker. We needed someone with a softer touch. Or at least the appearance of one. Egon had that."

Vladimir crossed the room holding a full glass of water. "Regardless, Erich never would have allowed tonight's tragedy. And he certainly would have gotten approval from Moscow before announcing that stupid new law."

"We received approval today," Jens responded. "But that involved another miscommunication. Moscow had seen an earlier version that only permitted *permanent* exit at *one* remote border location. They never saw the revised version that ostensibly permitted private travel at any border location."

Vladimir sat next to Matthias on the couch. "Well I can assure you, my superiors are furious. Even Gorbachev."

Matthias raised himself upright for the first time since Jens arrived. "I know Günter botched the announcement. But why open the gates? The government always makes promises it does not keep."

"Well, you had a second idiot at Bornholmer Strasse checkpoint," Vladimir said. "The senior officer in charge—a Harald Jäger—capitulated under pressure. He let people cross into West Berlin. Then other checkpoints followed."

"You cannot blame him," Hans said. "Thousands of screaming, angry East Germans descended on his checkpoint, demanding to cross after hearing Günter's announcement. And Jäger was instructed by his superiors not to use force because the Western media was everywhere. How can a handful of guards who cannot use bullets stop an angry hoard?"

"Which raises the question," Jens' glare bored into Vladimir. "Where were the Russian tanks and hundreds of thousands of troops East Germany has been housing since '53? What was the point of that!"

Vladimir sipped his water. "I asked my superiors for military intervention. I even pleaded. But they said Moscow was silent."

Hans shifted in his seat and crossed his legs. "Neither our government nor Moscow can stop what is happening without a blood bath. Can you imagine the scene of thousands shot at the border? The GDR would be shunned. We must accept, things are changing. The Party is losing its hold across the Soviet Bloc. Not to mention our government is completely broke. Without hard currency loans from West Germany, we would have collapsed long ago. We can no longer afford the infrastructure and subsidies that have held our system together." He shook his head. "It is over. Time to move on."

Jens gazed at the oil painting hanging on the wall above Hans. Two women dressed in long, loose blue dresses tended a vegetable garden outside a wooden dacha. The proletarian dream he never shared. He wanted a big house, a decent car, and power. A vision he had in common with Vladimir. And Jens had had it all, until tonight. He ran his hand over his face. The humiliation was more than he could stand.

"What now?" Jens asked. "Do we travel to Moscow?"

"Why would we do that?" Matthias slurred.

"Moscow took in German Communists in the '30s when the Nazi fascists were after them," Jens pointed out. "Now we need protection from Western fascists."

Vladimir pursed his lips. "Moscow will not do that this time. Gorbachev is weak. He wants good relations with the West."

Jens set his drink on a coaster. "Shit," he muttered. He propped his elbows on his knees and dropped his head in his hands. Where would he and Helga go? North Korea? Cuba? No. No way. He would not live in those hellholes. He would take his chances closer to home. He began creating a mental checklist of what needed to be done. He must access his balance at that Liechtenstein bank. Thank god he had had the foresight to stash some of the Stasi's hard currency in a secret account. And the discipline not to waste it on frivolous things like fragile Western shoes for his wife. He had enough money to buy a new identity for Helga and him, and a house somewhere outside the GDR. The thought of having to tell Helga almost made him sick.

Vladimir lifted a thin book off the coffee table. It was filled with inspirational quotes from Soviet leaders. He noisily flipped through it, which Jens found intensely annoying. After all, Vladimir would survive this just fine. It was a setback, sure, but hardly the end of his career.

After a time, the Russian set the open book in his lap. "This marks the end of a chapter, not the book."

"Stop talking in riddles," Matthias grumbled. "I hate it when you do that. I'm ruined. Jens is ruined. We are not in the mood for your stupid games."

Vladimir tapped the page. "Listen to these words spoken by Brezhnev, in his address to the Politburo in 1971, just as détente came into fashion." He cleared his throat and read aloud: " 'We Communists have to string along the capitalists for a while. We need their credits, their agriculture, and their technology. But we are going to continue massive military programs and by the middle 1980s we will be in a position to return to a much more aggressive foreign policy designed to gain the upper hand in our relationship with the West.' "

"What does that have to do with us?" Matthias threw up his arms.

"We follow Brezhnev's advice. We lay low for a while, like our German comrades in the '30s. Remember, they returned triumphantly in the '40s to set up the GDR. We lull the capitalists into complacency. But meanwhile we come up with a plan for revenge. A plan to regain power.

"What kind of plan? Are we going to build a super-secret military and wage a guerilla attack?" Matthias wiggled his fingers in the air.

Vladimir gave him a cold stare, but Matthias did not notice. Or care.

"No," Vladimir said. "We fool them into thinking we are all on the same side. They will let their guard down. It will take time for us to develop and execute our plan. And it will take patience . . ." His voice trailed off, like he was lost in his thoughts.

"And the four of us are going to manage whatever this is alone?" Jens asked, raising his eyebrows and tilting his head to the side.

"Of course not. We use our network. We must maintain contact with our Stasi colleagues as well as with our informants in Western governments and institutions. We will need them. And then, when the time is right, we return. With a vengeance."

"To what end?" Hans asked. "To put the Soviet Bloc back together? Who cares."

Vladimir scowled and shook his head. "Power. They will eat out of our hands. And we will enjoy every minute. And with power, comes money. If our plan is successful, we will have fat bank accounts to go along with it."

A glimmer of hope was sparked inside Jens. He imagined a villa like the ones he had seen pictures of in Italy. And his wife stepping her red stiletto heel out of the passenger side of his Maserati. The tight feeling in his chest loosened. He knew it was wildly optimistic, but he needed something to look forward to. He nodded and said slowly, "I like it."

Matthias straightened and turned toward Vladimir with the slightest hint of a grin on his face. "So my spy network may have a future after all."

Hans gave an annoying, staccato laugh. "Why not? Sounds like it could be fun."

Vladimir raised his tumbler and leaned over the table. "To vengeance."

They clinked glasses and threw back their drinks.

Backsliding

Andrew Hinshaw

IT WAS A mostly cloudless afternoon, save for a few striations smearing across the purpling evening sky, their edges blazing orange as they caught the dying rays of the setting sun. There were rolling green hills and a large, expansive lake. The air smelled crisp, almost like citrus. Despite Kenneth's daughter Samantha having poor taste in clergymen, she did pick a lovely location to have her wedding. Lily Lake Dock in the Rocky Mountains lived up to her praises; or at least praises Brandon had relayed secondhand, since Samantha hardly had spoken to Kenneth since her mother Christine's death two years prior.

Unfortunately, Kenneth could no longer bask in the beauty, as he'd just been escorted into the canopy tent by his son Brandon, who had convinced Samantha to allow Kenneth a brief speech. The tent was reasonably sized, given that there were only about thirty guests. It was longer than it was wide, with a slightly raised wooden stage in the back, just opposite the entrance. The entrance flaps were tied off on each side, giving it the look of an opened theater curtain. In between the wooden stage and the opening to the outside world were five tables. And oddly, due to lack of room or poor planning, the reception table was kept just outside the entrance.

In the far corner, just to the right of the stage, stood Kenneth. He leaned forward and sniffed one of the tent's transparent vinyl windows, then pulled his head back and exhaled sharply from his nose in disgust.

"Still off-gassing," he remarked to his son Brandon. "I told you to tell Samantha to ask for a used tent." Raising his spectacles, he leaned forward and flicked one of the window's fake plastic grilles. "And what's with this nonsense? Is anyone fooled into thinking this is an actual cathedral window?"

Brandon responded with a half-assed shrug that suggested he wasn't really listening. The boy had just turned thirty, but people often thought he was ten years younger due to his baby-faced features. And, when he wasn't donning the austere, stony gaze that he seemed to only reserve for his father, his default expression made it look as if he perpetually knew a joke no one else was privy to—eyes slightly narrowed and lips pressed together into a mild grin. Brandon also lucked out that he hadn't inherited his father's cleft chin, something Kenneth hid under his beard because it made him look a bit brutish, which was not so useful in the world of academia.

Brandon tugged at the bottom of his black tuxedo jacket for the fifteenth time, even though it was completely straight. Kenneth looked over his son's fine outfit. The damned thing was so crisp it looked as if it had been stitched that morning.

Brandon focused on Kenneth's tie. "Purple ducks?" Brandon said. "Really? You couldn't find a single plain black tie?"

Kenneth tucked his chin to look down at his tie and smiled fondly. He lifted the tie to examine it closer. "An amateur's mistake. That's actually the common loon."

"How fitting," Brandon said, reaching up to adjust it further.

Kenneth resisted the urge to bat his son's hands away. "I said it's fine." He noticed a sheen of sweat on Brandon's forehead. "Why are *you* nervous? I'm the one giving a speech at my disaffected daughter's wedding. It's not as if I'm meeting the pope. Though I'm sure Samantha's new surrogate father Pastor Porzio sees himself as such."

As if on cue, Porzio, the stumpy man who had officiated this farce, passed by them. He walked with limp wrists and his hands slightly raised, leading with his belly. The tails of his black robe drifted behind him like a cape.

"Does he really have to wear that damned robe?" Kenneth said in a slightly hushed voice, making a perfunctory attempt to avoid Samantha hearing him. "He's participating in the time-honored tradition of duping two young people into an outmoded social construct, not presiding over a murder trial."

Brandon glanced over at Porzio, who had taken a seat at the table behind Samantha. He turned his attention back to Kenneth's tie. "He officiated a wedding. What would he have worn instead?"

Kenneth pursed his lips and thought for a moment. "A body bag?"

Brandon snorted. "Just because yours and mom's marriage wasn't all *milk and honey* doesn't mean it can't be that way for others."

"I don't get what Samantha sees in that fraud," said Kenneth, ignoring his son's comment about his marital problems with Christine. "I thought I raised her to be more of a skeptic. And now she's latched onto him like some father she never had." Kenneth frowned in disgust. "I bet you he isn't even wearing anything under that robe."

"Well, you haven't exactly been dad of the year lately," Brandon said lazily while continuing to fiddle with Kenneth's tie. "She's trying. That's all that matters. Act like an adult for once and be insincere." He finally stopped messing with Kenneth's tie and stepped back to examine his work. "It'll have to do."

Kenneth glanced down at his suit. It was restrictive in all the wrong places and seemed to be designed to make him look like a paunchy, low-ranking mobster from the 1980s. Except for the sneakers, which were broken in and then some, having been stained green from one too many lawn-mowing sessions. Brandon had tried his damnedest to get Kenneth to wear dress shoes, but Kenneth had said he would only allow either his body or feet to be stuffed into something two sizes too small, not both.

Brandon went to take Kenneth's glass of wine but Kenneth pulled it back out of reach.

"You've had enough," Brandon said. "Your teeth are turning purple."

"Then they'll match my tie."

Brandon gripped Kenneth by his shoulders and gave him a stern look. Kenneth noticed how Brandon's baby blue bowtie brought out the crystal blue in his son's eyes. It was another lucky genetic roll of the dice; Kenneth had always been disappointed in the muddy brown color of his own eyes. They looked like stagnant water in a pothole. Or boiled shit.

"You have your mother's eyes," Kenneth said.

"And my father's receding hairline," Brandon said with a faint smile. Kenneth knew his son well enough to know that Brandon's quip wasn't just banter, but an attempt to derail the subject of his dead mother.

"I saw her again today," Kenneth said, doubling down. "On the way here. She was driving a Honda when we passed by that motor lodge in Estes."

"Mom never owned a Honda," Brandon said as he craned his neck to look at something over Kenneth's shoulder.

Kenneth narrowed his eyes and tilted his head to meet Brandon's gaze again. "How is it that you always pretend to be distracted when I bring her up?"

"You know why," Brandon said, his expression momentarily darkening. "Just tell Doctor Collins about it when you see her next. And I *was* distracted." Brandon jerked his chin, signaling for Kenneth to turn around and see what he was looking at.

Kenneth did as asked, looking through the opening of the tent. He saw a triangular tree outside with blue-green needles and a few people standing by it. It was just to the right of the banquet table. "Why are you having me look at a cypress? Or is that a spruce? Definitely a conifer."

"Not the tree," Brandon said, sighing. "The girl standing next to it in the purple dress."

Kenneth adjusted his glasses and spotted the girl, who was chatting with a few random people he didn't care to identify. The girl was shapely and looked to be in her late twenties, wearing a snug dress with a high black belt. Her blonde hair was pulled back into a tight bun and she held a champagne flute. She had large, round eyes and high cheekbones, and looked vaguely like a young Julia Roberts, at least from this distance.

"I'm pretty sure I had a fling with her back in college." Brandon chewed his cheek. "She was friends with Sam, but I didn't know they kept in touch. If only I could remember her name." He held a fist to his mouth and concentrated. "Vanessa. Victoria." His eyes widened. "Valerie!" A moment later, the joy melted from his face, replaced with uncertainty. "It for sure started with a V. Or had a V in it."

Kenneth raised an eyebrow. "Hoping to hit another home run?"

Brandon shrugged. "I'd take second base. Honestly, I don't think it ended well, so it might be better if she doesn't remember me. I think I passed out." He threw out some lazy jazz hands. "Tequila."

"Well, who knows?" Kenneth said, lifting his chin and breathing in through his nose as if he smelled something delicious. "The night is young and love is in the air."

Brandon snorted. "It almost sounded like you meant that."

"Well," Kenneth said, "I'd hate to deprive my son from engaging in a repeat sexual liaison that will likely leave you both awkward and depressed in the morning."

"Now you're talkin'." Brandon glanced over Kenneth's shoulder again. "Sam just tapped her wrist. Looks like you're up." Brandon locked eyes with Kenneth, his gaze growing stern. "Just stick to the script. Boring is better. Think platitudes and clichés—"

"—and glittering generalities, as Samantha's borscht-eating husband might say. Don't worry my boy, I've got this. Banality is like a son to me." Kenneth clucked his tongue and winked. He reached up and tugged at his collar, loosening the tie that Brandon had so carefully arranged. Then he spun around, stepped onto the stage, and stumbled toward the microphone.

The guests chatter continued as he reached for the mic. He gazed upon the small crowd, no more than thirty people spread out amongst the few tables in front of the stage. All of whom were dressed just as smartly as he was, well, save for his shoes. For a brief second, Kenneth felt like he was the presenter at one of Christine's loathsome outdoor Christian revivals. He thought about blotting the sweat from his brow with one hand, holding his other on high, and asking, "Canna getta amen?"

Instead, Kenneth brought the mic up to his bearded mouth and cleared his throat. The space beyond the slick wooden stage went silent, as several of the candlelit faces turned in unison toward him like a mob of meerkats. His daughter Samantha stared up at him, her hands folded neatly in her lap. She was seated in the center table nearest the stage and was adorned in a typical wedding gown with white lace and intricate pearl beading. For a brief moment, the lighting caught her just right and it reminded Kenneth of her mother. She had Christine's soft nose, her subdued cheekbones, her flawless, light bronze skin, and her shiny black hair.

She also had the same condescending glare that Christine had occasionally given Kenneth when she was still alive. It was the way a stranger might gaze upon a stray dog covered in its own excrement: with a mixture of pity and revulsion.

I don't need your pity, Kenneth wanted to say as he returned her spiteful glare. Then he thought about how Brandon had said Samantha was trying, and that he should, too. Kenneth fished Brandon's speech out of his pocket, but just as he was about to speak, Samantha reached up to her breast and plucked a cell phone from inside her bra and started checking her messages.

He stared at her a moment, disconcerted. This hardly seemed like the behavior of someone who wanted to mend fences. He glanced down at the folded piece of paper, massaging it in his hands for a moment, then stuffed it back into his jacket pocket. "First, I'd like to offer a toast to the most important person here." He held his wine glass toward Samantha, which still failed to cause her to look away from her phone. He then moved it a few inches to his left toward the liquor station, which was positioned against the tent's wall to Samantha's right. The station was draped in a fine black cloth and topped with an assortment of wine, beer, and spirits. A jaded bartender clad in black stood behind the table, looking like a cliché movie extra as he polished the inside of a wine glass with a towel.

"The bartender."

Samantha wedged her phone back into its boob pocket and looked up at Kenneth, giving him a generic smile that suggested she was completely checked out. Kenneth clucked his tongue then took a sip of wine, savoring it for a moment. He then started pacing. "I'd like to tell you all a story. So, Samantha was on sabbatical in Boston, and

Porzio, whom most of you already know—" Kenneth tried his best not to frown as he nodded toward the man, who remained seated behind and to the left of his daughter. The portly, crow-faced balding man had an oversized nose and hunched shoulders. He grinned at Kenneth, his sycophantic, shaded eyes matching his sycophantic, smarmy face.

"Well, Porzio here had invited Samantha and her soon-to-be over for spaghetti dinner. After saying grace, a guest turned to the pastor and asked," Kenneth looked down at his shoes, raised an eyebrow, adopted an exaggerated, high-pitched Bostonian accent, and said, "hey Pasta? Wouldja pasta pasta?" He chortled at his own joke, stopped pacing, and looked up at the small crowd.

No one laughed.

Kenneth glanced at Brandon, who returned his gaze with an eye-twitching, vein-in-his-forehead expression of constipation. Brandon slowly mouthed the words *the script*.

Kenneth clenched his teeth and reached into his jacket pocket again. He pulled out what he thought was the speech, but instead he found in his hands a tattered leather bookmark with a cross on it. He stared down at it, massaging the embossed lettering. Looking back up, he locked eyes with Samantha. The stern gaze she laid upon him felt as if Christine was using her daughter as a conduit from beyond the grave. First, it was just the eyes, but then the features started to change. The lines in her forehead hardened some, the bags under her eyes became a bit more pronounced. Her lips became less full and curved slightly downward. For a moment, it felt like Christine was looking right at him.

Kenneth looked away and spoke under his breath, mostly to himself, but the mic still picked it up. "It shouldn't be me standing here right now."

Samantha shot a concerned glance to Brandon, who was looming directly off stage, square-shouldered with his arms folded behind him like he was a maître d'.

Kenneth opened his mouth again to speak, but the words seemed to catch in his throat. His face flushed and his eyes began to sting. Suddenly the flimsy walls of the tent felt as hard as concrete. Walls that were closing in.

A concerned smile grew on Brandon's face and he started to step up onto the stage. Kenneth held out a hand toward his son, stopping Brandon in his tracks. He stuffed the bookmark back into his pocket and drew a trembling hand down over his graying beard, feeling the pain of Christine's passing blossoming in his chest, a pain just as raw as the day she died.

Clearing his throat again, Kenneth used his thumb to nudge his glasses up his nose. "When you first told me you were doing this," Kenneth said, holding Brandon's gaze for a moment before looking back at Samantha, "you remember what I told you?"

Samantha's lips formed a thin line and she ran her hand along the side of her head, pushing a black bang behind her ear. Her face was unreadable, her cold gaze more calculating than empathetic.

"I told you it was a bad idea."

To her right sat Nikolai, Samantha's new husband, sporting a charcoal suit jacket a little too shiny for Kenneth's liking. The golden-haired groom stared back at Kenneth with a placating grin that dimpled his boyish cheeks. He looked to his new bride, frowned a smile, and shrugged playfully, as if he were in agreement with Kenneth's appraisal.

"But then I met Nik," Kenneth said. He cast a warm gaze toward his new son-in-law. "And then I realized it was a *terrible* idea."

This garnered a single laugh that quickly transformed into a cough as someone lost in the crowd took a sharp elbow to the ribs.

Kenneth sighed and shook his head. His repeated attempts at levity were wasted on such a dull crowd. He ignored Brandon's fidgeting in his periphery and doubled down. "Seriously, an *anthropologist?*" He paused a moment to look at Nikolai before turning his gaze to Samantha. He cringed. "You marry a man who makes a living off of *conjecture?*"

Nikolai's eyes narrowed to match Samantha's, but he maintained his picture-perfect smile. "Some of us are content studying ze mating habits of winged rodents," Nikolai said, frowning dismissively. The boy had been in the States long enough to lose most of his Russian accent, but there was a touch still there. "While others are more concerned vith the scientific study of humanity—"

"Ah." Kenneth chuckled as he looked at the various faces in the crowd. "How adorable. At first, I thought you were a charlatan, but now I'm not sure you really understand what science is."

"Are you done, Kenneth?" Samantha asked, her flat voice making the question sound more like a demand.

Kenneth paused a moment, clenching his teeth. On the rare occasion she felt fit to speak to Kenneth over the last year, she had taken to referring to him by his first name. He struggled to hide how much it bothered him. "Oh, come on Samantha. I'm just razzing the boy. I'm his dad now, don't I have that right?"

Behind her, Porzio shook his head disapprovingly while glaring at Kenneth. He reached forward and squeezed Samantha's arm a bit too tightly, and for a bit too long. Then he whispered something into her ear and she reached over and patted his hand.

Kenneth raised his eyebrows. "Is there something you wish to add, *Pasta* Porzio?"

Brandon entered the stage and approached Kenneth, a fake smile plastered on his lips. He forced a laugh. "I think my father may have had one too many glasses of zinfandel."

"I'm sorry Samantha," Kenneth said, as Brandon attempted to take the mic from him. Kenneth refused to hand it over, instead holding it closer to his mouth, amplifying his voice and causing a shrill feedback whine from the speakers. "Maybe we could just chalk this up as practice for your next one—"

The last word was cut off as Brandon turned to look at the back of the stage and made a less-than-subtle neck-slicing gesture toward the DJ booth. *I got a feeling that tonight is going to be a good good night!* boomed from the two large black speakers standing atop posts on either side of the DJ.

As Brandon unceremoniously escorted him from the stage, Kenneth tried to give the DJ a cross look. Unfortunately, the pimple-faced, sideways-hat-wearing twenty-something was too busy hiding behind a gray laptop, twisting knobs on his soundboard. As if toggle switches and blinking lights amounted to any measure of musical talent.

After a brief walk past a couple tables covered in pristine white cloths and adorned with flowers, candles, and sweaty jugs of what Kenneth suspected contained only the best tap water, the two of them stopped at the tent's entrance.

Brandon rounded to face Kenneth. He glared at him, his face slack with subdued anger. Brandon held out a hand and raised his eyebrows expectantly. "What the hell was that? You know what . . . I don't care. Give it to me."

"Give you what?"

Brandon's eyes narrowed. "Dad, don't test me."

Kenneth sighed and wrinkled his nose. He rummaged through his pockets and pulled out an old Pop-Tart.

Brandon looked at the stale, lint-covered pastry then looked up at Kenneth, baffled. "Why?"

Kenneth frowned, struggling to remember. Then his eyes widened. "Ah, I think that was when you insisted I eat something on the way to your mother's procession." He sniffed the Pop-Tart and shrugged. "You'd think it'd look worse after twelve months. This thing might still be edible."

"Since the—" Brandon stared at Kenneth as if he were unable to understand what he was seeing. "Jesus. You wore the same suit you wore to mom's funeral to your daughter's *wedding*?"

"Don't use the lard's name in vain sonny," Kenneth said, wagging a finger and pocketing the Pop-Tart. "We wouldn't want to offend any faith-healers nearby with an Italian last name."

Brandon held his forehead as if he was developing a fever, then dropped his arm to hold out his hand again.

Part of Kenneth wanted to put the Pop-Tart in his son's hand but didn't want to waste a good joke on the tiresome bore Brandon had turned into. He dug in his other pocket, pulled out the microphone and slapped it into his son's waiting palm.

Brandon flipped the mic over and toggled the off switch for good measure, then handed it to a caterer and asked him to return it to the DJ. He placed one hand on Kenneth's back and gestured toward the buffet table with the other, just outside the tent. The long table was also clad in clean white linen, its many silver platters illuminated by dangling strands of string lights from the overhanging branches of the tree beside it. "How about we soak up some of that alcohol?"

Kenneth snorted, half amused. But in doing so, he smelled barbeque sauce and spotted some fresh-looking buns with a brick of white butter next to them. His stomach growled. He squared his shoulders and ambled toward the buffet, as if it were his idea all along. Having exited the tent, he noticed the temperature had dropped outside. He welcomed the cool air, given how snugly his suit fit.

Arriving at the buffet table, Kenneth glanced back at the DJ. Bass thumped from the speakers as a small mass of people coalesced onto the stage, their swaying arms and shaking butts bathed in strobe lighting.

"I helped that jerk set up and what does he do?" Kenneth turned to watch the crowd beyond the tables gyrating on the dance floor. Most of the tables were half empty now and the DJ bobbed his head with a big derpy grin on his face. "He cuts me off."

Brandon reached for a roll and raised an eyebrow. "I'm not sure if asking if he had the Moody Blue's Greatest Hits LP qualifies as helping."

"I should have stuck with my 'guy walks up to a mailbox' joke," Kenneth grumbled. He watched as Brandon spooned some twice-baked mashed potatoes onto a plate. Kenneth reached over and poked a finger into Brandon's food, sampling some of the cheese-covered glop. Its velvety texture and garlic notes were delicious, which just made him angrier.

Brandon grabbed another plate and jabbed Kenneth in the gut with it.

"Ow," Kenneth whined, grabbing his side. "You hit me right in the fat."

"What joke?" Brandon said, his tired gaze suggesting he couldn't care less about hurting Kenneth. "You mean the one with no punch line?"

Kenneth refused to take the plate and stared back, dumbfounded. "Its lack of a punch line *is* the punch line."

"How avant-garde," Brandon said, rolling his eyes. He slid the plate

Kenneth still hadn't taken underneath his own and started placing random items onto his plate. "You realize Porzio is Catholic, right? His title would be *father*, not pastor."

Kenneth grunted, a sharp exhale through the nose. "He's Episcopalian. That's like the generic diet soda of Catholicism. They don't care about honorifics. I could've called him Tim. Or Timmy. And Samantha only has one father, and it's not him. Plus, my joke wouldn't have worked if I had changed his title."

"It still didn't work," Brandon said, giving Kenneth a brief glance and raising his eyebrows. "Either way, I'm guessing it would've landed better than projecting your life's failures onto your daughter."

"Life *is* failure," Kenneth said, grabbing a dinner roll from Brandon's plate. "I keep hoping one day you'll realize that."

Brandon snatched his dinner roll back and glanced down at Kenneth's protruding belly. "Tell that to your liver."

"Oh, don't start with that shit," Kenneth scoffed. "We're at a wedding. You're supposed to drink."

"I'm pretty sure your doctor specifically said *not* to drink with your meds. But what the hell does she know? She only went to school for what, ten years?"

"I'm a doctor," Kenneth said, attempting to drink the rest of his wine only to realize the glass was empty. He held it up, frowning. "Why should her word supersede my own?"

"Tell me, how often do ornithologists prescribe psychotropics?"

Kenneth adopted an academic tone. "How often do they, or how often *should* they?"

Brandon rubbed the back of his neck and looked up at the darkening sky. "I don't know how you always drag me into these . . . *schizophrenic* sparring matches. I'm tired, dad. Your antics surely ruined my chances with V-what's-her-face, so can we please just eat and watch people dance and say a few kind words to whatever passersby and then go back to the hotel? We can even rent *March of the Penguins* and order some cheesecake."

Kenneth's eyes widened and he held up a pointing, accusatory finger. His words were hateful and slow, and he spoke through clenched teeth. "That movie is a pandering diatribe of anthropomorphic bullshit!"

Brandon held out a hand as if he were trying to calm a cornered stray dog. "Okay! Keep your voice down!"

Kenneth grabbed the roll from Brandon's plate and took a bite.

A tall, gangly, fedora-topped man surveying the smorgasbord on the other side of the table was not so sneakily giving Kenneth the side eye.

"Can I help you?" Kenneth asked with his mouth half full.

The man quickly shook his head, and was suddenly very interested in a large wooden bowl of Caesar salad at the far end of the table.

"Sure, get into a fistfight at your daughter's wedding." Brandon spotted a silver chafing dish with an assortment of fried chicken. He briefly ducked down, using its reflection to check his hair, and then put two drumsticks on his plate. "You already bombed on stage. Might as well lock it in."

Kenneth followed Brandon back inside the tent to an empty table a few feet from the entrance. He pulled out one of the table's rustic wooden chairs and took a seat. Brandon slipped out the second plate and placed it in front of Kenneth, and dropped one of the drumsticks on top of it.

Brandon took a seat to Kenneth's left, giving a kindly nod to the table to the right of them. An elderly woman with short curly brown hair and white roots was trying to smooch a spoonful of soup that wobbled precariously in front of her mouth. Next to her sat a bald man with a white goatee, whose slight tilt to the right made Kenneth suspect that the vodka tonic in his hand was not his first.

"You know I actually like the boy," remarked Kenneth, referring to Nikolai. "I just knew if I went after him it would upset Samantha."

Brandon used one hand to type a message in his phone, his face aglow in the dim lighting. He was only half listening again. "You and Sam are more alike than either of you realize."

Kenneth looked over in Samantha's direction, and to his utter lack of surprise, he saw Porzio had now moved to her table. The man's eyes briefly connected with Kenneth's, then he leaned over and made some comment to Samantha which caused the table to erupt in laughter. Porzio apparently thought his clever remark was so funny he had to grab his belly and double over, causing the light to glisten off his scalp between the lines of his thinning hair.

"I never trust a man with a comb over," Kenneth said. "It's like those fake grills on the plastic windows. You're not fooling anyone."

"Maybe he just doesn't give a shit?" Brandon said, continuing to mess with his phone.

"No," Kenneth said, still glaring in Porzio's direction. "He's hiding something, but too stupid to realize how obvious it is to everyone else."

Just then, Porzio looked over in Kenneth's direction again. He flashed a child-like smile and gave a small wave. Kenneth couldn't help but twist in his chair to look behind himself, thinking that maybe Porzio was waving at someone else.

"Did he just wave at me?" Kenneth asked, turning to look at Porzio again.

Brandon looked up from his phone. Porzio snapped his fingers at some young-looking waitress with a bouncy ponytail, signaling he needed a drink, then stood up and started walking in their direction.

Brandon's normally narrow eyes widened fully. "Fuck, he's coming over here, isn't he?"

Kenneth looked at his son and gave him a devious grin.

Porzio seemed to somehow float-waddle his way toward them, his black robe hiding his feet, making him look like an overweight poltergeist.

A muscle flashed in Brandon's clean-shaven jaw as he gave Kenneth a cutting glare. He pointed at Kenneth with his phone and spoke through his teeth like a ventriloquist, as if Porzio could somehow hear over the DJ's most recent overplayed bass-laden hip-hop song that Kenneth knew the words to despite having no idea who the artist was. "Don't you dare," Brandon said.

Kenneth held a hand to his chest as if wounded. "You should have more *faith* in your father."

Porzio arrived at the table, pulled out a chair, and sat down. "May I join you guys fa' moment?"

Kenneth rested his elbow on the table, then pointed quickly at Porzio with a quick twitch of his wrist. "You're one of those people who flicks their turn signal on after they've already started merging, aren't you?"

"I'm sorry?" Porzio said, his round face grimacing in confusion. Just then, the young barback showed up and placed a bottle of beer in front of him.

"I'll take a pint of vodka," Kenneth said, talking over Brandon who had attempted to tell the waitress they were fine. "And my boy here needs a sherry enema to remove the stick up his ass."

The youngster held her mouth open, uncertain what to do next.

"We're fine," Brandon repeated, giving her a dismissive waive.

Kenneth didn't have it in him to argue. Porzio leaned back in his chair to stare at the server's backside as she walked away.

"Actually, we were just getting ready to leave," Brandon said to Porzio, giving a quick glance to Kenneth. He paused, then added, "I did want to say you did a wonderful job officiating the wedding."

"Yes, that's very kind," Porzio said, returning Brandon's smile with a slimy one of his own. Porzio turned his attention to Kenneth, taking in a contemplative breath for a moment. "Mister Burman—"

"Doctor," Kenneth interrupted.

"Ah," Porzio said. "Zoology, right?"

Kenneth crossed his arms and leaned back in his chair. "Sure."

"I couldn't help but notice you were holding a bookmark with scripcha written on it when you gave your," he paused, holding a fist to his mouth and half coughing the word, "speech." After clearing his throat, he said, "I was curious what verse it was."

Kenneth realized he had removed the bookmark and was massaging it again in his hand in plain view. He silently cursed this unconscious reflex, but tried to shrug it off and throw a barb toward Porzio for good measure. "Oh, I think it was something about a wolf in sheep's clothing."

Porzio pursed his lips and stared at his hands as he slowly spun his bottle of beer on the table. He looked up to return Kenneth's gaze. "Matthew 7:15." He nodded, causing his second chin to wobble. "A good verse, though a bit timeworn."

The three of them stared wordlessly at one another.

Porzio glanced at the bookmark before Kenneth could put it away.

"Ah," Porzio's eyes brightened as he realized it was a different verse entirely. "That was hers, wasn't it?"

Kenneth's face twitched.

"Philippians 4:13," said Porzio, quoting the verse on the bookmark as if he were speaking now from the pulpit. " 'One can do all things through Him who strengthens me.' "

Kenneth grunted. "Except beat cancer." He shoved the bookmark back into his pocket, aware that his hand was shaking again. He looked away from Porzio, trying to locate the waitress to see about that pint of vodka.

"I just came to say—" Porzio started, reaching out to touch Kenneth's hand. Kenneth looked down at the man's hand atop his own. It felt cold, befitting a wraith.

"Mr. Burman," Porzio started again, now patting Kenneth's hand. "We all have our struggles. I fa' one struggle with understanding why so many of my flock are drawn to worldly pleasures, something I've never had any interest in."

Kenneth gave a tight-lipped smile, and then carefully but firmly used his other hand to remove Porzio's hand from his own. "Says the fat pervert drinking a Bud Light."

"Dad—"

Porzio held up his hand to silence Brandon. Brandon's eye twitched and he reeled back slightly; it was the first time Kenneth caught a glimpse of irritation from Brandon directed at someone other than himself.

"It doesn't take a leap a logic," said Porzio, "to think that your poor treatment of Sam is a reflection on ya' treatment of your late wife." He let out a slow sigh, bobbing his head in contemplation. "And there has to be guilt in that, given her death means ya' can't ever apologize, at least not in this life. What I'm getting at is, if you ever need me to bridge a conversation between you and Sam, I can do that. Barring anything uncouth, of course."

"Let me get this straight," Kenneth said. "You're offering to facilitate a conversation between me and my daughter?"

"God willing," Porzio said, a pious look on his face.

"How about you facilitate this." Kenneth rested his fist on the tabletop and flicked up his middle finger.

Porzio stared down at the gesture and sighed. He looked back up at Kenneth. "Before I go, I do want ya' to ask yourself one question: is this what Christine would've wanted?"

Kenneth's heart rate doubled and he realized he was grinding his teeth. He glanced over at Brandon and let out a sick, incredulous laugh. "Is he serious?" He looked again to Porzio. "Just who the hell do you think you are? You're nothing more than . . ." Kenneth paused, his anger interfering with his ability to insult the bastard, ". . . than a sanctimonious elephant seal masquerading as a holy man!"

"Dad!" Brandon said, standing up.

Kenneth hadn't realized he had gotten to his feet as well. He also hadn't realized he had grabbed the drumstick and was brandishing it like a billy club.

Porzio remained seated, his eyes fearful and his hands lifted defensively, but behind it all was a look that left a sinking feeling in Kenneth's gut: the man was struggling to hold back a small, satisfied smile.

Kenneth looked around and realized that several people had stood from their seats and were watching them, including Samantha and Nikolai. Apparently, they had noticed Kenneth's outburst, despite the DJ's most recent ear-bleeder techno song that sounded like someone had trapped a cat in an aluminum trash can and was rhythmically whacking the top of it with a broomstick.

Kenneth slowly sat back down and placed the drumstick back on the plate.

Porzio stared at him for another moment, then stood up, the small grin on his face slipping away before he turned to face Samantha. He began to walk away when Kenneth leaned over and said to Brandon,

"Ever notice how the back of his neck looks like a package of hot dogs?"

Porzio stopped, then turned toward them again, as if he'd watched one too many episodes of *Columbo*. He took a few steps and rested a hand on the back of the chair he had just been sitting in and leaned forward, his eyes squinted. "Proverbs 18:2: 'A fool takes no pleasure in understanding, but only in expressin' his opinion.' Maybe your relationship with your late wife and daughter would be better, if ya' took that to heart." He returned Kenneth's tight-lipped smile from earlier. "Food fa' thought."

At this, Porzio turned on his heels and headed toward Samantha's table, the pitiful stump of a man waddling off like a pudgy penguin. He arrived at Samantha's table and gave her a hug. She took a sip of wine and Porzio gave her a sympathetic frown, rubbing her back.

Brandon remained standing. "I think it's time to leave."

Kenneth didn't move.

"Dad?" Brandon said, clearly concerned. He snapped his fingers in front of Kenneth's face.

Kenneth batted his son's hand away and said through his teeth, "His sit-down air stinks."

Brandon frowned, clearly still concerned with his father's mental state. "His what?"

"His sit-down air. You know, like when you're talking to someone and they smell okay, but then they sit down and you get this funky deluge of onions, malted barley, and lies." Kenneth eyed his empty wine glass sitting on the table.

"You know what I think?" Brandon placed his hands on the table and leaned forward. "I think Porzio planned that whole thing, and you fell for it hook, line, and sinker."

"What if he's right?" Kenneth started to space out, his vision blurring slightly as if he were looking down a long tunnel. "I was too focused on my career. It was always about me and never about her. And now I have no one to share it with."

Brandon's eyes softened. "You have your children. And you were there for Mom, in the end, when she needed you."

Kenneth glared at Brandon, feeling his face flush in anger. "A pig's bladder and a tube," he said flatly.

Concern transitioned to confusion on Brandon's face and his eyes unfocused. It gave him the appearance that he was having what Dr. Collins would refer to as a dissociative episode.

"Doctors," Kenneth continued, "would fill the bladder with tobacco smoke and then insert the tube into the rectum of someone thought dead."

Brandon rubbed his eyes, stretching the skin out underneath them, looking exasperated. "What are you even saying right now?"

"What I'm saying is," Kenneth said, struggling to keep his voice steady, "your attempt at placation is based on the supposition that I'm a fool." Kenneth turned his attention to the elderly couple. "Hey Mildred, can you or Cecil spare a cigarette?"

The old woman adopted a curmudgeonly look of disgust and lifted her oversized baby blue purse against her chest as if it were body armor.

Kenneth started to stand up and Brandon grabbed his arm. Kenneth jerked his arm out of Brandon's grip, knocking a few flowers out of the vase as he did so. "Would you stop doing that!" He then straightened his jacket and rolled his neck. He briefly closed his eyes and took a deep breath, then released it over five seconds. "I'm not going to even say anything to Porzio. I'm just going to go congratulate my daughter and her new husband."

Brandon shook his head. "Sam doesn't want to talk to you, Dad. Hasn't she made that abundantly clear?"

"Why are you defending her?" Kenneth asked. "It's not like she's treated you all that well, either."

"We're all handling Mom's death differently," Brandon said. "Sam's a control freak, you're a drunk, and I spend all my time not getting laid."

Kenneth blew out some air and rolled his eyes.

Brandon bit his lip. "You do realize Sam's had her own shit to go through? You lost a wife. She lost a mother *and* a child."

"Oh, give me a break," Kenneth said. "She used the death of a fetus as an excuse to not see her dying mother on her final days. And now that parasite Porzio is fanning the flames of her delusion."

Brandon held up a fist and twisted his neck the way one does when they're trying to contain a string of hateful words. "Did you ever consider that maybe she knows Porzio's a scumbag and she's just using him to fuck with you? Do you know how much work it was for me to persuade her to allow you come to this in the first place?"

Kenneth scoffed. "She sure seemed chatty back when I was paying her tuition."

Brandon rolled his eyes. "Riiiight. That's it. There's no other possible reason why she's not talking to you." He straightened and threw his hands out, shaking his head and feigning confusion. "Like, I don't know, say the time you showed up to her church group wearing a 'smoke meth and hail Satan' T-shirt. Or when you gave Barkley milk instead of water the entire week Sam was out of town."

Kenneth guffawed. "How was I supposed to know that stupid poodle was lactose intolerant?"

"Who feeds a dog milk?" Brandon asked, blinking and shaking his head as if he'd just been slapped.

"Maybe I should've fed it *honey* instead," Kenneth said. He then looked to Porzio and felt his fingernails dig into his palms. The swindler once again had a meaty hand on Samantha's shoulder and she and Nikolai were yukking it with him like he was family.

"Your mother wouldn't have put up with Porzio's shit," Kenneth said.

"Don't," Brandon warned, rounding the table and placing himself between Kenneth and Porzio.

Kenneth smirked. "Don't what?"

"You *know* what!" Brandon hissed through clenched teeth and pointed down at the ground. "I'm tired of you using her death as an excuse to behave like an asshole."

"He's the asshole!" Kenneth said as he jabbed a finger toward Porzio. "He's the asshole!"

The elderly couple at the table next to them started to get up, though the woman had to reach out to steady her husband, Mr. Leaning Tower of Pisa. Kenneth gave a bow toward them and swirled a hand in an excessive flourish as if he were an actor at the curtain call. He jabbed himself in the chest with a thumb, returning his attention to Brandon. "I'm her father and it's my duty to protect her." He pointed in Porzio's direction, over Brandon's shoulder. "And she needs to know this *man of the cloth* is a phony."

Brandon didn't budge. Instead, he adopted a wide stance and crossed his arms like a bouncer not allowing an unruly patron into a bar. Kenneth realized Brandon wouldn't let him waltz over to Samantha without continuing to be a petulant obstruction, so he looked down at the mostly full glass of water on the table in front of Brandon's seat. He leaned toward it and knocked it on its side, spilling the water over most of the table and saturating the white cloth underneath. "Now look what you've gone and done."

Kenneth tried to juke right but Brandon moved with him, ignoring the water. Brandon also gave up trying to keep his voice down. "Tell me this: when have you acted like a father to either of us in the last year? You think I wanted to play babysitter all goddamned night?"

"And there we have it," Kenneth said, tilting his head. "Dr. Collins would refer to that as *displacement*. You don't care about my relationship with Samantha. You're just angry you'll be sleeping with your hand tonight."

"Who cares if he's a phony?" Brandon said. "The man *means* something to Sam right now. You know, your daughter? The girl that was just married an hour ago?"

Kenneth held his son's belligerent gaze for a moment. He then raised his hands in surrender. "Fine. You win." He turned around and started to walk back toward the reception table, but Brandon moved with him, circling again to block his way.

"I'm literally headed in the opposite direction," Kenneth said.

"Uh huh," Brandon said.

"I have to pee."

Brandon didn't move.

"Want to come along?" Kenneth asked. He massaged the back of his neck. "You can rub my shoulders. You know, help me relax. Get the stream going."

Just then, a finger attached to a freshly manicured hand tapped Brandon on the shoulder. Brandon clenched his jaw and his eyes danced back and forth as if he were trying to glean Kenneth's true intentions. He finally turned around and flinched.

"Brandon?" the young Julia Roberts doppelganger said. "It's me, Vivian. Remember we had poli-sci together."

"Vivian," Kenneth said warmly as he moved beside Brandon and reached out to shake her hand, internally thanking her for having impeccable timing. "Brandon *did* remember you," Kenneth added, with a playful grin. "He just assumed you wouldn't want to talk to him due his father's shenanigans on stage earlier."

Brandon held up a finger as if to counter. "Technically true—"

"Well, I for one thought you were hilarious," she said to Kenneth, snorting. She finished the remainder of the champagne in her glass, leaving some lipstick on the rim. She lowered her voice to a loud whisper and leaned in toward them. "I'm ashamed to admit these weddings are such a slog I always secretly hope something entertaining will happen. Just once, I want to go to a wedding where the disheveled ex-lover barges in, breathlessly objecting on the basis of some past indiscretion."

Kenneth stared at her a moment and felt his lips grow into a genuine smile. This girl looked nothing like Christine, but damn if she didn't have the same mischievous sense of humor she'd had. "I like this one."

She smiled back at him.

Kenneth put a hand on his stomach. "Alas, I must excuse myself to the lavatory. Too much wine."

Vivian cocked a seductive eyebrow at Brandon. She nodded toward the bar. "Wanna get a drink?"

Brandon made a series of involuntary gestures, such as opening his mouth and not saying anything, then closing it and holding up a finger, only to close his hand, drop it, and sort of shake his fist, halfway pointing with his thumb.

It looked as if the boy was having the weirdest seizure anyone had ever seen. Kenneth bit his lip, doing his absolute best to hide his enjoyment while he watched Brandon squirm. Ah, the unexpected company of a beautiful woman versus trying to keep his crazy dad under control. The poor kid had no chance. Kenneth slapped Brandon on the back and squeezed his shoulder. "You two catch up. I'll be right back."

Before Brandon could say anything, Kenneth tucked his hands in his pockets and whistled while strolling atop the fresh grass. He passed the buffet table and took a few more steps to the outdoor restroom. It was a portable trailer resting on tires with two sets of aluminum stairs leading to the respective restroom doors. Thankfully, neither looked occupied.

The music stopped, and the small crowd behind Kenneth started clapping. He turned to see Porzio stepping up onto the stage. He lowered the stand to his pitifully short height and tapped the mic three times. Kenneth winced at the knocking sound it created.

Porzio opened his arms, welcoming the crowd. "Everybody out there havin' a wicked good time tonight?" Hoots, hollers, claps of hands and clanks of wine glasses filled the air.

Kenneth turned toward the bathroom again. He nasally repeated Porzio's words as he walked up the steps and pushed the door open. The speech echoing in from the reception area was disgustingly sentimental. He talked about how he had met Samantha. How they had been shopping at the same farmer's market where Samantha insisted on paying for some tomatoes she'd accidentally squashed with her oversized purse.

Porzio punctuated the end of his teachable moment with, "It's whatcha do when no one else is lookin' that counts."

"How apropos, you sanctimonious prick," Kenneth said to himself as he jammed the bathroom's rubber trash can underneath the silver door handle, barricading the door. He wandered past the sink then checked underneath each of the two stalls to the left of it. Certain he was alone, he dug into his jacket pocket. The Pop-Tart spilled onto the floor as he pulled out the smaller backup microphone he'd swiped earlier when talking to the DJ. Kenneth banked on the fact that DJ Crotchling hadn't bothered cutting the feed to the secondary mic. He walked into the first stall and sat down on the closed toilet seat. Finding the small switch on the bottom of the mic, he flicked it on and brought the mic to his mouth, grinning as he heard a small pop from the speakers outside.

"Paging Pasta Pederast," Kenneth said, stuttering as he started to crack up at his own joke. "You're needed in the bullshit department."

Kenneth flinched as he heard a loud crash to his left. He leaned forward just enough to peek past the stall divider and see the trash can on its side. Its contents were strewn across the glossy black tile. Behind it stood an enraged Brandon, hair tousled, his face red as a baboon's ass.

"Give it to me!" Brandon snarled, spit flinging from his lips. "Now!"

Brandon charged him.

Kenneth reached for the door and tried to close it, but Brandon was too fast, bashing the stall door open and nearly hitting Kenneth in the face.

Kenneth gripped the microphone tightly to his chest with both hands as Brandon attempted to wrench it from his fingers. Kenneth started screaming the lyrics to a song that Christine used to sing in church, his words harsh and bombastic, "Blessed be the name of the lord! He is our rock! He is our sword!"

In the struggle, Kenneth and Brandon's legs became tangled and Kenneth fell forward, landing halfway out of the stall. He managed to break the fall by landing on his side, but just as he rolled onto his back, Brandon landed on top of him.

Brandon straddled him and continued to claw at his fingers, but Kenneth held tight onto the mic as if he were fighting a robber trying to take his gun. Brandon gave up and instead grabbed Kenneth's tie and yanked hard, pulling Kenneth's upper body off the floor. Brandon's mouth formed into a savage snarl and he pulled his hand back, balling it into a fist. There was madness in his son's eyes he'd never seen before. A small part of him yearned for his son to strike him.

Kenneth leaned up and screamed into Brandon's face. "PASTA PASTA PASTA!"

"Stop!" a voice rang out from the doorway. Kenneth and Brandon both looked to see Samantha standing there, her cheeks red and her dark hair pulled back in a ponytail. Her arms were crossed and she stared down at Kenneth, her eyes cold and a grimace of disgust on her pretty face. "What the hell is wrong with you?"

Kenneth stared back, unwavering. "How lovely it is that I finally get to talk to my daughter on her wedding night."

She shook her head and gave a quick, dismissive shrug. "Well? You've got my attention now. What would you like to talk about?"

Kenneth hadn't expected that response. He was at a loss for words. He rubbed his forehead and stammered. "I just—Samantha—" He looked over at Brandon, who had gotten off him and was seated on the floor, leaning against the stall divider. "Brandon and I were discussing untrustworthy hairdos and hot dogs and that funk you get sometimes when someone sits down and then we started talking about your mother, and it got my head all screwed up, and—"

"We all miss her," Samantha said, a brief expression of sorrow breaking through her icy glare. "You don't have a monopoly on suffering."

"I know—I just . . ." Kenneth tried hard to get his thoughts together. "It's just that . . . *shyster* Porzio. Your mother would've seen right through him—"

"No, you don't get to do that." Samantha shook her head. "This isn't about your issues with God. This is about your own selfishness."

Before Kenneth could respond, Samantha's eyes flicked over to Brandon. "You were supposed to control him."

To Kenneth's surprise, Brandon rolled his eyes and looked up, banging the back of his head against the stall. "Figure out your own shit. I'm done playing intermediary. You're both assholes. Just leave me the hell out of it."

At this, Porzio entered the bathroom.

Kenneth held an open hand toward the man. "What, are we stuck in a joke right now? So a quack walks into the bathroom at a wedding—"

Porzio placed his hand on Samantha's lower back and asked, "Can I do anything, Sammy? Shall I call security?"

"*Sammy?*" Kenneth said, curling his lip as if he smelled something rotten. "Hey dingus, I'm literally lying on the floor of a bathroom." Kenneth wagged his hands and exaggerated a fearful tremble. "Ooh! So threatening!"

Porzio walked over to loom over Kenneth. "You are a godless man, Mr. Burman. Your behavior tonight has been reprehensible. It is clear to me that you are a toxic force in Sam's life, one that I don't think she should tolerate any further."

Porzio turned, his robe swinging as he did so. "Sammy, let's leave this poor soul alone to think about—"

Kenneth grabbed the man's robes and yanked as hard as he could. The robe became taut against the man's body, but his extra weight and forward momentum worked to Kenneth's advantage. There was a brief noise, sounding like paper being torn in half, then a loud pop. Porzio's robe loosed itself from the man's body, scattering buttons on the floor and revealing a completely nude man underneath.

Kenneth's mouth fell open and he pointed at the soggy excuse for a man. He looked over at Brandon and triumphantly exclaimed, "I told you!"

Porzio panicked and placed one hand over his crotch and his arm across his chest.

"Oh my god," Brandon said, holding his forehead but unable to look away. He then focused, moving his head forward. "Is that a tattoo?"

Kenneth tried to glimpse the tattoo but Porzio crouch-ran back over to Kenneth to grab his torn robe. He yanked it from Kenneth's hands and wrapped it around his body like a black toga. "This is outrageous!"

Samantha covered her nose and mouth with both hands, as if she were going to sneeze. She let out a small hiccup.

"Are you happy now?" Porzio asked, pointing back at Samantha. He turned and started to walk toward her. "You've ruined your daughter's wedding night!"

Samantha dropped one hand and used the other to cover her mouth. There was a small line of mascara running from the corner of her eye.

Porzio froze in place, then reared back, horrified.

Samantha wasn't crying. She was laughing.

"*You*—" he hissed, his voice full of betrayal.

Samantha uncovered her mouth to apologize, but covered it again when her attempt at speaking turned into a guttural sound in the back of her throat caused by her failure to stifle more laughter.

Porzio swept his gaze over the three of them. "Clearly the apple hasn't fallen as far from the tree as I previously thought." He did a small shimmy as he adjusted his robe-turned-toga. He held his chin high, and just before leaving, he said, "You will be hearing from my lawyer."

"You're Christian, forgive us!" Kenneth yelled as Porzio stormed out of the restroom. But just before the man exited, Kenneth glimpsed the tattoo Brandon had mentioned earlier. On one of Porzio's pasty-white butt cheeks was the red, uppercase B of the Boston Red Sox logo, and just below it was written, *#winning*.

Just as the door closed, Samantha burst out laughing again, doubling over. It was infectious. Brandon started to chuckle, then Kenneth joined in. He laughed so hard it devolved into a series of coughs, causing tears to stream down the sides of his face.

After a joyful moment, it all died down with a few more chuckles before the room went silent. Brandon reached down to grab Kenneth's slightly bent glasses, which had spilled to the floor during their struggle. He gently flexed them back to shape and held them toward Kenneth.

Kenneth waved them away and wiped some tears from his cheeks. "Your mother used to sing those god-awful songs," he said, referring to the song he was screaming while fighting Brandon for the mic earlier. He failed to hide a small sob, then half chuckled at the unintentional pun he had just made.

"I know, dad," said Samantha, wiping the tear from her eye as she gave him a sad smile. "I remember."

Contributors' Notes

LYNN BEMILLER lives and writes in Southern California, inspired by her forty years as a physician, and nearly as many as a wife and mother. She holds a certificate in novel writing from Stanford and is working on her second novel.

NELL PORTER BROWN is a long-time journalist—and new fiction writer—in Cambridge, Massachusetts. A staff writer/editor at *Harvard Magazine*, she focuses on alumni profiles and New England-based arts/culture, history, gastronomy, and travel. She is also earning a master's degree in creative writing and literature, and is available for freelance editing and writing projects. Contact her at nell_porter_brown@harvard.edu.

KATE M. COLBY writes paranormal fantasy novels, as well as the Desertera steampunk dystopian series. Her fiction has been published in regional magazines, won local awards, and been taught in college courses. In addition to pursuing a master's degree at Harvard Extension School, Kate enjoys wine tasting, playing video games, and doting on her feline familiars. Learn more at katemcolby.com.

ELIZABETH COLEMAN lives in San Francisco with her husband and two extremely spoiled cats. She writes across genres, and because life is better with a little bit of magic, her stories usually contain elements of the fantastic. She is currently pursuing a certificate in feature film writing from her alma mater, UCLA. Connect with her at elizabeth-coleman.com or @ thelizcoleman.

VICTORIA FERENBACH is a retired interior designer. She lives in New York City.

JENNIFER FICKLEY-BAKER lives in Florida with her husband and two sons, and has been a writer for more than twenty years. She focuses on thrillers and ghost stories with a historical twist. Her first short story, "The Haunting at Darlington Boardwalk," and her first novel, *The Widow of Harteforde*, were written under the mentorship of author Seth Harwood.

ANDREW HINSHAW resides in the Midwest with his girlfriend, two cats, and a honey badger masquerading as one. Once a trance DJ and dog food lineman, he now works in a field more suited to his background in psychology. He spends his free time rereading the Darth Bane Trilogy, looking stoic in grayscale photographs, and participating in online workshops hosted by author and instructor Seth Harwood. He's published short stories in *The Scarlet Leaf Review* and *Oyster River Pages* (the second of which, "Abigail," was nominated for the Pushcart Prize).

JEANNIE HUA has been an attorney for twenty-six years and a genius writer in her own mind since birth. While awaiting her genius to be discovered, she's an MFA candidate at the School of the Art Institute of Chicago and has a law practice in Nevada in criminal defense and special education law.

ANDREW C. PETERSON is a writer currently working on his thesis for a master's degree in creative writing and literature at the Harvard Extension School under the tutelage of author Seth Harwood. He is a frequent lecturer at the annual Tolkien at UVM conference. Andrew is an avid reader, writer, and possible book hoarder who lives in Boston. Learn more at inkbringer. com.

J.L. PRICE has recently made the move to fiction writing after spending most of her work life writing academic pieces and teaching. When she isn't working and writing, she loves to spend time with her husband and two kids enjoying places of natural beauty. She is particularly fond of the mountains of Wyoming, where she loves to hike, bike, camp, and fish (which for her means reading a good book on a nice rock by the water).

ALYCE WERDEL lives with her husband in San Francisco, where they raised three children. In a former life, she was a partner at the international law firm, Baker & McKenzie, and was a frequent speaker and author on global equity compensation. She is a graduate of the University of Notre Dame Law School and Stanford University, where she played on two NCAA Championship tennis teams. Her husband always told her she had an active imagination, so she decided to try fiction writing. This is the prologue to her first novel, *Vengeance*.

ELIZABETH WETMORE'S fiction has appeared in *Epoch*, *Kenyon Review*, *Iowa Review*, and other journals. Her debut novel, *Valentine*, was named a best book of 2020 by *The Washington Post*, *BuzzFeed*, and *Texas Monthly*. After debuting at No. 2 on the *New York Times Bestseller List*, *Valentine* won the Chicago Writers Association's Book of the Year and was a finalist for the Crook's Corner Book Prize. The French translation was a finalist for the 2020 Grand Prix de Littérature Américaine. Born and raised in West Texas, she lives with her family in Chicago.

www.ingramcontent.com/pod-product-compliance
Lightning Source LLC
Chambersburg PA
CBHW022045240626
47154CB00007B/2566